CLOUD INVASION

R-D SERIES, BOOK TWO

CONNIE SUTTLE

Print Second Edition (2018)
Print ISBN: 1-63478-060-4
Print ISBN-13: 978-1-63478-060-5
eBook ISBN: 1-93975-931-5
eBook ISBN-13: 978-1-93975-931-3

Published by:
SubtleDemon Publishing, LLC
PO Box 95696
Oklahoma City, OK 73143

Cover art by Renée Barratt @ The Cover Counts

To Walter, Joe, Larry, Lee, Dianne, Sarah and Mark.
Thank you.

ACKNOWLEDGMENTS

As always, this book is the result of collaboration. If it weren't for the support of my editor, my cover artist and my beta readers, it would be less than it is. All mistakes, as usual, are mine and no other's.

About the Author:
Connie Suttle lives in Oklahoma with her husband and a conglomerate of cats. They have finally banded together to make their demands, which has proven disconcerting to all humans involved.

You may find Connie in the following ways:
Facebook: Connie Suttle Author
Twitter: @subtledemon
Website and Blog: subtledemon.com

R-D Series:

Cloud Dust

Cloud Invasion

Cloud Rebel

Latter Day Demons Series:

Hot Demon in the City

A Demon's Work is Never Done

A Demon's Due

Seattle Elementals Series:

Your Money's Worth

Worth Your While*

BlackWing Pirates Series

MindSighted

MindMage

MindRogue

MindMaster*

Black Rose Sorceress Series

The Rose Mark

Rose and Thorn

Black Rose Queen

Queen of Thorns and Roses

Future Wars Series

Buffer Zone

Black Zone*

Other Titles from SubtleDemon Publishing:

Malefactor

Transgressor

Underhanded*

by Joe Scholes

*Forthcoming

CHAPTER 1

otes—Colonel Hunter

"What the hell is that?" I stared at the exposed spine of the clone pretending to be the President's Chief of Staff, Hal Prentice. Richard Farrell asked me to look at what he'd found in the course of the autopsy.

"That's the reason Corinne couldn't bring him down. Rafe destroyed the device when he broke his neck."

The device, made of metal and electronics, was fused to the clone's spine at the base of the neck. "I imagine it kept the clone's brain and heart working when Corinne attempted to shut them down," Dr. Farrell explained. "The X-rays revealed sensors in both organs. When the device and the victim's neck were broken, everything stopped functioning. There's something else, too."

"What? Tell me it's less terrifying than this," I pointed at the device.

"I believe it was transmitting a signal somewhere—both audio and video. Whoever was on the receiving end has been watching the President for a while."

"And has seen all of us in meetings with the President, no doubt," I said. "Whenever this clone was present, he knew who the President met with and probably what they were discussing."

At that moment, I wanted to hit something. Or someone. This could be the ultimate spying weapon—capture or kill anyone, replace them with a clone who could see and hear everything around them, then transmit that data to a waiting master and the world could be had for the price of a bit of gadgetry.

"Has the President been informed?" I asked.

"I have a meeting this afternoon. She'll see a slideshow and not the body. It's anybody's guess whether the real Hal Prentice is alive or not."

"How's Corinne?" I asked the next question on my list. I'd been in meetings all morning and hadn't gotten an update.

"I left her with Shaw and Rafe. I believe she's waking, but I can't guarantee it, yet."

"We need her," I muttered. I felt bad about that, too. The minute she was capable of walking, she'd be put to work again and that wasn't fair in any sense.

We'd been terrified she'd die after Prentice's clone shot her, but the drug had been administered quickly. So far, her body remained alive and responsive, and the scans Farrell ran showed brain activity.

"We need her help with this," I nodded toward the device clinging to the clone's spine like a creature from a horror movie.

"I wouldn't mind it, either, but we have to take things slowly," Farrell replied. "We've never given the drug to the same person twice, and the physical change we've seen already was somewhat unexpected."

"It's only her hair color, as far as I can tell," I huffed.

"I've checked her eyes. They're a brighter blue," Farrell said.

"If those are the only changes, then we should consider ourselves fortunate."

"I'm concerned about her talents."

"You had to scare me worse than I already was, didn't you?"

Ilya

The rest of us woke after a few days, when it became apparent we'd survived the drug. Even Corinne woke faster the first time. This time, three weeks had passed. I was grateful for the scans and other tests Dr. Farrell ran, indicating she was alive.

Still, I was terrified for her. And for me. I spoke to her often and lately, I begged her to open her eyes.

The different hair and eye colors? They meant nothing to me as long as she woke.

"Ilya?" she croaked.

Yes, I'd been far away in my thoughts and failed to see her eyes open.

"Cabbage?" I was up and gripping her hand quickly.

"You okay?" she asked.

"I am more than okay," I responded. "You, however, sound much like a frog in a dry pond."

"Water?" Bright blue eyes blinked hopefully at me.

"Immediately," I said, and shouted for the nurse.

∼

Corinne

Rafe sat on one side of my bed, James on the other, while James spoke with Auggie on his cell phone.

"Yes, she's talking. I don't think she's ready for a marathon," James said. "Rafe says her grip is weak."

Yes, the Ukrainian mountain had tested my grip with his hands. I hope he took that as a sign that I wasn't up to lifting weights, running or being smeared across a mat during Krav Maga lessons.

"Colonel Hunter has photographs," James said after covering the cell phone with his free hand.

"Of course he does. Tell him he's a slave driver."

"I think he already knows that. He said sorry at least three times," James blinked at me before going back to his conversation with Auggie.

"Honey, how is Laci?" I asked.

"Colonel Hunter, she's asking about Laci."

"Laci's fine," James relayed the answer.

"Cool. Awesome. Tons of other adjectives," I leaned my head against the pillow.

"Colonel Hunter says we can move, now that you're awake."

"Great. Where are we moving?"

"He says he'll tell you himself when he gets here."

"Joy."

Rafe laughed.

"I was afraid to let you see this earlier," Rafe said, handing a mirror to me. I already knew my hair color was different—the white-blonde lengths hung about my shoulders and I couldn't miss *that*.

"Your eyes are brighter, but that's all I can see—for now," he grinned. "Want me to brush your hair or do you feel strong enough to do it?"

"I'll try," I said, accepting the hairbrush from his hand.

"Look who's awake," Leo Shaw strode into the room.

"Why Dr. Shaw," I muttered, attempting to pull the brush through long, tangled hair, "Whatever brings you here?"

"You should know the answer to that," he grinned. "I'm just glad you're still with us."

"I'm glad you're glad," I shrugged. "Can I have vegetable soup?"

"I'll order it now," he pulled his cell from a pocket and dialed a number.

"You don't want chicken?" Rafe asked.

"Honey, the thought of eating meat sort of makes me feel sick," I sighed. "I'm not sure I can eat it anymore."

"Is this another change?" he sat on the side of my bed and trailed fingers down my face.

"I think so. This is just—so weird," I muttered.

"Then we'll make a menu that will ensure you get plenty of protein. Will it bother you that I continue to be a carnivore?"

"No. Not at all. I just don't think it's for me, now." I looked past Rafe and stared out the window of my room—I was up on a second story somewhere and eventually realized it was the ugly building in Arlington.

"Why here?" I asked.

It took a moment for Rafe and Leo Shaw to understand what I meant.

"Because that thing posing as the Chief of Staff knew about the other building," Leo explained. "We moved out of there the next day. Maye and Nick are elsewhere; we brought you here because it was easier to set up a hospital room for you and get necessary supplies in. Rafe refused to go with Nick and Maye, so you're both here with us under heavy guard."

I took a moment to digest what he'd told me. "Any idea where we'll be moving?" I asked.

"Not yet. The President and Colonel Hunter had a private meeting. I believe they came to a decision, but because of the instability of the situation, they haven't shared with anyone else." I could tell Leo wasn't exactly pleased about being excluded, but I figured he'd know soon enough.

"We have to get you moving," Rafe said, lifting my hand to his lips and kissing it. "We missed you, cabbage. Too much."

"Push harder." I had a new slave driver. His name was Marcus and he was a sadist posing as a physical therapist. He'd shown up shortly after lunch and started working with me right away.

I was pushing my hands against his as hard as I could, but that much force and energy wouldn't have given a fly a mild concussion.

"Colonel Hunter wants you able to walk out of here in three days," Marcus grunted, forcing my hands against my chest.

"Then why are we working with my hands?" I asked.

I should have stayed quiet. He started on my legs and that was agony. I resolved never to argue with Navy Lieutenant Marcus Cargill again. By the time he was finished with me, I wanted to ask whether he was bucking for brownie points with Auggie or just looking for a promotion.

The question was moot—he wanted both those things. I'd seen it in his face. If torturing me might get those things, then he was willing to do whatever it took. Rafe was absent, so he agreed with Auggie on getting me prepped and out the door to our new hiding place.

That didn't mean I wouldn't add Marcus and Auggie to my verbal ass-kicking agenda.

"How's the patient?" Auggie walked in wearing a huge grin.

"August Hunter, I swear I'd kick your ass right now if I were able. Then Mr. Cargill's ass for following your orders too strenuously." I pushed Marcus' hands away with my foot and swung both legs over the edge of my bed.

"Are you trying to do that now?" Auggie almost giggled. For a Colonel who also happened to be Secretary of Defense and Director of the Program, that was totally inappropriate.

"Jerks. Both of you. You're banished." I lifted a hand weakly to enhance the royal command and slid off the bed. Yeah, my legs shook, but I was standing.

Marcus thought to put me back on the bed. I moved out of his way so quickly it even surprised me. Auggie just gaped for a moment before closing his mouth.

"I know where you're taking us," I shook a finger at Auggie. "I need windows. End of statement."

~

Notes—Colonel Hunter

"James, we're moving tomorrow. Pack up all unnecessary equipment and be ready at oh-six-hundred tomorrow morning. We're flying out of here on a cargo plane." I stalked past James' desk on the way to my own to let the President know.

Marcus and I had followed Cori on her way to the kitchen. She wobbled several times on the trek down the hall, but she made it to the elevator and then to the first floor. She appeared to get stronger as she went, and managed to search through meager supplies in the pantry for coffee and a granola bar.

Marcus, my choice to bring into the Program as an assistant for Shaw, shook his head at Corinne's miraculous recovery.

"Get used to it—especially from her," I whispered while Corinne settled on a barstool with coffee in hand while crunching on the granola bar.

"Is Cori better?" James asked, pulling me away from my thoughts.

"Cori walked to the kitchen and helped herself to coffee and a granola bar," I shrugged. "Marcus is undeniably impressed."

"Then I guess we're moving. I already arranged to send all of her stuff ahead," James informed me. "It'll be set up and waiting when we get there."

"We need windows."

"I already looked into it, and the crew is ready to go if you say the word." James handed a sheaf of mechanical drawings to me.

"I want this, too," I said the minute the drawings soaked into my mind.

"I think they can arrange for all the offices to be modified."

"Then do it," I nodded. "We would be up the creek without Corinne, and if they're doing hers, it won't be such a big deal if they do the rest."

"I like the fact that they can be camouflaged," James agreed, taking the papers back. He'd had the information for two hours and already he had things ready to go. "I put Maye, Jeff and Nick on notice, so they're packing."

"What about Rafe?"

"He was ready to go in five minutes; he's just waiting for Dr. Farrell to give the okay to move Cori. You know he won't budge without her."

"I won't budge without her, either. The President doesn't want to go anywhere without Corinne's advice. We're all crippled after the Chief of Staff thing, and that's probably not the half of it."

"What about Laci?"

"She's seeing Dr. Shaw at least once a day."

"Not good," James shook his head.

"We're seeing him together once a week," I admitted. "She feels abandoned and left out, but there's not a lot I can do about it if she doesn't want to live within the confines of the Program. We're trying to compromise on a few things. At least she knows Corinne isn't a threat to us or to anybody on our side—she had a long talk with Rafe."

"She needs to get to know her. Cori wouldn't hurt anybody who didn't deserve it."

"I think she knows that, now. If that were the case, we might all be dead."

"Yeah. No wonder she wouldn't tell anybody." James shivered. "I think Becker was lucky he lived as long as he did."

"She let Nick take him down, like she knew that would help Nick get over things," I said.

"She probably did know that. This is a secret we have to keep, and I think we need to let Cori decide when and where somebody dies, if it's necessary. She's not an assassin—no way, no how," James said.

"You're right," I agreed. "The President knows to keep that information under wraps—I just worry about what the enemy may know through that fucking device attached to Hal's clone. At least he knew to stay out of Cori's way, because she'd see it in him. The rest of us, though, we saw Hal regularly. That doesn't include the President's confidential statements to him, or the messages he had from her. The equipment he carried may have delivered all of that right into waiting hands."

"I need to see that thing," James said. "Is somebody examining it?"

"Farrell put a team together," I shrugged. "We should have a complete report in about a week."

"Will he send the information to us?"

"That's what I asked for."

"Good. Thank you, Colonel Hunter."

~

Corinne

I still wasn't up to packing the following morning; I didn't have much to pack, anyway. Several sets of pajamas, a hairbrush, lotion and toothbrush. Everything else was loaded on a cargo plane somewhere.

The Pacific Northwest hadn't been a blip on anybody's radar as a place to hide the Program, so I imagined Auggie and the President chose it because of that. It might be the last place the enemy expected us to go.

Rafe stuffed my meager belongings into a small bag and zipped it up while I swung my feet over the side of my bed and watched him work. Thankfully, Marcus had left us alone; he was probably in a dungeon somewhere, planning more torture for me.

"James is bringing something for you to wear—all you have is pajamas," Rafe pointed out the obvious.

"Good. I hope it's comfortable," I said. "Shoes, too?"

"Of course. I can't wait to dress you in blue to match your eyes," he walked toward me and took my face in his hands. "An evening dress, perhaps, or a nice blouse." He leaned in to kiss me.

"You taste good," I said.

"Thank you. Do you want something else to eat?"

"No, the pancakes filled me up," I said. I'd had those with a glass of milk, and only finished about a third of what was placed in front of me.

"Do you still love me?" he leaned back to ask, his dark eyes begging me to say it was so.

"Honey, that's the only thing that brought me back," I said.

"Just what I wanted to hear," he murmured before kissing me again.

Flying in a military cargo plane was now on the list of things I hated. We were buckled into four rows of seats and the rest of our belongings, which hadn't already been sent ahead, were packed in crates and boxes and tied down behind us.

Sitting up that long was extremely uncomfortable after a while, and there wasn't any place to lie down. If Rafe and James hadn't sat with me, I might not have made it. Eventually, we landed at a naval airbase on Whidbey Island north of Seattle.

Our transfer to the new facility was done by helicopter after that, under a cloudy and darkening sky.

~

Ilya

I held Corinne close after the helicopters landed and we were allowed off. The facility had been excavated into the southern side of Mount Pilchuck, located north and east of Seattle, with only two camouflaged windows facing southwestward. I imagined that if we looked through those windows hard enough on a clear day, we might see Puget Sound.

At the summit of the mountain lies a fire lookout, and on the western side a popular hiking trail meanders upward. Where the facility was located, the mountain was much more inhospitable, with steep sides, rocky cliffs and pines lower down that jutted into the sky.

At one time, a ski resort was located not far from the western edge of our new facility. It closed in 1979 after a combination of weather problems resulted in a lack of snow and a subsequent refusal by the Forestry Service to renew the lease.

Sometime after that, the resort was destroyed by a mysterious fire. I didn't wish to investigate the cause or the outcome—I had no interest in it, after all.

"You need warmer clothing," I murmured against Corinne's hair when she shivered against me. She wrapped her arms about my waist and buried her head against my chest. The ride had been torture for her, and the ensuing helicopter flight only added to her misery. She needed to lie down.

"Let's get her inside," Dr. Shaw walked up beside us. "She needs rest."

We followed Colonel Hunter as he walked toward a thick, steel door, painted to match its rocky surroundings and nearly hidden behind pines and plants. It required a code and an eyescan to get inside. It made me wonder about Corinne's ability to defeat the security system in place, and whether it had been modified to prevent that.

An elevator stood at the end of a wide entry; we rode it to the main floor, where all offices and suites were located. At that moment, I hoped we'd have a kitchen.

~

Notes—Colonel Hunter

Cori was asleep on her feet when Rafe pulled her down the hall toward their shared suite. "We'll have a meeting in the morning, when she's awake," I said and opened the suite door for them. Rafe lifted her and carried her inside. I closed the door behind them and walked toward my new office.

The facility had been built after the attack on Fort Stevens in 1942 by the Japanese. Originally, it was built as a command center in World War II in case of further attacks, but it was never finished—the end of the war came. It sat there, an empty bunker, until nine presidents ago, when it was selected as a potential spot for local military personnel in case of an attack during the cold war.

That idea was abandoned the minute the wall fell outside East Germany, so it sat empty again, until the President considered it as a retreat for the Program. Recently, as in the last eight weeks, it had been modified to accommodate the Program. Thankfully, Madam President hadn't shared that information with Hal—she'd come to me and I'd secretly enlisted Navy engineers for the cause.

It was nearly finished, a few windows and upgrades notwithstanding, and we had a tunnel, complete with electric vehicles to drive through it, which ended in a ranch farther down the mountain.

I found it amusing that our exit hole was located near a resident's home, converted from an old train caboose. While I had no desire of my own to live in a converted train caboose, I silently applauded the inventive repurposing of the abandoned car.

From the exit, we could take one of the waiting SUVs if we needed to drive to Seattle or anywhere else. Several military agents were set up to treat the property as their own and guard the tunnel entrance. They were already in place, and some of them would act as bodyguards for us if needed.

Shaw worried that some of ours would get cabin fever, being so far from everything. An occasional outing would be allowed, unless we were under lockdown. Laci was also being moved—to a nice house in Seattle. I promised I'd see her at least once a week.

I wanted the others to visit the city, too, to eat out or shop. They'd have guards with them, watching from a safe distance. Once Corinne approved the personnel we'd brought with us, I was hoping to loosen the restraints we'd worn closer to the Capital.

～

Ilya

Shaw arranged for sunlamps to be installed in every suite until the engineers and their staff could cut windows in the side of the mountain containing our rooms. That would take time.

I made sure Corinne was covered warmly after putting her to bed. I sat beside her, toying with the tablet Colonel Hunter had given me— several dozen photographs were loaded on it and I was checking them first to see whether I recognized anyone before Corinne looked.

I considered, too, what Baikov might be doing and where he could be at the moment. If I knew anything about him (and I did), then he was likely plotting death and destruction for someone.

"Honey, stop obsessing. I can feel it in my sleep," Corinne mumbled.

"Cabbage?" I set the tablet aside to scoot into position beside her. "How's my darling?" Pulling her against me, I settled her head onto my shoulder.

"Tired," she lifted her hand to cover a yawn.

"That plane ride was too much," I grumbled. She was already asleep again when I tucked a strand of pale blonde hair behind her ear.

~

Notes—Colonel Hunter

"Corinne's sunlamp burned out this morning," James informed me when I walked into our shared office, stifling a yawn.

"She can have mine," I said. "What happened? Those things are new."

"Just got a bad one, I guess—hardly anybody else has used theirs, but she had it turned on this morning and it just went out. She changed the bulb, but that wasn't the problem."

"Was she writing when it blew?"

"Of course. Rafe said she sneaked out of bed, went into her office next to their bedroom and sat down at the computer without waking him. She was writing when he got up an hour later. Here are those photographs you gave her, with notes," he handed a tablet to me.

"She got those done, too?" I scrolled through the photographs, reading the short blurbs she'd sent. Several had crimes listed beneath the photographs; a few had lists of evidence to gather to prove their guilt. None of them were clones—at least she hadn't identified them as such.

Two of them were members of Congress. I was least surprised about them and gave a snort when I read their information. Their crimes were of the white-collar variety, and I wondered if Madam President would even bother to investigate.

"Nothing about the enemy," I said. "Dr. Farrell says the autopsy on the lizard woman makes for interesting reading. He's forwarding that information to us later today."

"Did he give you anything at all about her?" James asked.

"He says the DNA shows she's mostly humanoid, but he's still trying to get a lock on the rest of it."

"How can that happen?" James asked, his mouth settling into a puzzled frown. "Gene splicing?"

"I don't think that's it," I said. "He and I have a guess, but we can't prove anything at this point."

What I didn't tell James was that I knew significantly more about the Program now than I did a month ago. Farrell and I'd had several discussions, and the more I learned, the more it concerned me.

I felt we were lucky that Corinne survived a second round of the drug. It had never been attempted twice on anyone else, because the death toll on the first round was much too high. Actually, where she was concerned, I considered that we'd hit the drug lottery twice and didn't want to jinx it by discussing her survival.

Conversations with Farrell and his medical team were ongoing, too, about the clones. How they were made, how quickly they were made—we had too many questions and too few answers where those were concerned.

We'd done autopsies on the Becker clones, first. They'd all been identical to him in every way. Farrell had some theories, but without testing them, we couldn't be sure.

A research lab for our new location was in the process of being built. The moment it became operational, Farrell and his team would move in. I considered that I might have to put a rush on the windows —we needed natural sunlight.

"James, what about a patio or outside garden?" I asked.

He blinked at me—I'd gone from one subject straight into another, which made absolutely no sense.

"You mean, build that while they're cutting windows?"

"Yes. We can camouflage it with plants, trees and such. We can't open the windows they'll build. This will allow us outside air every day."

"I'll ask the engineers to draw up plans."

"Have them design it so the audio and video can be easily turned off and on."

"Will do. Anticipating private conversations?"

"Don't you think we need someplace for that?"

"Probably." He reached for his phone.

"Good. Keep me informed; I have a call with the President this morning, to discuss this." I held the tablet aloft.

"I'll see that you're not disturbed, Colonel."

"If Corinne or Rafe decide to disturb me, send them in. The President wants to speak with them, too. Eventually."

"Yes, sir."

Corinne

Our suite was three thousand square feet and included my office, a study for Rafe, a huge bedroom, a kitchen and a dining area. The dining area included a long table with seating for eight. I imagined Auggie had been instrumental in arranging that.

We had plenty of storage, plus an extra bedroom and bathroom. The kitchen was everything Rafe and I could want, with a huge island and six barstools lined up along one side.

"Only oatmeal?" Rafe lifted an eyebrow at me. We'd made eggs, sausage and toast for him, but I'd made a small portion of oatmeal for myself.

"It's all I want," I shrugged. "I'll ask James if he can order protein shakes for me."

I knew we had the bugs turned on in our suite when James arrived ten minutes later to help himself to leftover eggs and sausage while I made fresh toast for him.

He used his tablet to order bottles of protein drink for me in several flavors while he ate. "Want more OJ?" I lifted the bottle in James' direction.

"Just coffee," he said. I made a fresh cup and set it at his elbow.

"How are you feeling?" he asked.

"I'm better than I was yesterday. Thanks for getting me a new sunlamp, by the way. I'll try not to break this one."

"How soon can we make arrangements to go to Seattle?" Rafe asked. "I owe my cabbage dinner," he added, coming to a stop behind me and kissing the top of my head.

"Can I come?" James asked hopefully.

"Of course, if it will mean one less guard, no matter how discreet," Rafe grinned. "We much prefer your company."

"If you say Colonel Hunter and his wife can come, I think I can make it happen soon," James said. "Very soon."

"Then make it happen," Rafe agreed.

"I'm all for that," Auggie walked into our kitchen. "Thanks for the information, Cori," he nodded to me. "The President may have other photographs soon. I have a feeling you'll be seeing some of the crime bosses from drug cartels."

"She thinks they may be involved in some of this?" I asked.

"It's possible," he shrugged.

"Yeah. It's possible," I agreed. There was another question I wanted to ask, and it involved the handful of people who'd survived the drug in Montana. More and more, that was on my mind and I figured the President hadn't told Auggie what happened to those people or where they were.

That, of course, could turn into a huge mistake.

CHAPTER 2

C orinne

Nick and Maye joined us for lunch; Jeff tagged along with them. I guess Auggie had this planned ahead of time, because he and James showed up, too, with Leo Shaw right behind them. Then, Marcus came looking for everybody else and decided he wanted soup and a sandwich.

"We have an appointment at two," Marcus reminded me.

"Did you get special classes on day-ruining?" I asked, handing him a plate of food. "James, we'll need to restock the pantry soon," I said, turning to him.

"On it," James said, pulling out his tablet.

"I got an A in day-ruining," Marcus grinned and bit into his ham sandwich.

"You're too competitive," I pointed a finger at him.

"Have to be the best," he agreed.

"Uh-huh. How long do you intend to torture me? Besides, you should consult with Rafe, because he can give you pointers on that sort of thing, in addition to honing your Krav Maga skills."

"An hour. He can teach me Krav Maga?"

"I can," Rafe confirmed with a nod. "Let me know when you have an hour or two to train on most days. I'll take care of it."

"You're moving pretty well today," Leo said, nodding in my direction. "How do you feel?"

"Good," I said.

"When do you think you can start running and training with Rafe?" Auggie asked.

"I'll let you know, Colonel Hunter," Marcus said.

"I will temper his assessment with my own," Rafe interjected. I could tell he was a bit annoyed with Marcus. Well, I was a bit annoyed with Marcus, too. He needed to consider his patient and not his brownie points, as far as I was concerned.

"How about I tell you when I'm ready?" I told Auggie. "I'll let Leo know, too, so we'll all be on the same page."

"I'll take all reports from all sources in a week," Auggie said, ending the debate.

"Good enough," I said. "Anybody want ice cream?"

"I hear you're pretty special," Marcus said while putting me through my exercise torture later.

"I don't think of myself as special in any way," I grunted as I lifted five-pound weights and held them until he said I could let my arms down. "The next time you're a hostage of terrorists and watch a bunch of people die, come see me. We'll talk special then."

"Dr. Shaw told me," he said. "After Colonel Hunter said he could."

"Of course he did," I muttered, dropping my arms when he gave the signal. I was sweating, and we'd only done fifteen minutes of exercises. "Is there any chance we can get in a pool and do exercises there?"

"There's no water in it, yet," Marcus offered a smile. He wanted to see me sweat.

The bastard.

"When will there be water in it?" I hefted the weights again.

"Maybe next week. Okay, let your arms down—we're done with weights for now. Get on the treadmill. I'll see how far you can walk."

I could have walked farther, but that would only make Marcus ask for more next time, so I settled for two miles.

Leo saw me after I'd showered and dressed.

"We haven't talked yet about you getting shot a second time and getting the drug a second time," he settled into the comfortable chair across from mine in his new office.

"We haven't talked about you being schlepped from pillar to post after all the bombings and moves," I countered.

"This session isn't about me," he said, but he smiled anyway.

"I thought about not coming back," I said.

"What made you decide to?" I could read the unasked question behind that—he was surprised that I thought I'd had a choice in the matter. Oddly enough, this time, that's exactly how it was.

"Rafe," I shrugged. "I came back because he wanted me to. I was worried about how all of you would see me now—that in your eyes, I might be a monster, able to kill on what some might think a whim. That has never been the case, but you might not understand that."

"I can see how you might think that," he said. "But Colonel Hunter and I trust you with our lives; you've saved them often enough. Maye and Nick have been briefed, and we've discussed your abilities in a few sessions. Both agree—without you, we'd all be dead."

"That's not a light burden," I pointed out. It wasn't. I felt responsible for so many people and so many things, now. It ramped up my anxiety to another, much higher level. After I'd wakened this time, Dr. Shaw hadn't put me on any drugs for my anxiety or PTSD. I knew he wanted to see how things stood before recommending anything.

I didn't want any of that, and didn't intend to take anything he prescribed. No, I wouldn't recommend going against doctor's orders for anyone else. Things were different for me, now, and I had personal checks and balances to ensure that all those internal things were managed without the use of medication—for the most part. In fact, I was doing exactly that while talking with Leo.

I recalled vividly the pain in my chest and the last rush of fear as I fell when Hal Prentice's clone shot me. I knew I'd die. Leo had an injection of the drug ready. He and Auggie had made plans for such an emergency, and had needles ready for Rafe and me.

Rafe hadn't needed another injection; his shields held and Hal Prentice's clone never had a chance when Rafe broke his neck, in addition to breaking the device that kept him from dying when I'd attempted to kill him.

"I think those devices are really expensive," I blurted, startling Leo.

"What devices?"

"The kind Hal Prentice's clone had attached to his neck. That's why none of the others had one that day. The enemy placed that one where it would do the most good."

"What brought that up? Just curious—I'm very interested in what you have to say about that—Colonel Hunter will be as well."

"I was just thinking about that day, what happened, what I saw in Hal's clone, why he didn't die—what it felt like to almost die a second time."

"Corinne, it was barely two seconds after you said that wasn't a light burden. You shifted gears really fast."

"Sorry—I know it's confusing," I said. "But all of it raced through my mind that fast."

"Is this another change?" he asked.

"Maybe, although things always tend to run through my mind—it's part of being a writer."

"Then let's talk about Sarah Fox and Carol Dane," he said. "Do you feel like three people?"

"No. The other two are façades. Just names I use to keep from losing all my work and income, in case I have to change identities again."

"That's important to you?"

"Very important to me," I nodded.

"Are you willing to tell me who you were before?"

I knew he wanted to know before, and hinted at it several times, but this time, he'd come right out and asked. "That's a complicated story," I sighed. "And one I'd prefer to only tell once. Can we wait until Rafe and Auggie are here and I'm in a better place emotionally? That way you can all hear it at the same time and ask all your questions during the session."

"I'll arrange it whenever you're ready," Leo nodded. "How do you feel, now? Shaky? Have bouts of depression or anxiety?"

"In some ways, yes, but I think I'm better equipped to handle those things this time."

"Are you sure?"

"I think so."

"I'll let you go for two weeks with no medication, but at the first sign of those symptoms returning, we'll consider prescribing something."

"That sounds fine. I hope you won't have to make the effort."

"While it would please me greatly to know you don't need it, I have reservations," he said.

"I know you do," I agreed. "I hope they prove to be unfounded."

"Is there anything else you'd like to discuss?"

"Marcus," I said.

"What's wrong with him?"

"He's an ambitious overachiever," I said. "While most people would see that as a strength, it sort of sours when he's trying to please Auggie by pushing me into the ground. His priority, as I see it, should be his patient and not necessarily his boss or his desire for an important promotion."

"I'll have a word with Colonel Hunter. Perhaps he should tell Marcus exactly what he needs to do where you're concerned, instead of having thoughts of pushing you too hard in order to complete his assignment early and move up."

"Thank you. I just want his focus to be on the right things, for the right reasons," I said.

"As do I, but if it's August he wants to please, instead of me, then the word needs to come from Colonel Hunter."

"Tell Auggie I'll take the blame for this, as long as Marcus doesn't try to take it out on me afterward."

"I imagine that Rafe may have something to say about it, if that happens."

"Just tell Marcus that it's for his own good, and I can fight my own battles, thank you."

"I see," Leo focused his gaze on me. "You're not threatening him, are you?"

"I sure hope not," I said. "But he either needs to get his priorities straight, or he needs to find another way to kiss Auggie's ass."

"I'll give that some thought before going to Colonel Hunter," Leo said.

"Thank you."

❧

"I hear you don't like Marcus," Auggie stormed into the suite while Rafe and I were having dinner later.

"I like Marcus fine. He just has no sense of humor and he wants your job," I pointed out as tactfully as I could. "Want dinner?"

"What?" Auggie stopped in mid-stride. That was a shame; he had a really good walking snit going when he burst into our kitchen.

"You can see it, can't you?" Auggie took a seat at the kitchen island, where we'd sat down to eat. Rafe didn't say a word, but I could tell he was somewhat amused.

"Yeah, I see it, all right," I mumbled before cutting into my tomato and cheese omelet. Auggie pulled a bowl from the cabinet and dipped beef stew out of the slow cooker.

"I can rough him up," Rafe offered.

"No. That's not a good idea," I said. "I just think Auggie needs to talk with Marcus and let him know that in his line of work, it's the quality and not the speed of recovery that matters."

"What should I say about his grasping for a higher position?"

"Tell him how long it took to get where you are, and you didn't do it by cutting corners or trying to impress people. You worked to get the job done right," I pointed out.

Auggie stared at me for a moment before shaking his head and pulling crackers from a sleeve Rafe placed in front of him. The paper crackled as he extracted six crackers and set them beside his bowl while he considered what to say.

"I should have known you can see that stuff," Auggie said. "I always did that because it was the right thing to do and not because of what anybody else thought or said."

"And that's why I love you," I said. "Not like Laci does—but as a good friend."

"Cori, she knows that. She said it was stupid of her to even consider you any kind of rival."

"I know." I hunched my shoulders. It had taken her more than six years to realize I wasn't competing for her husband. I'm sure she thought I took up too much of his time, but that couldn't be helped. He liked his work and I'd done my best to take as little of his time as possible.

There wasn't anything I could do about the hours of research and investigation he did when he wasn't herding me around. Now, he was Secretary of Defense and Director of the Program. That only complicated his life further, in my estimation. Auggie was a workaholic; that was a well-known fact.

Laci still hadn't realized that it didn't mean he didn't love her, or intended to ignore her. It was just the way he was made. Where he needed to improve, I think, was the quality of the time he spent with his wife.

That was his business, though, and none of mine. I sighed again at life's complexities. "When will the pool be filled?" I asked, changing subjects.

"In three weeks. I'll have James keep you informed. The water is piped up the mountain, and the pipes are small, because they were installed more than half a century ago. It'll take time," he shrugged.

"Is the water source protected?" Rafe asked.

"As much as it can be. Nobody wants another Montana."

"Or another Georgia," I said. "At least those directly responsible are dead. We just don't need somebody stepping into their shoes."

"On another note," Auggie said, "Madam President wants secret feeds of some of her meetings to come to you, Cori, so you can tell her if anyone at the meeting needs to be watched."

I knew what he didn't say—the President wanted to know if any of them needed to be dead, too. She expected me to take care of it, if the case were severe enough. I'm sure she expected to be informed if any of them wore an apparatus like Hal's clone did. She thought someone else would have to be sent after those.

That remained to be seen.

"She isn't worried that I might hear sensitive information?"

Auggie snorted at my question. After a moment, I could see his point. I could see just about anything I wanted to know by looking at someone. The only one I couldn't see—or find—was the enemy.

"Do you suppose there are clones of Mary Evans?" I asked. That also weighed on my mind, and I was very worried that the answer was yes. She was too good at what she did for the enemy; I couldn't imagine that he'd let her be caught so easily if he didn't have a replacement for her.

"Why do you ask? And that sent a chill up my spine, just so you know," Auggie said.

"Well, look at it this way—all those Becker clones? They were smarter and more determined than the original ever was. What if it's the same with the Mary Evans clones? That they're better than the original?"

"Fuck." Auggie buried his face in his hands. "We've had a report. I didn't know whether to take it seriously or not," he said.

"Now it's my turn to say fuck," I grumbled. "There's another one out there already, probably reassuring the enemy's clients that all is well in murder and mayhem land."

"Do you think he could be funding the Iraqi insurgency?" Auggie asked, letting his hands drop. His dark eyes reflected his concern.

"I wouldn't be surprised," I said. "What's the latest estimate? Half a billion? A billion, maybe, pumped into that organization? That money has to come from somewhere. It may be funneled through other sources, but it could ultimately come from a single source. Where was the sighting of the Mary clone?"

"Greece, near the Bulgarian border."

I felt Rafe tense beside me, but he didn't say anything. Baikov likely figured in this somewhere, and Mary Evans' clone had probably arranged a meeting there. "What do you suppose Baikov is cooking up?" I asked Auggie.

"No idea. It makes me wonder what he's trading for what he's getting," Auggie said.

Rafe snorted; it wasn't a happy sound. "Does that mean that the Russian crown jewels are next? Or something better?" Auggie turned his attention on Rafe.

"It could be almost anything, but bear in mind, the Russians have their hands on the drug—I'm sure you've figured that out already. Perhaps Baikov is trading that for whatever he wants."

"Where the hell did he get it?" Auggie snapped.

"Ask Corinne. She was far ahead of me on that." With that statement, he rose from his seat and stalked out of the kitchen.

"You know where the drug came from," Auggie accused, his eyes narrowing as he rapped his knuckles against the granite island.

"I have very good guesses," I said. "And I don't think they're wrong."

"We need a meeting," Auggie rose abruptly. "With Farrell and the President."

The meeting was scheduled in a week, and it wasn't just Dr. Farrell and the President who were involved. Eventually the Directors of the FBI, CIA and the Joint NSA-Homeland Security Department were included.

At least Leo was invited, too, even if Marcus fell into a snit because he wasn't. He had no idea what it was about, but wanted to be included anyway. He was a prime example of a little knowledge being a dangerous thing.

Meanwhile, Auggie had given permission for an evening trip to Seattle, so Rafe and I could have dinner out. James, of course, was going, as were Auggie, Leo and Laci. At the last minute, Maye, Nick and Jeff were added, then Marcus included himself. We had reservations at a nice restaurant downtown, in a private room with a view of the bay.

"I intend to make love when we get back," Ilya murmured against the nape of my neck before we left our suite.

"I missed you," I sighed and leaned against him.

"I have missed my cabbage in my arms, calling out my name," his lips wandered down my neck.

"Honey, you may have to stop or we won't get to dinner."

"You want me that badly?" I could hear the smile in his voice.

"I can't think of any woman who wouldn't want that. I'm first in line," I added.

"You are the only one I allow in line," he turned me in his arms before covering my mouth with his.

You say the best things, I sent to him.

I mean all of them, he returned.

Ilya

"You hear me?" I asked as we stepped off the electric vehicle and walked toward the back end of a large barn. That's where our tunnel ended and the farm property began. Another vehicle waited there for us, ready to transport us to Seattle.

"I do," Corinne said. "I heard you before I woke this time. That's what brought me back."

"Good enough. I assume you do not hear all my thoughts?"

"Only those you send in my direction."

"Good. Very good."

"You can keep your mystery," she looped her arm in mine. I watched her smile and couldn't help smiling in return.

~

Corinne

Mushroom ravioli was my choice for dinner. It was delicious. I just wished I'd gotten to eat as much as I wanted.

Instead, Baikov chose to make his presence known, and while it offered Rafe the gift of revenge, it effectively killed the one possible link I had with the enemy.

Sure—ask how I got us to Crimea. Auggie sure did afterward, and he was there, the rat.

It started, I'm sure, as an attempt to make Ukraine into the enemy. Somehow, Baikov arranged for Russian missiles to fall into the hands of those posing as Ukrainian rebels, who then arranged to fire those same missiles into Crimea.

I was only two bites into my meal when the images flashed across my brain. Baikov should have stayed at home, that day. I transported everybody at the table (including Laci) to an underground bunker southeast of Ivanivka. Computer consoles surrounded us and Russian troops disguised as Ukrainian civilians were seated at those consoles, preparing to launch missiles from a site just outside the Crimean border.

The resulting deaths and destruction would be catastrophic, and all of it blamed on Ukraine. That would cause immense problems down the road, from economic sanctions to an outright takeover by Russia, with nobody willing to stand in the way.

Baikov was there, barking out orders in Russian, which, surprising even to me, I understood. He was telling them to fire the missiles.

I'll never forget the next few minutes as long as I live.

Ilya shouted at the three men sitting at computer consoles to stand down. When they didn't, Auggie, Maye and Nick made sure of it. Baikov pulled a gun and fired at Ilya. It turned out to be the wrong thing to do.

Baikov had the strangest expression on his face as he died, Ilya's eyes boring into his while his neck snapped audibly in Ilya's hands.

Laci, who'd grabbed my arm, stared at the mayhem—and the dead Russian General—in alarm.

"It's okay, they were trying to blow up Crimea," I told her before rubbing her back. The other three were still alive, and I didn't think it was a good idea to kill them in front of Laci. Leo came to Laci and pulled her away while James helped restrain the prisoners.

"I'm assuming you can get them back with us?" Auggie lifted an autocratic eyebrow in my direction, daring me to argue.

"Where do you want to take them?" I asked, ignoring his anger.

"I'd like to take them to Matt Michaels. As soon as possible," he snapped.

It was my turn to raise an eyebrow. Matt Michaels wasn't the name the Director of the Joint NSA/Homeland Security Department was born with, but that was his secret, not mine. "If that's what you want," I agreed. "Are you ready now?"

"I wish I could destroy this site," Ilya interrupted with a snarl.

"Let me do it," I shrugged.

"You can do this?" Ilya wasn't buying it. He muttered something in Russian, and it made me mad. He thought I was delusional for thinking I could destroy the thing.

At that moment, I almost let him see what I might do. I reined in that impulse and did it the safe and effective way.

I turned the whole thing into sand, computers and missiles included.

Yes, they'd called me a witch the last time. I knew they were right —in a way.

This time, nothing could be farther from the truth.

"What the fuck?" Nick muttered as computer consoles became white sand that puddled about his ankles, much like a dry sand castle pounded by a shovel.

"So much for my delusions, huh?" I snapped at Ilya, before transporting everybody, prisoners and Baikov's body included, to Matt Michael's office in Silver Spring.

~

"What the hell?" Matt Michaels stood and stared as all of us appeared in his office. "Auggie, I'm assuming you can get yourself home from here?" I gave him a look that said I was pissed.

"Laci," I added, "I can leave you here with Auggie, or I can take you to Seattle. Your choice."

"I'll, uh, stay here," she quavered.

I didn't blame her—if I'd been at the mercy of someone else who'd just done all the things I had, I'd be shaky, too.

"Corinne, stay here," Auggie demanded.

"Now see, I'm this close to telling you to fuck off," I said, holding a thumb and forefinger half an inch apart. "Bye."

I disappeared.

No, I didn't go back to my suite in the side of a mountain outside Seattle. At least not right away. I wanted a sunny beach somewhere, and I found it in Australia.

~

Notes—Colonel Hunter

"I don't know what the hell just happened," I said, drinking coffee from the cup one of Matt Michael's assistants brought to me. "She knew, somehow, and she went, only she took all of us with her. I still can't explain how she did that. Baikov was with three men disguised as Ukrainian rebels inside a bunker. They were about to fire missiles into Crimea. They had enough firepower to cause a lot of damage."

"So Ukraine would be blamed for starting a war while leaving the country ripe for a Russian invasion, after which the country would be taken over and added back into Russia with no qualms or quibbles from anyone else. Right?"

"It seems that way," I muttered. "I have no idea what Rafe said to her, but it set her off. She turned the whole bunker, computers and missiles included, to sand. I saw it. Still don't believe it, but that's what happened."

"Sand? Interesting choice," Matt leaned back in his chair. The leather squeaked softly as he shifted his body into a more comfortable position.

"You're taking this surprisingly well," I observed.

"Do you need something stronger to drink?" Matt lifted a bottle of bourbon from a desk drawer and offered it to me.

"Hell, add it to the coffee," I held out my cup.

~

Ilya

"What did you say to her?" Dr. Shaw asked quietly. We waited in a room down the hall from Director Michael's office, where there were chairs, sofas, a coffee machine and a small refrigerator filled with soft drinks.

Leo Shaw sat beside me, sipping coffee and watching everyone else —after calming Laci Hunter.

"I said—in Russian—that she was delusional if she thought she could destroy that bunker. It was built of concrete and steel walls, ten feet thick. It would even survive the blast of the missiles it housed, if they were aimed back at it. I had no idea what she was prepared to do. I understand that my words made her angry. I should have kept my mouth shut, instead."

"We haven't touched on all the changes that may have occurred with her," Shaw said. "It's obvious she understood what you said. Has that happened before?"

"No. She couldn't understand what I said before."

"Then this is certainly different. I'll update her file."

~

Corinne

After a while, I transported myself back to Seattle and paid the check at the restaurant. I got an order of the mushroom ravioli to go, along with a replacement order of what everybody else had, too, before leaving all of it in the fridge inside Rafe's suite.

I was about to choose my own suite, and he could live alone if he wanted. Actually, the suite I wanted didn't exist, yet. I took care of that. When I was finished, it was built into the outside rock wall of the mountain, past the last suite of rooms, which belonged to Maye. It was larger, more comfortable, better furnished, had a huge kitchen and pantry and not a single bug in it.

Any bugs that Auggie thought to put in it wouldn't work, either. I made sure of that. I'd handed Baikov to Ilya on a plate and he saw fit to insult me without asking questions. I shouldn't have been that angry, but I was.

I figured they'd get a flight back later that night or early in the morning; I didn't care which. Who knows how many people in Crimea might have died, and Ilya called me delusional.

"Fuck," I muttered aloud. Yeah, I'd probably overreacted, but his words had hit me wrong. I realized I was tired and out of sorts, so I grabbed a sunlamp from storage, turned it on and sat beside it until I fell asleep.

CHAPTER 3

*C*orinne
It took Auggie half an hour after he got back to the mountain to figure out I had a new, separate suite. He banged on the door after that.

I went to let him in.

"What the hell is this?" Auggie flung out an arm, encompassing my new digs.

"My suite. What else would it be?" At least this one had a wall of windows, all camouflaged on the outside so nobody would realize there was anything except rock there.

"You did this?" He blinked at our surroundings.

"I did this. Tell Rafe he can kiss my ass for calling me delusional, too. Want coffee?" I headed toward the kitchen.

"Corinne, you can't just haul off and do everything you want," Auggie walked behind me as I strode toward the kitchen.

"Really? Seems to me Rafe got what he wanted, last night," I snapped, shoving a pod into the coffeemaker. "A whole bunch of folks in Crimea are still alive today. I guess that's what they want, too. I'm sorry Colonel August Hunter didn't get exactly what he wanted, last night." I jerked a cabinet door open and pulled a cup off a shelf. Slamming it under the brewer, I hit the button to make coffee.

"Corinne, look. I don't know how hard that was for you," Auggie attempted to placate me. "I have no idea. Rafe won't talk to me. Laci is terrified. Marcus is still in shock. James, well, James thinks that was the coolest thing he's ever seen."

"Uh-huh." I handed the cup of coffee to Auggie.

"Cori, we have to talk about what you did last night. About how it was done. How long you knew you could do that. What else might be possible."

"No."

"No?"

"I don't want to be used," I said. "The President has good intentions, but she won't be able to help herself."

"Okaaay," Auggie seated himself at my kitchen island. "What do you want from me, then?"

"I want you to trust me. To believe me when I tell you something. That's what I want."

"Is that what you wanted from Rafe last night? For him to believe you when you said you'd destroy the bunker?"

"Yes. Look, I realize I overreacted—I'll admit that. But he didn't give me the benefit of the doubt. I don't know why that bothered me so much, but it did."

"Tell me," he said, making himself comfortable on the barstool, "do you know why things are so different this time?"

"It's a natural progression," I said. "That's all I feel comfortable saying right now. I hope it doesn't go any farther than you and Leo."

"The suite is nice," Auggie said and sipped his coffee.

"It's what I wanted," I replied.

"I can see that. The rugs are nice."

"Wool, power dyed and woven," I said.

"Power dyed and woven?"

"It means I used energy to do it, instead of people."

"Corinne, I almost spit a mouthful of coffee across your floor."

"I'd clean it up if you did."

"The windows are very nice. I assume they're invisible from the outside?"

"Even with the lights on," I agreed.

"Fantastic." He drank more coffee.

"Want a burrito?" I asked.

"You cooking?"

"No, I was thinking about going to Texas to get one."

"Cori, please stay here. You'll give me a heart attack if you don't."

The knock on my door almost gave both of us a heart attack. I left Auggie in the kitchen and went to let Rafe and James in.

"Nice. Very nice," Rafe said as he followed me to the kitchen.

"Before you ask," I held up a hand, "I think it was low blood sugar. Too much energy expended and not enough reserves."

"I accept your apology," Rafe said.

"Good."

He and James helped themselves to coffee before finding the food in the fridge; I'd transferred it there after completing my new home. That resulted in a flurry of microwaving, after which they sat down to a nice meal.

"Did you pay for this?" Auggie asked.

"I did. And the stuff we didn't get to eat, too, plus a nice tip and a promise to never go back there again."

"I'll fix that," Auggie grumped. "This chicken is good."

"Suit yourself," I shrugged.

Notes—Colonel Hunter

I left Corinne's new suite when the call came from the President.

It wasn't good news.

"What do you mean, they escaped?" Making sense of what Madam President shouted over the phone was impossible—for at least the first ten seconds. All I could understand initially was the word "escaped."

"Sixteen survivors that we had in quarantine escaped," she slowed

34

her speech and calmed her temper. "We had them locked in and cared for. They all got out. I need you, Farrell and anybody else who might help with this mess. Please tell me Corinne can help. This is disastrous."

"Why?" I asked. "Why is this disastrous?"

"Because they're not human, and some of them—some of them defy explanation."

It angered me that she'd left us out of that loop from the beginning —that she'd taken control and hidden the survivors away. At first, I imagined it was to keep them away from the general population until they could be reintroduced into it without revealing the drug or the Program.

Later, I began to imagine other, more terrible things. This announcement brought the worst of those imaginings to life.

"How did they escape?" I asked.

"I don't know. I don't understand any of this. We thought they were responding to the care they were getting, but evidently, that wasn't enough."

"Is there any trail to follow? I'll bring Nick," I offered.

"Bring all of them. We can't find a trail to follow, but I'll take anything I can get."

"I hope you have records and images to help Corinne," I said.

"We do, but it's so classified, I almost didn't get to see them."

I wanted to curse. I didn't. At least not aloud. This spelled one thing to me—the CIA Director was in this up to his hairline. He and the Joint Chiefs had likely colluded to keep me out of this after they took charge, and almost left the President out of it. Now it was exploding in their faces. If the situation didn't sound so serious, I might have laughed at their faux pas.

"I'll get my bunch together," I said. "We'll be there before you can blink."

Corinne

Ilya was in the middle of being amorous when Auggie commanded everybody to pack for a trip to D.C. He was knocking on our door two minutes later, asking if I had enough energy to get everybody to D.C. without hurting myself.

"I can," I said, "But I need fresh air and something to eat afterward."

"I'll see to it," he nodded curtly. "We have an emergency, you understand, or I'd fly everybody back."

"I know."

I turned to Ilya, who allowed Rafe to come to the fore. "I'll have a bag ready in ten," he said and loped toward the door. He was just as frustrated as I was that we'd been interrupted.

"The President didn't give me much," Auggie sighed when Rafe shut the door behind him. "It doesn't sound good. I think she's saving the bad stuff for when we get there."

"I was worried about this," I said. "It didn't help that we were cut out of it. I think Dr. Farrell should have been consulted at the very least, but bigger dicks wanted to control this." I spoke mainly of CIA Director, Merle Askins; Auggie understood that. While we both thought of Askins as a boil on America's butt, everybody was secretly afraid of him.

"While I wouldn't agree openly with you under most circumstances, I'm agreeing with you now," Auggie said. Worry clouded his dark eyes as he shook his head at the state of affairs and what might wait for us when we arrived at the White House. "The President should have asked us. She didn't. Now, we're expected to do cleanup."

"Doesn't sound like an easy job," I pointed out.

"I don't think it will be. They can't find a trail to follow. That concerns me. A lot."

"Do you know where they were?" I asked.

"No idea. We'll have that information when we get there."

"Then I'll be ready in five," I said and took off toward my bedroom.

～

Matt Michaels and a woman I hadn't met before were already in the Oval Office when we arrived.

"You know Director Michaels," the President made introductions. "This is one of his best agents, Opal Tadewi."

"I hear you can see things about people just by looking at them," Opal held out her hand.

I shook and nodded. *Your secret is safe with me,* I sent to her. She blinked once, telling me she heard and understood.

"I can work with her," Opal jerked her head in my direction, telling Director Michaels that she felt she could trust me.

"Good. I've been briefed on the Program," Director Michaels nodded to Auggie.

"It was my choice," the President said, holding up a hand to keep Auggie from arguing.

"He knows how to keep quiet," I acknowledged when everything went silent for a moment. Maye released a troubled sigh.

"Where are we going?" Auggie asked, following the second uncomfortable silence. Nobody liked the fact that someone else knew about the Program. I suppose almost being killed on several occasions will do that to you. I didn't say it, but future threats against our lives wouldn't come from Matt Michaels.

"You're going to Las Vegas," the President said with a sigh. "Actually, outside Las Vegas is where they were kept, but you'll be staying in Vegas until you find a trail to follow."

Rafe turned slowly toward me, offering the slightest of nods. He and I were thinking the same thing; we just didn't say it aloud. Area 51 was too much of a cliché. We were headed somewhere else.

After all, you can hide a secret location near a bigger, badder-looking secret location. Everybody looks for the big one, when they have no idea that the smaller one exists.

"There's transportation ready, and anything you didn't pack can be had in Las Vegas," the President said. "The facility director will brief you when you get there."

I could see she was tired and angry. Angry that this had blown up in her face. She'd allowed the CIA and Joint Chiefs to have these survivors, possibly in the hope of creating another arm of the Program.

Auggie was pissed, too—as Secretary of Defense, he'd inherited the Joint Chiefs, who'd always been at odds with him. They were more loyal to the CIA Director than to Auggie, because Merle Askins had more power and bigger guns.

Now, the President worried that she—and they—may have unleashed something that couldn't easily be caught or contained. I had worries, too, and they included hers plus a few of my own. Mine were ultimately worse.

"What do you expect us to do with them, if we find them?" Auggie asked quietly.

"Kill them if you can," she whispered.

∾

"We don't have much time; I hope this works," Auggie said as we trooped into a Denny's near the air base. Opal was with us; her luggage was now in one of our borrowed SUVs.

"Cabbage, what are you hungry for?" Rafe rubbed my back.

"Eggs, cheese, fruit," I shrugged. At least the day was fine and sunny. I ignored the hot part.

"Oatmeal, too?" Rafe grinned.

"Maybe. I'm hungry after toting you around," I wrinkled my nose at him.

"I can understand that," he agreed.

A waitress led us to three tables shoved together. We sat down and ordered drinks. An hour later, we were loaded onto another military transport heading to Nellis AFB in Nevada.

∾

Notes—Colonel Hunter

Once I was seated on the plane across from Shaw, I opened the classified e-mail sent from the President. No pictures were included—

not the important ones, anyway. I only saw photographs of the damage caused during the escape.

"What the hell can do that?" I placed my tablet in Leo Shaw's hands. It only took a moment before his grim gaze met mine.

"If that were Tokyo, I'd have a good guess," he said. "This isn't Tokyo, and I sure hope we're not dealing with something that size."

"Something that size would be hard to lose," I pointed out. "What if it's much smaller and much more difficult to locate?"

"Even scarier," he nodded before leaving his seat and settling on the empty one beside me so he could study the photographs easier. "Do we know if they acted together, or whether one or two got the others out?"

"I'm concerned that somebody else may have gotten them out," I muttered. "I think Cori is worried about the same thing, she just won't say it."

"If Corinne is concerned, then we certainly should be," Shaw said. "She hasn't been wrong yet. Whatever these survivors became, we should have been allowed to help. If there was any way to communicate with them, then Corinne might have reached them. I can't help but think we could have helped. Now, we have orders to kill them."

"That concerns me, too. Besides, the Joint Chiefs need taking down a notch or two over this. Whether the President will see the need for it is questionable."

"I believe Hal's clone may have advised her on this," Shaw jerked his head at the photographs on my tablet. "Therefore, he may have had a good guess as to where they'd be taken. I wonder if Madam President considered that."

"I think the CIA Director and the Joint Chiefs are so smug in their perceived invincibility, they may have advised her against moving these. Obviously, they thought them well-contained."

They had. Steel doors more than a foot thick, which had been ripped from their hinges, attested to that. "They're either on their own and can cause damage that way, or they're in the hands of the enemy, and we've all seen what he's capable of doing," Shaw said.

~

Corinne

"Cabbage, we're here." Rafe squeezed my hand to wake me.

"What? Oh." I'd been far away in my dreams and wasn't particularly pleased about waking in the extremely hot state of Nevada.

I blinked sleepily as I followed Rafe and the others off the plane, while our luggage was taken off the aircraft and loaded into three waiting SUVs.

"Cori, you look half asleep," James came to stand beside me while Auggie and Leo decided who was riding with whom. Rafe, Opal and I ended up with Auggie. Nick and Maye went with Leo; Jeff rode with James, Richard Farrell and Marcus.

I'd seen Marcus eyeing Opal—she was beautiful; an American Indian with long, black hair and dark eyes. I caught her eyeing him a couple of times, too, and I wouldn't want to be Marcus if he attempted to touch her without permission.

Just the thought of it made me smile.

"What?" she turned a lovely smile on me.

"Oh, just thinking about Marcus and how much trouble he might be in if he doesn't keep his hands to himself," I said.

That made her laugh. "You're right," she said. I knew without a doubt that Opal had no yearnings toward Marcus, and hoped he didn't learn the hard way just how dangerous she could be.

"We don't have much information on you," she said. "I saw dossiers on everyone else in the Program, with permission from the President." I could almost hear Auggie and Rafe's ears perking up at Opal's question. "The President said she wouldn't give your information to anyone—that you could tell us or not."

"I almost died in the terrorist attack on the Louvre," I shrugged. "The drug kept me alive."

"You were there?" Her dark eyes widened at the idea that someone actually survived.

"It's a long story," I said. "Do we have water in the car, Auggie?" He'd let Rafe drive and was sitting up front with him.

"Some in the cargo area—they sent a cooler," Auggie said.

"Okay." Unbuckling my seat belt, I reached over the seat to open the cooler. The minute I put my hand on one of the bottles I knew. *Don't drink any of the water*, I sent to everyone in our party. *It's laced with ricin*, I added.

Auggie's cell phone rang immediately. "James drank some of the water," Jeff reported.

"Pull over. Honey, pull over," I was terrified in an instant.

Dr. Farrell was already using the ability he had to heal James when we pulled over to the side of the road. I jumped from the SUV and ran back to James' vehicle. Richard's hands were on James' chest while he sent power coursing through James' body to reverse the poison's effects.

I placed my hands on James' chest, too, only it was my goal to neutralize the poison. Richard felt my presence and turned to blink at me, astonished by what I was doing. He could feel it in his hands— that the poison was changing composition to something that wouldn't harm anyone.

"Cori? Will I be okay?" James' voice wobbled when my work was done and I removed my hands.

"Honey, you are one hundred percent okay now," I said. "You wait till I find whoever put that shit in your water, though. They have a big surprise coming, and it won't be a good one, either."

"I'm with her," Richard pulled away and nodded in my direction. "Colonel Hunter, how long is our drive from here?" He turned to Auggie.

"It's less than an hour away," Auggie said, blinking in the bright sunlight that bore down on us.

"Is everybody on the same page—don't drink the water?" Dr. Farrell asked. Everybody nodded. "Good. Whoever did this wanted to thin the herd. We're not going to let that happen."

"I order it not to happen," Auggie said. I could tell he was pissed— we could have lost James and nobody would be happy about that.

"Can I ride with you?" James reached out to touch my arm.

"Honey, you can do whatever you want right now," I said.

"Good." He climbed out of the back seat of Jeff's SUV and put his arms around me.

Honey, I know that was scary, I sent to him. *You're okay. Dr. Farrell and I wouldn't let anything happen to you.*

"I'm glad you checked the water," James said as I pulled him toward Auggie's SUV.

"That makes two of us," I confirmed.

Not far from Devil's Hole Road, just outside the triangle it forms in one area, lies an underground facility owned by the U.S. Government. Its entrance is hidden beneath an old, tin-roofed barn, sitting next to an old ranch house, its exterior hiding the more modern facility located inside. Fences, with *Private Property, trespassers will be introduced to our guns and dogs* signs hanging everywhere, greeted us as we drove across a cattle guard and onto the property.

"Why the hell do they need a cattle guard?" Opal asked as our SUV bounced across it, the tires clunking over metal pipes and shaking the vehicle annoyingly. There certainly weren't any cattle anywhere—it was desert, with nothing for a cow to eat until you reached parts of California.

"It's wired—it tells them we're coming, and if they weren't expecting us, our tires would have been cut and guards would have shot at us," Auggie said.

"Good news all around," Opal muttered. I laughed.

Ten minutes later, we parked in the barn, where nothing around us resembled the inside of a barn. A modernized metal building surrounded us, while the heavy, steel doors leading into the hidden facility were undergoing repairs—two welders were outside working on them. This was the survivors' final point of escape, looked like.

"I'm not detecting much scent," Nick walked about the interior of the barn, sniffing.

"There probably isn't much to detect," I sighed. "Auggie, one of them knew how to shield, I think, so they wouldn't leave that kind of a trail. It's anybody's guess how they got away, once they were outside this barn."

The facility director chose that moment to appear. He walked up to Auggie and held out his hand. "Pete Dumont," he introduced himself. "I wish I could welcome you under better circumstances, Mr. Secretary."

Pete Dumont had thick, reddish-brown hair that refused to allow any comb to tame it. Streaks of silver ran through the mess of it, indicating that Pete was in his mid-fifties. His green eyes begged Auggie to be friendly, if not nice. Pete felt personally responsible for the escape of sixteen no-longer-human detainees.

"I hope you have images and information on what it is, exactly, we're supposed to track," Auggie gruffed.

"I do," Pete said. "I'm sorry you didn't have this information before, but I was ordered not to reveal it until now."

That meant, in English, that CIA Director Merle Askins ordered it. He'd been placed by Madam President's predecessor, which automatically rendered him suspect in my eyes. Plus, he was a conniving bastard. Everybody said so, just not to his face.

It meant, too, that Merle was likely hiding a ton of excrement from Madam President. Yeah, that pissed me off. You can't ask questions about things you don't even realize exist.

"Merle Askins strikes again," Opal whispered beside me as Pete turned to lead us into the facility.

"You got that right," I whispered back.

"Cori," Auggie handed a fistful of photographs to me after he looked at them closely. Pete stood nearby, sweating as Auggie, wearing his Secretary of Defense hat, swore at the images before handing some of them to me, first.

Rafe sat on one side, Opal on the other, so all three of us looked at what sixteen humans had become after surviving the drug.

"The youngest one is the most dangerous, I think," Pete sighed. "As a human, he was nineteen. Here's his photograph, before and after."

Auggie looked, shook his head and handed it to me. Rafe drew in a breath beside me. In one photograph, Kevin Riley smiled as his senior class photo was taken. In the other, the creature that formerly was Kevin Riley stood over the carcass of a disemboweled cow. His muzzle, if you could call it that, was bloody from eating the animal from the middle outward.

Sharp, obsidian scales covered his body, while his eyes glowed golden as he fed. Claws on all six legs were evident, although he only employed the first two to feed himself.

"I believe that's a carryover from his human existence, only using his front set of legs to hold his lunch," I handed the photograph to Rafe. I was more than done looking at it and the next one of him, which showed him holding the cow like most humans would hold a chicken leg.

That's how large he'd become; that a cow—in proportion, anyway—could be eaten like a chicken leg.

"He liked showers after eating, so we let the fire sprinklers clean him and the blood up at the same time," Pete muttered.

"Cori, can you tell us what that is?" Auggie asked as Rafe passed the photograph to Nick and Maye.

"I know you're familiar with the dinosaurs in Earth's history," I sighed.

"That's no dinosaur I've ever seen," Pete protested.

"It isn't, because you didn't grow up on a world a thousand light years from here," I said.

CHAPTER 4

*C*orinne

    I was forced into a semi-private meeting with Auggie after our meeting with Pete ended. Only Auggie, Leo and Dr. Farrell were allowed into this meeting. The Program was about to be blown wide open, and I wished that Rafe could be beside me while I explained what I'd known for a while.

"What did you mean when you mentioned a world a thousand light years from here?" Auggie began. I could tell his blood pressure was about to rise dramatically if he didn't get a quick answer.

"It's what the Program—and Cloud Dust is all about," I said. "We didn't manufacture it here."

I watched Richard Farrell's face as he turned it away from me. He suspected, he just didn't have enough evidence to make a conjecture. Good scientist that he was, he wasn't about to make a wild claim without substantiation.

"Where, then? Russia?" Leo Shaw asked. He still wasn't getting it.

"Oh, they have it too, just from separate incidents. I will say that they've taken its uses to the extreme, though."

"Corinne, stop talking in circles and explain this. Now." Auggie thumped his fist on the table, making Richard jump.

We'd been allowed into a private meeting room inside the underground facility, and I'd already taken care of the bugs planted there before saying anything.

"The original drug, which looks like dust to anybody who doesn't know, by the way, came from extraterrestrials. We got it once—in 1947. The Russians got it twice, in 1969 and 1986."

"Reported crashes," Richard mumbled while he stood and raked fingers through his hair.

"How does it work, then? Why was it there? Do you have any ideas?" Auggie asked. I could see that he struggled with the information, just as the others did.

"Have you ever wondered how someone from so far away might live long enough to reach Earth, if they didn't have a faster-than-light drive on their space ship?" I asked.

"Not really," Leo shook his head. Auggie just stared—he was attempting to piece this puzzle together.

"They had the drug," I hunched my shoulders. "It's called Cloud Dust because it looks like dust and it—and the spaceship—came from the clouds above us. I figure that when the pilot or pilots got to the end of their lives, they'd take the drug and have another life to live. The problem with all this, of course, is that it was engineered for their race. If another race gets it, interesting things happen."

"Oh, my God," Auggie covered his face with both hands.

"You're telling us that this is instant reincarnation, or as close as you can get to it?" Richard asked, turning worried eyes in my direction.

"Yeah. Only sometimes, that reincarnation should have happened on another world. In a different atmosphere, maybe. Or under water. Who knows? The ones who die? It's because they're reborn in the wrong place."

"Holy Christ," Leo breathed.

"What about the clones?" Farrell asked. "Can you explain that?"

"I think that was an accidental discovery," I said. "People—lots of people—have the same blood types. Take Becker, for example. Somebody with the same blood type, getting Becker's dust-infected blood, will become exactly like Becker. It's like a copy machine, regularly spitting out identical images, it just has to pass from an original survivor of the drug. The recipient's blood recognizes the same blood, and then the drug takes over. It can happen in a matter of weeks, as you've already seen."

"And blood can be kept frozen for a lengthy period of time," Richard nodded. "If the enemy loses one servant, as long as he has their blood, he can make as many copies as he wants."

"I don't want to imagine an army of Beckers," Auggie said.

"I'm hoping we killed off the last of him," I shrugged. I didn't want to tell them the other things I knew—Armageddon could come soon enough, and from more than one direction.

"They know, now?" Rafe asked as I walked into the room where he and the others waited for me. Auggie, Leo and Richard had gone off to have a phone conversation with Madam President. I didn't envy them.

"Yeah. As much as they need, anyway," I said.

"You know something?" Maye asked.

Yes, but we can't discuss it here—there are bugs and unfriendly employees, I replied to Maye's question.

No surprise, she sent and nodded at me. Too bad for Merle Askins that he couldn't bug mindspeech. We could call him a bow-legged twat in mindspeech and he'd never know it.

Why are you smiling? Maye's eyes narrowed as she watched the corners of my mouth curl.

I just called Merle a bow-legged twat in my head, I returned.

Maye started laughing.

"What's going on?" Opal asked, her dark, unblinking eyes studying me.

I called Merle Askins a bow-legged twat, I sent to her and the others.

Nick slapped a hand over his mouth before the guffaw could escape.

∾

Notes—Colonel Hunter

The call took place outside, far from any bugs. I hoped that someone, somewhere, wasn't bugging my phone while I spoke with the President.

"That's what Corinne said?" Madam President asked. She wanted to believe Corinne, who'd never lied to us yet, but the news was so far-fetched as to fall in the realm of pure speculation.

"It's what she said. It makes sense, I suppose, but I still can't wrap my head around it."

"And Dr. Farrell thinks it's plausible?"

"Hell, Corinne just confirmed his suspicions," I replied. "According to him, everything went back to that time, and he'd done enough research to know that the scientists initially working on the drug were stationed in the Southwest. If I'm right, that's when this bunker was built. It's been upgraded all along, but the original building dates back to the late forties."

"That's true," Madam President sighed and went silent for a moment. "If the Russians have the same thing, and they've done all this," she hesitated again. "Damn. This is outrageous. I can't believe my predecessor put so many lives in danger."

"Do you think he'd gotten wind of the experiments going on in Russia? Did he think he needed his own army to combat what they were building?" I asked. "Rafe didn't know about this, but Baikov likely did," I added.

"Does this mean that the enemy, whoever he is, may have come from those experiments? Could he be Russian?" she asked. "This President hasn't been in power very long, but he seems bent on following in his predecessor's footsteps. I hoped things would be different after the last one died, but that wasn't to be."

"No idea about a Russian connection, but we'll start looking at likely candidates," I promised.

"You still have sixteen survivors to track," she reminded me.

"I know, but that trail may lead to the same place and the same person," I pointed out. "If he took them, after getting them out, somehow, we may be in a world of trouble. Did you see the photographs of that giant, well, whatever it was? Corinne says it's a dinosaur of sorts from another planet."

"This is a nightmare," the President mumbled. "And it happened on our watch."

"I like to think that we're where we are, because we're the right people for the job," I said.

"I sure hope you're right, because you know what might happen if you're not."

"Let's not think about that for the moment. We have a job to do, and I need to get my people on it ASAP."

Corinne

"Cori, where do you think we ought to start looking for that thing —and the others with it?" James flopped onto the uncomfortable sofa beside me. No furniture inside the bunker looked as if it were begging to be lounged on while reading a book.

Leo Shaw had taken charge of the bottled water from our vehicles, and ordered the lab inside the facility to analyze it for the poison it contained and look for fingerprints or residue. That made me happy and kept Pete's employees occupied at the same time.

The only records we had concerning the water were of the delivery made by the vendors who supplied Nellis AFB, where we'd picked up the vehicles. James had worked on tracking down their suppliers before they'd gotten the cases of water, and ordered all deliveries picked up so they could be examined for contamination.

Auggie didn't want word of the poison leaked if he could help it, and worried that we'd been targeted specifically by someone wanting all of us dead. It was a valid thought, and one I considered exploring.

The other thing that came to my mind was this—were they testing us? Testing me, perhaps, just to see if I'd find it before anybody died?

For the moment, Auggie wanted information on James' poisoning to remain with us, and everybody we'd had contact with would be watched carefully. He depended on me for that, knowing I'd see it in them if they were guilty.

I considered letting Rafe, Nick or Maye know first, because they wanted a few pieces of the one responsible and I wasn't about to stop them. Auggie, Leo and Richard walked in together.

"Cori, is there anything to find here?" Auggie asked.

"No," I shook my head. "There's no trail to follow and wherever they are, something is hiding them. They won't find anything helpful on the water, either, except that it contains ricin, which we already knew. Dinosaur Boy and his entourage could be far away by now."

"Something that large can't be transported in a normal vehicle," Rafe pointed out. "The others, yes. The dinosaur creature? Absolutely not."

"Let's go back to Vegas; I'll send messages on the way, asking about any unusually large trucks traveling through the state around the time of the escape," Auggie said. "We have other problems to solve, too, and we need to get on that before suspects disappear."

He wanted whoever attempted to poison us—bad.

James rode back to Vegas with Rafe, Auggie, Opal and me. "Do you think we'll find that thing?" Opal asked along the way.

"I hope so," I said. "At this point, I'm not sure he remembers much about who he was before, because the animal is taking over."

"I'm supposed to have records e-mailed to me on all of them," Auggie said, peering around his front seat. "We didn't see all the photographs, or hear everything," he added.

"I know," I nodded. "I think they were afraid of us. Somebody told them what was coming to inspect their facility."

"You mean who, don't you?"

"That's not what I read," I replied. "Several of them thought their lives might be in danger, because there was a killer among us."

"Were they talking about me?" Rafe asked. He was driving, so he didn't turn to look.

"No, honey. They were thinking about me."

"Who the fuck told them that?" Auggie exploded. "They shouldn't have information on any of us."

"You know, I think I'd like to know the same thing," I said. "What I do know is this—they'd gotten an anonymous e-mail from somebody, telling them I could kill with a look. No description, so they had a hard time figuring out whether it was me, Opal or Maye, but they knew it was a woman."

"So they didn't know where the message originated?"

"No," I shook my head at Auggie. "But I intend to find out."

"This complicates things. I hope they think it's a lie, now, since nobody died back there."

"That's not exactly true," I said. "Not now, anyway."

"What the hell?" Auggie snapped.

"One of them knew what was happening. I didn't kill him. The creature he had locked in a closet did it when he opened the door to release it. It's dead, too, by the way—the others shot and killed it before it got away."

"I may kill somebody before the day's over," Auggie growled.

"So only fifteen are left?" Leo asked when we settled in Auggie's suite at a high-rise in Vegas. "Did you know about the one left behind, Corinne?"

"I did, but the guy intended to let it loose on us if we said we suspected as much. This way, he's dead and it's dead. There are fifteen others."

"He wanted it to kill us if we pointed a finger in his direction?" Auggie shook his head.

"That was the plan. He was the inside man, letting Dinosaur Boy know that somebody was waiting on the outside to give him anything he wanted, including a nice, new home, if he'd agree to scare the bejeezus out of people and devour a few, now and then. I think he liked that idea, so one was chosen to stay behind to protect the mole while the rest followed Dinosaur Boy out the door."

"Did the mole know where they were going?"

"He had no idea, but I figure you'll find the fat bank account he left behind—if you get to it fast enough."

"Fuck," Auggie cursed and went to stand by the floor-to-ceiling windows of his suite. Las Vegas was beginning to light up around us, but the noise of the streets didn't reach that high. I was grateful. I had enough worries and honking horns, engine noise and screeching tires would likely wear on my nerves. Opal was the one to contact Matt Michaels, who turned his attention to the dead man's bank deposits.

"Cabbage, are you all right?" Rafe stood beside me as I studied Auggie's tense shoulders and Las Vegas through his window.

"Tired," I shrugged. *James could have died again, if that thing had gotten out of its closet. Leo, too, they were closest to it. The rest of us could have killed it, but the damage would be done.*

Why did it kill its keeper, then?

It was pissed because he didn't let it out soon enough. He was still afraid one of us would kill him, so he waffled.

Were you intending to tell us?

You know, this is the first time we've really had a mental conversation, I pointed out.

Didn't want anybody to know, he gave me a wink and a grin.

Yeah, hoping I'd trip up, huh?

Answer my question, he said, still grinning.

Yes, I intended to tell you and Auggie when we got away from there, so he could be arrested the next time he left the compound and the monster could be contained. He removed that option—and himself—from the food chain, making it so much easier for everybody.

Saved all of us time and trouble, Rafe agreed. *Where should we go next?*

I need time to think about that, okay?

Auggie's cell phone rang. The President was on the line, telling us to go back to the Pilchuck facility. We could plot and plan from there just as well as we could from Vegas.

I agreed with her—someone had tried to kill us with ricin-laced water. James was afraid to drink anything now, unless I told him it was safe. Whoever had planned that nasty little surprise likely had clearance and more than enough flunkies to do the job—flunkies who had no idea what they were doing, other than following orders.

"Take us home, Cori," Auggie said, his words sounding flat and weary after he ended the call with the President.

"Yeah," I said and did just that.

~

"You really can see Puget Sound from here," Rafe's arms dropped around my shoulders as we gazed out our window. It was closest to the southwest, and the day, surprisingly, was clear.

The Sound was there, shining far in the distance—a swath of blue beneath a setting sun. "I want to make love to you, right here," he pulled me toward the sofa that faced the window.

"Yeah," I breathed against his mouth. "Let's get naked."

His fingers lifted my top as he backed me toward the comfortable sofa I'd supplied for our suite.

After that, it was a frenzy of clothing removal. I unbuckled his belt. He unzipped my jeans. After a while, you'd have thought piranhas were stripping anything other than skin away from us. Ilya's mouth was all over mine, and then traveling down my body as he pulled me onto the sofa.

The first time was fast. Frenetic. The second—slow and decadent. Both times were exactly what we wanted.

~

"Cori, can you get me to the house in Seattle?" Auggie walked in with James right behind him. "Laci wants to cook dinner for me, and I think James needs a glass or two of Scotch."

"Yes and yes," I nodded to Auggie and James. Rafe pulled the open bottle of Macallan from the liquor cabinet and dropped ice cubes in a glass before pouring a generous portion for James.

Laci lived in an older, richer part of Seattle, referred to as Upper Queen Anne. The house was a three-story, built in the early 1900s, with plenty of gingerbread decorating the exterior. It also had an exceptional view of Elliott Bay. I hoped she liked it—I'd have loved it, provided it were in a place with more abundant sunlight.

"Are you ready now, or want to have a drink first?" I asked Auggie.

"I'll have a drink," Auggie sighed. My guess was that he wasn't looking forward to this meeting with Laci—I imagine she was more than tired of his life being constantly on the line.

Rafe poured a second glass and handed it to Auggie, who downed it immediately and held out his glass for another shot. Rafe pulled me against him as we watched Auggie and James drink—they both had personal worries and I hoped Leo Shaw intended to see both of them —at length.

"James, why don't you stay for dinner," Rafe offered. I intended to ask, but he beat me to it.

"I'll be back in a minute," I gave James a hug. "Ready?" I asked Auggie.

"Yeah. Let's go."

~

Notes—Colonel Hunter

I figured Laci would ask for a divorce again. She didn't. She didn't even point out that I tasted like Scotch when she kissed me. I'll admit I spent a moment, immobile and shocked as hell before recalling that I should put my arms around her.

"I missed you, baby," I kissed her temple before moving down to her earlobe.

Cori had dropped me outside the front door, so I'd used my key to get in. Laci found me in the foyer, punching the code into the alarm. That's when she'd pulled my head down for a scorching kiss and I eventually reciprocated.

"I heard there was dinner, too," I whispered in her ear. "I like the appetizer so far."

"Wait until dessert," she breathed against my ear.

"I'm ready for that, now," I said as she took my hand and led me toward the dining room.

We had the best dinner—Laci fixed everything I liked, including strawberry shortcake. The sex afterward?

Sex hadn't been that good in forever. I felt like I was twenty again. It made me want to buy her something—a piece of jewelry or spicy lingerie. I'll admit, my brain was stuck on the spicy lingerie.

"Do you like it here, baby?" I asked after we'd shared a short nap.

"I do, actually." She gave me a genuine smile—I always knew when she wasn't telling me the truth. "Nelda and Ray take me down to Pike's Place when I want to go. They have the most amazing fresh flowers there," she said. "I got the fish there, too, that we had for dinner. I even like the crowds—it reminds me of when we lived in New York, except for the huge house and the better view I have here."

Nelda and Ray were her assigned day guards. Others watched the house at night, but they stayed out of sight. Nelda and Ray were stationed in the house next door, and I could tell Laci liked both of them.

"Dr. Shaw suggested that I come see him once a week at the facility for my appointments," Laci said, leaning in to kiss me. "He says it wouldn't hurt for me to spend a night with you, just like you come to spend a night with me every week."

"You want to?" I was surprised, but tried to hide it.

"I think I do. I wouldn't mind seeing Corinne and Rafe—I hear they're very good cooks. I'm a little upset that James could have died, too, so I'd like to see him."

"Did Ray tell you that?"

"He and Nelda keep me updated as much as they can. I want you to keep Corinne as close as you possibly can—and Rafe too. I think they can save your life if that kind of thing ever happens again."

"You should hear Madam President talk about the same thing," I huffed and rolled off the bed.

"Where are you going?" Laci demanded.

"To the john. And then to the fridge to get more shortcake. You almost wore me out, woman."

"I'm going to the kitchen first," she slid off the bed and headed for the door.

"Don't eat it all," I called after her and grinned on my way to the bathroom.

Corinne

"I can't move," James mumbled, leaning back on the sofa. I didn't tell him that earlier, Ilya and I had sex there. We'd been neat about it, at least. "You have such a great view," he added, staring at Seattle and Puget Sound in the distance.

We'd served chicken cordon bleu for Rafe and James, with plenty of vegetables for me. They'd polished off all the chicken, along with the Italian cream cake for dessert.

"I'm not carrying you to bed, but you're welcome to the second bedroom," Rafe offered.

"Really?" James turned to Rafe.

"As long as you pick up after yourself."

"I always do." He pretended offense.

"Honey, this place is plenty big enough," I shrugged. Rafe knew, as did I, that James was still in crisis mode. It would take a while, with Leo's help, to get him back to normal. James was a good fighter—with an enemy he could see.

Somebody had tried to poison him, and he'd never suspected anything like that. It had thrown him—just as it had several others. He'd gone from trusting the military he'd worked for to distrusting almost everyone.

James needs to have sex, Rafe informed me in mindspeech as we watched Auggie's assistant rise and wander toward the extra bedroom.

Any suggestions? I asked.

Not now—nobody in the program is suitable, Rafe responded. *Leo still has the list, but there's nobody there for James.*

I understood what it was like not to have anyone support you so intimately. Without Ilya, I wouldn't have come back at all. *James needs somebody who cares about him,* I returned. *Not just a casual fuck.*

Relationships take time, he reminded me. *A casual fuck may help in the interim. Men aren't wired like women,* he wrapped his arms about me. *Even gay ones.*

Are you being philosophical?

I'm being horny. I hope you're feeling the same way. We can have meaningful sex in our bedroom. Or on the table. Or on the rug in the media room. Your choice.

Rug?

Excellent choice.

~

Opal

I'm getting notification of some seismic activity in the Seattle area, Matt's text read.

Not unusual for this part of the world, I replied.

Just putting you on notice, he sent a smiley face with his second text.

Really? You're using smiley faces? I thought it was in your job description that you could never, ever use smiley faces in official communications.

I have a special dispensation from the President.

You do not send smiley faces to the President, I pointed out.

Nah, I send frowny faces to her.

Why are you concerned about seismic activity? I was back to the original subject.

Something just feels off, he said. *Keep your eyes, ears and fast little feet on alert,* he added. *Anything new with Corinne?*

Not yet. I do get the idea that she'd do anything to protect everybody here, me included.

I'm still marveling at what she's done so far. I just wish we knew what we're up against—she wants this enemy as much as we do.

She does—I can see it in her face, I tapped into my phone. *Look, I'll keep you updated. Go save the world or something.*

I would, if there weren't so much paperwork involved.

Always a comeback, I said and shut off my phone.

~

Corinne

Ilya and I were in the throes of climax when the earthquake hit Seattle, and while it barely rocked Mount Pilchuck, it did major damage to parts of the city near Elliott Bay.

CHAPTER 5

Corinne

"Power is out in much of the city," Auggie muttered while pulling on a clean shirt and stomping through the command center. I understood that, even before he'd called me on his cell ten minutes earlier, saying he wanted me to come for him, Laci and Laci's day guards.

"Laci, why don't you let James take you to Auggie's quarters," I said while Auggie barked orders at subordinates.

"Will we be all right?" Laci's voice quivered in fear. I understood then that she'd never been in a substantial earthquake.

"We're fine where we are, and if that changes, I'll get us out of here," I promised. "Go with James. We'll keep you updated. You may want to see if the TV is working in his suite—just to see what they're saying on the news stations."

"Will that help?"

"You bet." I smiled and hugged her. "Ask James for a tablet, and send messages to let him know what's going on. Take Nelda and Ray with you."

"I'll do what I can," she promised.

Rafe, Maye, Opal, Nick, Marcus, Leo and Auggie stood near the bank of computer screens, looking as if they were ready for a football huddle to plan their next move. Auggie nodded his thanks to me for giving Laci something useful to do before turning his attention back to the monitors. Nelda and Ray ushered Laci from the room, leaving me to join the huddle around computer screens.

I hadn't contributed yet, other than to pull Laci, Auggie and the other two away from Seattle, where things were going crazy. I knew, and she'd likely hear it on the news soon—part of the sea wall had been crushed, allowing water to rush into a section of vulnerable and unstable land at the waterfront.

Yes, they were attempting to replace the old, wooden sea wall with concrete and steel, but not all of it had been done. Now, parts of underground Seattle, a popular tourist attraction and extra storage for many businesses, was filling with water and flooding anything near the wharf.

I was afraid to use my talents to search for the number of dead. Pike Place Market and other businesses along the water were off-limits—not only was the power out, officials were afraid everything would crumble beneath visitors and traffic.

Many were learning for the first time that the waterfront section hardest hit was landfill—and poor landfill at that.

The most important thing I understood, however, was this—an earthquake hadn't caused this damage. I needed to get Auggie and Leo away so I could explain what I knew. Fixing the problem, too, was going to be a lot harder than anybody might think.

"Corinne, are you coming?" Auggie barked in my direction. The meeting was about to take place and I'd been lost in conjecture land.

"Coming," I trotted toward Auggie, who herded everybody else toward a secure meeting room.

Rafe pulled me onto the chair next to his at the wide table, which took up most of the floor space inside the room. Auggie and Leo sat at the head of the table, while the rest of us scattered around it.

"We don't know much," Auggie sighed. "We're still getting reports on the damage and we may not know for days how extensive it is."

"Auggie," I half-lifted a hand.

"Cori?" Auggie turned toward me. "You know something? Wait. You always know something." He massaged his forehead, as if he were expecting me to announce the end of the world.

"It's not the end of the world, but some of the residents might feel that way," I said. "Our escaped dinosaur is now holed up in the Seattle underground. The enemy turned him loose in the ocean, where he can swim happily and feed on endangered whales, et cetera, but he needs a moist cave to call home so he can sleep off his meals."

"What the holy hell?" Auggie stared at me as if what I'd told him was the last thing he'd ever imagine.

"Remember they told us at the facility where he was kept that he liked being sprayed with water? He's amphibious. Unless we can find a way to either capture or kill him, he'll likely go after boats in the bay to add variety to his new seafood diet. He has a taste for human flesh, now. I think the enemy fed a few people he didn't like to DB."

"How the fuck did he get from Nevada to here?" Auggie exploded.

"I don't know how he was taken to the ocean, but nobody was looking for a giant tanker on the water. Somehow, he was transported to California, and I'm beginning to worry that they're using the same method I do to move things around. I think the enemy has tapped the talents of those he took from Nevada."

Auggie and Leo went quiet. Both had their eyes trained on me, as if I'd had something to do with all this. I didn't. I had a few suspicions, but without being able to locate the enemy, I was in the dark, just as they were.

"Cabbage, are you saying that the enemy knew what their talents might be?"

"I think he did—or suspected. He probably thinks he hit the lottery when he lured the fifteen away like he did. Somehow, he suspects we're in the area, too. That's why Dinosaur Boy is living beneath the wharf in Seattle. He knows we'll turn to that problem, which will likely mask the plans for his next activities from us."

"Dinosaur Boy is a distraction?" Leo asked quietly.

"I believe so. The enemy thinks we'll be so caught up in trying to get DB out of his hole—and secretly, I might add—to hide the program from the population, that we'll ignore the signs of his next big plot."

"Which is?" Auggie blinked at me, silently begging me to know what that plot might be.

"I have no idea," I shrugged uncomfortably. "It's the same as it always was—I can't find him or any trace of him. Something is blocking all that."

"Should we move?" Jeff asked.

"I don't think so," Rafe replied before Auggie could say the same thing.

"Let the enemy think as Corinne suggests—that all our resources are focused on DB," Auggie nodded. "Yes, we'll be working on that problem, but we'll bring in another team to help with that. Meanwhile, we'll go back to hunting the enemy full-time, beginning with our sightings of the Mary Evans clones."

"You've found more?" I asked. I knew the answer before Auggie had a chance to say yes.

∾

"You're telling me that monster is beneath Seattle?" Madam President was pissed. Auggie insisted that Rafe, Opal and I be in the room while he and Leo attempted to explain what we knew to the White House.

"It looks that way," Auggie admitted. "We've sent divers down, and there's one huge breach in the sea wall. He went right for the wooden part, Madam President. The wood farther down is fine. I've seen preliminary photographs from the diving team. They found evidence of huge claw marks."

"What's the likelihood that he'll pop up from beneath the streets?" Madam President moaned.

"We don't know what his orders are, or whether he was given any instructions past making his home beneath the wharf area," Auggie shrugged. "I don't want to panic the people, but how else are we going to get them away from danger while we attempt to contain or kill this thing?"

"I worry that he'll be seen in the bay," Rafe pointed out. "Once that news gets out, along with a few cell phone photographs, the truth will be splattered on every television screen whether we want it to be or not."

"This is a nightmare," the President shook her head. "Ms. Tadewi, have you contacted Matt with this information?"

"We spoke earlier," Opal confirmed.

"Does he have a team prepared to go to Seattle? I want him working on this, too."

"He may come himself, and bring others with him," Opal said.

"Then tell him he has my blessing to do whatever it takes to keep the population safe and get rid of this menace at the same time. The same goes for you, Colonel Hunter. I understand that you think this is a diversion, but I beg you to cooperate as much as you can with Director Michaels while you search for the enemy's next plot. I have a call scheduled to the former President, to ask if he may know anything we don't."

"Madam President, will that be a video call?" Auggie asked.

"Yes."

"May I have a recording of it—audio and video?"

"Of course. Why do you ask?"

"You know the former President has shied away from the cameras since he left office. I'd like Corinne to take a look. She may see something that he is reluctant to tell you."

"I'll do what I can." Madam President ended the call. Auggie had done what I'd wanted to do—ask for a current image of the former President. After all, he's the one who'd approved the drug for use on volunteers. I wanted to know exactly what he knew about the Program.

"Honey, I'm starved, and I need to sit with the sunlamp for a while," I mumbled the moment Rafe and I arrived at our suite.

"Let's do both—I feel the need for some light in my life," he agreed.

"What shall we fix for breakfast?"

"Oh, my God, what time is it?" I looked up at him.

"Nearly seven in the morning. It's really foggy out."

"Breakfast?" James walked in, a hopeful expression on his face.

"What do you want, hon?" I asked. "How are Laci and her guards?"

"She finally went to bed when it looked like the ground wasn't going to shake again. The same news, shown repeatedly on television, put all three of them to sleep. I found quarters for the guards, so we're okay for the moment."

"Good work," I rubbed his back. "Want eggs, omelet, ham, pancakes —what?"

"I want ham, pancakes and eggs," he said. "And then a bed, if Colonel Hunter doesn't come looking for me."

"I'll see what I can do," I said. "Come on, you can make coffee while Rafe and I do the rest."

Leo arrived in time to get fresh pancakes, and then the others dribbled in. *I'm beginning to wonder why we have a cafeteria*, Rafe sent as he surveyed the crowd at the table.

Let's hope everybody else inside the mountain doesn't find out, or they'll be here, too, I replied.

"Auggie, you look like you've been in a war," I rubbed his back when he sat beside me and accepted the plate of food Rafe handed to him.

"Yeah. At least Laci is asleep. That makes my life marginally better."

"Small miracles," I agreed. "We'll take 'em."

"She'll be staying here with me until the mess in Seattle is sorted," he went on, his words grim. "She probably won't like it, but that's all there is unless she wants to stay with her parents again."

"I don't think she wants that," Leo offered.

"I just don't want her to feel trapped here with me," Auggie said.

"Nobody's trapped here," I said. "If she wants to go somewhere, I can take her."

"Cori," Auggie warned.

"Yeah."

Rafe snorted.

~

Ilya

We slept for six hours after breakfast before Colonel Hunter woke us with a message. Madam President had her conversation with the former President, and we had a recording to view.

"Wake up, sleepyhead," I nuzzled Corinne's cheek before planting a kiss on her temple.

"Ilya," she grumbled, "let me sleep."

"I would like nothing better than to keep sleeping with you," I said. "But Colonel Hunter is calling for our presence."

"Slave driver."

"Me?"

"No. Auggie."

"Come, cabbage. We have time to shower and make a sandwich before we go."

"All right."

She wasn't happy, but she sat up in bed and forced her eyes open. "See," I smiled at her. "You can wake up when necessary."

"It shouldn't be necessary."

"It is. Come along. My cabbage's leaves looked wilted. A shower will remedy that."

She slid off the bed and walked toward the bathroom, cursing in several languages while she wobbled along. Some of those words sounded alien to my ears.

Half an hour later, we were in Colonel Hunter's office. James had arrived ahead of us and he looked concerned.

"What's wrong?" Corinne asked.

"Colonel Hunter thinks Merle Askins has been playing everybody," James mumbled.

"Why?" I asked.

"Because former President Phillips doesn't know very much," he frowned. "We think Merle may have been secretly in charge of the Program, and signing off on everything without President Phillips' knowledge."

"Get in here," Auggie appeared in his office doorway. "There's only one way I know to get to the truth of this."

Corinne, James and I walked into Colonel Hunter's office. James shut the door behind us, then took a seat next to Corinne. That left him between us. I didn't care—I think he felt safer that way.

Colonel Hunter pointed a remote at the screen hanging on the wall. Images of the current President were shown while she spoke with Former President Phillips on a screen inside the Oval Office.

"Hello, Madam President," President Phillips' image said.

"Holy, fucking hell," Corinne exclaimed.

"What?" Colonel Hunter demanded, hitting pause on the player.

"That's not President Phillips," Corinne stood and hugged herself. "That's the real Hal Prentice."

~

Corinne

"I'm on the most secure line available," Madam President assured us. "What do you have? Was he not telling the truth?"

Warily I watched Madam President as she did the same—she had no idea what was going on. I was almost as confused. "Madam President, the person you spoke with earlier isn't former President Phillips."

"You're joking."

"No, ma'am, I'm not," I assured her. "That's Hal Prentice. He's been posing as President Phillips since before Phillips officially left office. One of Hal's clones, made before the extensive surgery Hal had to look like President Phillips, was acting as the Hal Prentice you hired as your Chief of Staff."

"Where the hell is the real President Phillips?" the President snapped.

"No idea," I said, "but now I think we can put a name to the enemy."

~

"Madam President didn't tell Phillips—or the one posing as Phillips—what she was really calling about," Auggie informed us later, after we'd ended our call with the White House. "She told him it was about foreign policy instead, in case anyone was listening. She caught him off guard when she casually asked him about the Program."

"Should we bring the real Hal Prentice in?" Rafe asked. I watched his hands—they were fists and his knuckles were white. He was furious.

So was I.

"That will only tip our hand," Auggie said. "I think we should let him believe we still don't know. Instead, I suggest we have him followed and monitor any communications. That call was placed from Northern Ireland—Madam President had it tracked. Now, I don't need to tell you who else we've seen in Ireland, recently. Granted it was Ireland and not Northern Ireland, but it wouldn't be difficult to travel from one to the other."

"Mary Evans," Rafe growled.

"Do you think Hal Prentice has control of the Mary Evans clones?" James asked.

"It's possible," Auggie agreed. "At this point, I'm not prepared to rule anything out."

"Hal has enough political experience to accurately predict every move made by the White House," I said. "His clone was likely feeding information to him all along, with important information being passed along to whatever President Phillips is now."

"What do you mean?" Auggie whirled in my direction. "Fucking hell," he said when he understood what I meant. "He saw the Program as a way to live forever, didn't he?"

"Maybe," I shrugged. "I imagine he saw the possibility of becoming more than what he already was, too. All the survivors of the drug are special in some way."

"So he wanted to be a superhero," Auggie huffed. "Instead, he's public enemy number one."

"When he was in office, his detractors would have said the same thing while he was still himself," I pointed out. "What I can't get a handle on is what's keeping him hidden from all of us. I can't figure this out."

"If he has allies in the armed forces, or is still in bed with the Joint Chiefs or Merle Askins, then it could have been easy to get those survivors away from Nevada," Auggie muttered.

"Under the cloak of official government business," James agreed. "Nobody would have asked questions. I'll look into military transports, ground and air, in Nevada," he added.

"This gets worse as it goes along," I said. Rafe unclenched a fist and reached out to hold my hand. I understood what he was thinking— he'd refused to approach the former President while he was in office —instead, he'd held on, hoping his disease wouldn't take him until Phillips' successor came to the White House.

He hated President Phillips. If we learned that Phillips was acting as puppeteer in all things governmental in the U.S., Rafe would be furious. Truthfully, I'd be just as furious. Phillips' every move while President had been made with a cavalier attitude, regardless of who or what was damaged or destroyed in the process.

"Do we have any word out of Russia?" I asked. "Have they announced Baikov's disappearance?"

"I believe they'll sit on that, since they're expecting a newsbreak any day from Ukraine, announcing that they captured or killed Baikov while he was attempting to start a war. For now, I don't believe they know what actually happened in that bunker."

"Maybe we ought to give them that information," Rafe dropped my hand and stood.

"Perhaps we should," Auggie said, his brow furrowing as he considered the idea.

"It's my guess that all this is connected, which means Phillips was in contact with Baikov. That also means that Phillips may have been controlling the current Russian President, since he's danced to Baikov's tune for two years, now," Rafe added.

"What the fuck does he want?" Auggie asked, tossing out a hand. "I can't for the life of me figure this out."

"I'm worried that he's in contact with the mother ship," James whispered.

"Honey, you're forgetting that he's a megalomaniac. There's no way he'd call the mother ship and let them take over, when he can do it himself," I said.

"You think he will?" Auggie's dark, worried eyes bored into mine.

"It's possible," I said. "So far, he's managed to get what he wants, except for Rafe and me. He still considers Rafe to be the bigger threat."

"Because I want him dead," Rafe hissed.

"Honey, you have my blessing to make him as dead as you want," I said.

"You'll be assassinating a former President," Auggie said.

"You don't want this?" I stared at Auggie in disbelief.

"I want it," he said. "I just thought I'd state the obvious."

"Look, right now, Hal Prentice is the former President—in everybody else's eyes. If we leave him alive and go after the real former President, who's going to say it was an assassination? Especially since nobody will recognize the real former President. If he's like everybody else who survived the drug, he no longer looks like himself."

"Fuck. He could look like anybody and we'd never know," Auggie exploded.

"Here's my question—did he get the drug through our Program, or through the Russians?"

"You keep making this worse," Auggie turned to James, who'd posed the question. I was glad he'd asked, because I had the same question going through my mind.

"Do you know how we can find that out?" I turned to Rafe.

"My contact in the Russian government was killed outside a D.C. bar," Rafe sighed. "At least his killer was taken down shortly after."

"After Corinne pointed him out," Auggie said.

"Did you do that, cabbage?" Rafe pulled me against him.

"Yeah—I guess I did."

"Thank you." He leaned in to give me a kiss.

"You're welcome." I smiled when he pulled away.

Auggie's phone rang. He answered it after looking at caller ID. Madam President was on the line again.

"We have a Mary Evans sighting reported in Ireland again," she said. "I want Corinne there immediately. Rafe, too. Matt wants Opal to go, so put a team together. I want this sorted out. I want Hal connected to all this. I want to know what information he has from this office."

I could tell the President had thought hard about all the implications after our phone conversation. She was beginning to think perhaps Hal and the former President were pulling strings—just as we'd discussed.

"Get your things together, cabbage," Rafe said. "I know a place we can go, if you'll take us."

"Great—another cloudy country," I said. "Why can't they hole up in a sunny place for once?"

~

Notes—Colonel Hunter

"Do you think Cori has SAD—Seasonal Affective Disorder?" James asked. "She has her sunlamps—plural—turned on most of the time inside her suite."

"I think it may be tied to the changes this time," I said. "Leo thinks the same—what if she belongs on a world where sunlight is prevalent? Wouldn't that make a difference?"

"Yeah, I guess it would," James agreed. "I guess I just worry about her."

"So do I. I'd still be trying to get out of Seattle and back up this mountain if it weren't for her. We'd still be in the dark about Hal Prentice and President Phillips. Look, Rafe will be with her. They're a good team. Besides, you and I have to work with Matt Michaels on the DB problem."

"It'll be like getting a cockroach out of his hiding place beneath a baseboard," James muttered. "He'll come out when he wants to and not before."

~

Corinne

Rafe's destination was Dublin. Actually, it was a hotel on the outskirts that had once been a mansion. It was now renovated and housing wealthy guests.

"I know the owner," Rafe breathed against my hair as we walked up the steps. Opal, Nick and Maye were right behind us.

"But," I began.

"Really. Don't worry," he smiled. He and I walked up to the front desk. "I'd like to speak with Katya," Rafe said.

"Right away, sir," the clerk said and walked through a door behind the desk. Moments later, a lovely young woman appeared. "Take care of that phone call, Daniel," she ordered the clerk. Daniel the clerk nodded and disappeared through the doorway.

I think my breath stopped for a moment as I blinked at the hotel's owner. *Don't give her away*, Rafe warned.

Yeah. I remembered to breathe again as Ilya's daughter offered both of us a beautiful smile.

Our party was given an entire wing to ourselves. "We can go to the smaller kitchen anytime," Rafe pulled me close. "I told Katya about you when I was here before. She couldn't believe I'd finally found someone."

"I couldn't believe she was happy to see me," I said. "I was relieved to see that she wanted to meet me, instead of only thinking I'd replace her mother."

"Her mother has been gone for a very long time," Ilya said. "Since she was four. She doesn't remember much. What she does remember is her older brother—who is also dead."

"Yeah." I'd seen that, too. Ilya and Katya had wounds that might never heal and a justified grievance against the Russian government. "I'm sorry, Ilya."

"You have wounds, too," Ilya pulled me against him.

"Yeah."

"Katya wants me to be happy. She knows you make me happy."

"I'm glad she knows her father is alive," I mumbled against Ilya's chest.

"I'm glad she's away from Russia and Ukraine," he breathed against my hair. "She has Irish citizenship. She just can't go back to either country, or they'll imprison her. They know who her father is and also know, thanks to Baikov and Phillips, that I'm still alive."

"We need to take care of that situation," I said. "There's no way I want to lose you. No way."

"I have no intention of being lost," he pulled me tighter against him. "Just as I have no intention of letting you go."

"What about Katya? Is someone watching out for her?"

"There are several, one of whom is her husband," Ilya said.

"Is he as badass as her daddy?"

"Almost," the corner of Ilya's mouth curled into a smile.

"Gotcha. I have the most badass guy on the planet," I said.

"Just remember that," he said and laughed.

"Here's the latest on the Mary Evans sighting," Auggie informed me on the video call early the next morning. "You'll have to be discreet," he added. "She's shown up twice at the same coffee shop. It's frequented by tourists, so she may be meeting someone there."

"Do you have more photographs?" I asked. "None of the people in this one are connected in any way."

Rafe was looking over my shoulder at the photograph Auggie held in his hands. It had been taken two days before by British Intelligence. They were still hot on the trail of anyone who might lead them to the stolen crown jewels.

"Do the Brits know about the cloning?" Rafe asked.

"Top level clearance only," Auggie said. "I worry about the information supplied—it came from the CIA and may be tainted."

"Get me a recent photograph of good old Merle," I said. "If you wouldn't mind."

"I'll see what I can do," Auggie agreed. "In the meantime, have a cup of coffee at this coffee shop, just to see if anybody stands out."

"We will," Rafe responded. "This morning."

"Ask Maye and Nick to tail you," Auggie said. "Just in case. Opal stays behind at the hotel, monitoring your movements. She has tags for all of you."

"What's the range on the tags?" Rafe asked.

"Twenty miles. That means a picnic in the countryside is out of the question."

"You take the fun out of everything," I complained.

"You're not there to have fun."

"See my previous statement."

"Cori."

"Yeah."

The coffee shop wasn't far from Trinity College. I stared longingly down the street that led to the entrance, but Rafe drew me away.

"Coffee, cabbage," he murmured. I went with him. The day was fine if a bit cool and the coffee shop was crowded when we arrived—the perfect place to pass information without really being seen.

Somewhere behind us, Nick and Maye would stop to look at souvenirs—many shops near Trinity College served the tourists crowding the area. That meant it wouldn't be unusual for tourists or foreigners to have coffee in our targeted coffee shop.

Rafe and I had to stand at the end of a substantial line to get coffee. Each of us casually scanned the crowd while we waited. The small tables inside and out were all taken—there wasn't anywhere to sit, once we placed our order.

Rafe's hands squeezed my arm when someone stepped out of line ahead of us. Either she realized we were there or she'd gotten tired of waiting.

A Mary Evans clone walked away without glancing in our direction.

CHAPTER 6

*C*orinne

I'm on her, Maye informed me after I sent a mental communication. *Nick is right behind me,* she added.

Rafe had stepped away to call Opal, who'd relay the message to Auggie.

I'm going after her, too, I sent to Maye. *I'll get in front of her, you take her from behind.* I did my relocation trick, landing on a sidewalk as our target moved swiftly in my direction. Rafe was screaming in my mind to come back when the Mary clone cast a swift glance over her shoulder before she came to a standstill feet away.

Yes, I no longer looked like myself. Instead, I'd chosen to employ the power I had to create a disguise. I now looked like General Baikov.

"Ah," she began speaking rapidly in Russian the moment she turned toward me. "There are people following me. We must get off the street." She stepped forward and took my arm.

I relocated both of us right back to Maye and then to Rafe, taking care to appear as myself instead of Baikov—I didn't want to be attacked while delivering the enemy into their hands.

Rafe cursed as he grabbed the Mary clone. She attempted to fight him, but that was useless—he pulled a weapon I'm sure his daughter had supplied and held it discreetly against the clone's back while Maye held her arms.

Tell Nick to meet us at the hotel, Rafe sent a curt mental message. *Get us back there as quickly as you can.* He wasn't happy with the way I'd taken matters into my own hands.

Clone Mary didn't want to walk; Rafe and Maye pulled her along as if she weighed nothing until we reached an alcove in a nearby building. That's when I relocated the four of us to the hotel.

"She doesn't have one of those devices, and is bug free," I informed Auggie ten minutes later. "Want me to bring her to you?"

"Yeah. Matt Michaels is here, now, so I'll let him have her after you tell me everything you can see in her."

I didn't tell Auggie that she hadn't been bug free when I found her —I'd employed my talent to get rid of it, first thing. I figure somebody was cursing somewhere when she vanished from their radar.

"There's a Baikov clone," I sighed, flopping onto a chair in the meeting room back at the Program facility. "She was expecting him when I showed up looking like him."

"What the hell?" Rafe snapped. He still wasn't happy that I'd gotten as close to Mary as I had—he worried I could have been hurt or worse.

"That's why she stepped out of line at the coffee shop," I continued, ignoring Rafe's anger. "He was supposed to meet her there and he was late. Half an hour, almost. She went looking for him. That clone may still be in Dublin, but I can't say for sure."

"Where else would he be?" Auggie asked. "If he was supposed to meet her?"

"No idea," I shrugged. It was a lie, but I couldn't tell Auggie the truth.

What do you know? Rafe sent.

Your son-in-law did the Baikov clone in, I responded. *Want to tell Auggie that?*

Good for him and hell, no, Ilya grinned at me, his anger momentarily forgotten.

"Corinne, did you see any other Baikov clones?" Auggie interrupted my mental conversation.

"No. I'm still trying to figure out how there's a Baikov clone to begin with," I said. "If the original got the drug, he should have changed. I'm not sure what to make of that."

"Does Mary Evans take two know anything?" Leo asked.

"No. She thinks the Baikov in Dublin is the original, so it's likely that the Russians had him as a backup for the one we killed. There may be others, for all we know."

"Too bad we don't have the other one." Matt Michaels, who sat beside Opal at one end of the conference table, shook his head.

"I think we ought to start looking for more Baikov and Mary clones," Maye suggested. "I can't believe they're cranking them out this fast."

"Where did Baikov come from?" I asked Rafe. "What's his background? When was he made general?"

"You're thinking this may go back farther than we suspect, don't you?" Richard Farrell asked.

"I'm not willing to dismiss any possibility at this point," I said.

"I know what the official reports say on Baikov, but I don't recall him coming to power or into the public arena until the end of the last regime, just before the current President took power. He's been pouring lies into the Russian President's ear ever since." Rafe had already done his homework on Baikov.

"You'd know," Auggie agreed.

"I have that photograph you asked for," Auggie said, tapping the tablet in front of him. "I want you, Matt, Rafe, Richard and Leo with me while we discuss that over coffee."

Nick and I want to see you and Rafe too, Maye sent.

I know. I'll ask Opal to join us, I returned.

~

"This was taken just this morning—he had a meeting with the Joint Chiefs," Auggie said, turning his tablet around so I could see the photograph. We sat in Rafe's and my kitchen, drinking coffee.

"Score," I sighed. Whoever had taken the photograph managed to get the Joint Chiefs in the frame, too.

"What do you see?" Auggie asked.

"I see collusion," I said. "He's been in contact with Phillips all along, as have the Joint Chiefs. The trouble is, the Joint Chiefs think Hal is Phillips, now. They have no idea what Phillips currently is—or where he is. Their initial goal is to make Madam President look bad," I said. I was terrified by other things I saw, but hesitated to give out that information.

"How will they go about making the President look bad?" Matt Michaels asked.

"Well, making her look bad may be an understatement," I amended. "They intend to discredit her completely. They'd love to shove her out of the White House now, by exposing the Program. That's the first purpose in getting the fifteen survivors away—and planting Dinosaur Boy beneath Seattle. DB may surprise them with how little sentience he has remaining to do as they ask. Every day he's on his own allows the animal to take over. Askins thinks they'll tie Madam President to the creation of DB when he causes havoc in Elliott Bay, although she had little to do with it."

"This could blow the Program wide open," Auggie said. I could tell how angry he was. Not only would Madam President fall if Askins succeeded with his plan, but everybody she'd appointed, including him, would fall with her if this news went public.

I had visions of bombers scrambling to shoot DB, all while the media had a field day with a situation that should only happen in science fiction movies.

"What is the former President's goal in all this? He can't run again," Leo began.

"Remember he likely looks very different now, and with Hal

Prentice posing as him, he has easy access to the White House," Rafe observed.

"He has another agenda, you can bet on that," I said. "Whether it's the White House or something more than that, I don't want him to succeed."

"So Askins and the Joint Chiefs are still blindly following Phillips," Rafe muttered. I think he was just as angry as Auggie about the entire mess. "In order to take charge again, we have to be eliminated. What do you suppose they intend to do with us and the Program as a whole?"

"Isn't that obvious?" Auggie huffed. "They want us dead. They've tried several times already. Two facilities have been destroyed, and we've lost good people already."

"Is it because he knows he can't bend us to his will, like he did with Becker?" Leo asked.

"How much time do you think we have, before DB makes his presence known?" Auggie changed the subject, directing his question to Richard.

"He'll come out when he's hungry enough. We've recorded small tremors already, so we may only have hours, at best."

"Hours before we're exposed?"

I'd never seen Auggie so angry. We were getting hit on multiple fronts, which left those in charge scrambling for a solution. "I think I can do something about this in the interim," I said.

"What?" The same question came from nearly everyone in the room. The only one who hadn't (wisely) expressed skepticism in that single-word question was Rafe.

"Move DB," I shrugged. "Sure, he's amphibious, but he needs land to make a nest. He's also a short-range swimmer, capable of bursts of speed but not for long distances. It's enough to catch large, slower-swimming prey—like the whales he's gulping down like candy."

"How are we going to move that behemoth?" Auggie threw his hands in the air. "We can't do it—Askins and his allies will be all over us in a heartbeat, with the media right behind him."

"I didn't say we," I snapped. "I said I. Me."

"Where the hell do you intend to take him," Matt asked.

"Someplace safe," I shrugged. It was my hope that the disappearance of DB would throw Merle Askins and his cronies into a tailspin—I didn't intend for DB to be found again.

By anybody.

I worried, too, about the other survivors. What plans did Phillips have for them? After all, it was natural to worry about the biggest and baddest, when the others could be just as destructive in different ways.

At least we knew where DB was. I had no clue where the others were. Likely with Phillips. "I wonder what name he's using now," I mused.

"Corinne, perhaps you'll come back to Earth for a moment and tell us what the hell you're talking about?" Auggie said.

"Phillips. He can't be using his own name. It has to be something else, now. The Mary clone didn't know it," I added.

"Perhaps that's by design," Matt said. "You see he's allowing the originals to be killed off and replaced by clones."

"So the originals may have known what he calls himself. The new ones don't." Leo shook his head. "Corinne, what do you need to take DB out of here? How quickly can you do it?"

"I need two hours alone," I said.

"Where?"

"I can't tell you."

"I don't like this," Rafe frowned.

"Fine. You can come. Everybody else stays here."

"Wait," Rafe held up a hand.

It was too late; I'd already transported us elsewhere.

"Cabbage, why are we sitting on top of Christ of the Andes?" He sounded so calm. He was anything but.

"Because it's nice and sunny here."

"The wind could blow us right off," he said, peering over the edge of the statue at the ground far below. "There are plenty of sunny spots elsewhere."

"I wanted to come here. I figure we need all the help we can get."

"There are tourists down there," he said.

"Are you afraid of heights?"

"Not unless I have nothing to hold onto," he gritted.

"I'm keeping us up here, and the tourists can't see us," I reassured him. "Remember, you didn't want me going alone."

"I'll reconsider next time. Are we here for the full two hours?"

"I can see you're going to complain about this the whole time," I sighed. "Let's go."

"Much better. Much, much better. Is that Kilauea?" We stood atop hardened volcanic flow and watched as a trail of fiery lava meandered down a hillside on the Big Island of Hawaii.

"Yes. Volcanoes fascinate me," I said.

"I've always been interested," he squinted to see the lava flow better.

"Here." I held out my hand—a pair of binoculars dropped into it. "You can see better this way."

"How do you do this?" Ilya had arrived, accent and all.

"It's what I am," I shrugged. "Like you are what you are."

"Better," he took the binoculars and held them to his eyes. "I can see the top crust breaking apart to allow the molten lava through. Thank you for bringing me here, cabbage. I like this."

"Ilya, someday I want a house in a place like this. Where you can see trees, water and maybe a volcano, without another house being ten feet away." I said.

"I want that, too. If we weren't tied to the Program at the moment, I would see that you had exactly what you want."

"I appreciate your willingness to get it for me," I said. I could see the sun shining on the water in the distance, past steep cliffs that called the lava flow toward them. Volcanic rocks stood in the water just past the cliffs, looking sharp and forbidding in sunlight.

"Have you been to Hawaii before?" Ilya lowered the binoculars and turned to give me a smile.

"Years ago. For an anniversary."

"Ah. Do you miss him?"

"At times. He was sick when we went to the Louvre—it was the last thing on his bucket list before going home to let the disease run its course. They tortured him before they killed him—in front of me."

"You have your vendetta, just as I had mine. Baikov is dead. A Baikov clone is also dead. I hope there are no others to kill," Ilya sighed before pulling me against him. "I am sorry, cabbage, that parts of our lives have been so similar."

"I know." We both had loved ones to avenge.

"So." I watched as Ilya's mind worked behind beautiful, dark eyes. "The former President—the one we hunt, knows who you are because you were made before he left the White House," he said.

"And, as he was already plotting and planning while the real Hal Prentice posed as him in the White House, he's responsible for all those deaths at the Louvre."

I wondered how long it would take him and Auggie to come to the proper conclusion. "I just never saw the President before he left office —it was during the last few weeks of his term and he went off the radar afterward. I'm sure Merle and the Joint Chiefs kept him informed as to what a disappointment I was to everybody."

"But now he knows how formidable you are."

"I'm sure he's plotting ways to take us, still," I said. "Why do you think I haven't explained to anybody all the things I can do?"

"This is worse than I imagined," Ilya rubbed his forehead before gazing into the distance. "We have to stay alive, my love. This man must be destroyed."

"Yeah. I feel the same way. I just can't find the fucker to get rid of him."

"He wants to destroy you, because you'll know him, no matter what he looks like," Ilya concluded.

"And he knows you'll stand beside me until the bitter end."

"At least he recognizes the truth of that," Ilya pulled me tighter against him.

"Yeah."

~

Notes—Colonel Hunter

"She'll be back," Matt Michaels assured me.

"How do you know? You don't know her like I do," I snapped.

"Then you tell me—will she be back?"

"Yeah. She still has ten minutes." I'd checked my watch again, just to make sure.

"If the enemy is Phillips, and I'm pretty convinced it is, he wants her out of the way," Matt said casually. We sat in my office, with the door shut and James guarding the door. "After all, if he intends to make a bid for the White House again, or any position of power, really, Corinne will know it's him. Whatever he decides to do, she'll know it's him."

"And she can announce what he is to the world," I grumbled. "For all the good it will do."

"With Askins and the Joint Chiefs working against her," Matt shrugged his agreement. "Ricin in the bottled water was an opening volley, I think."

"That means we have to have a private agenda," I said. "I'm hesitant to let the President know all our movements. Anybody could be listening."

"True. This is the biggest mess," Matt agreed.

"Hi, Auggie." Corinne and Rafe appeared in my office, looking fresh off a holiday. "Where were you?" I demanded.

"Hawaii, watching the lava flow from Kilauea," Rafe answered.

"You know, Auggie, I'll do your windows when I get back," Corinne smiled.

"Where do you intend to send DB?" I asked.

"I hear Alaska is a good place to go, and it's really close to Russia. You can practically see Russia from your back door, you know."

"Cori."

"Yeah."

She disappeared, leaving me to stare at Rafe, who barely looked perplexed.

Corinne

Although streets were blocked off from the wharf in Seattle, tourists were still coming—most of them snapping photographs of the damage to streets and businesses beyond the blockade with their phone cameras. It was easy to get lost in that crowd, especially since I no longer looked like myself. I could have been anyone at that moment—just a tourist carrying a cell phone, dressed in jeans and a fleece jacket.

I stopped at the spot nearest where DB was beneath the ground— he was hungry; I understood that. I'd timed it to coincide with his feeding schedule, too. Where he was going, he'd find plenty of fish, few whales and lots of water mostly free of fishing vessels.

I had to use the same talent I'd employed to bring binoculars to Rafe, except in reverse. Instead of pulling something to me, I'd be sending it away. Before I did that, I took a moment to scan the crowd.

That's when I saw her—a Mary clone. She was here, waiting to report to her superiors about any efforts made to contain DB. That information would likely go straight to Askins and his cronies, and then on to the next one in line.

She knew DB was about to leave his nest to feed.

She knew.

I also saw something else in her, although she was relatively new at this—she'd been staying in Vancouver, and had plans to get on a cruise ship.

I always wanted to see Vancouver.

Shielding my hand to keep her from knowing, I held up the cell phone and snapped several photographs before sticking it in my pocket and tending to business.

The moment the ground rumbled beneath our feet, I mustered all the energy I had and transported DB north of the Bering Strait.

"Corinne?"

It took several minutes for me to understand that Rafe was attempting to get my attention.

"Huh?"

I'd used up my last bit of energy to transport myself back to Auggie's office.

"Thank God."

That was Leo's voice. Standing behind Leo was Marcus. I didn't appreciate his presence at all. If I'd been able, I'd have sent him right back to his quarters, just as I'd sent DB to Alaska.

"DB is somewhere near the Bering Strait," I said, attempting to get a hand to cooperate. "I have pictures of a Mary clone down by the wharf. She was waiting to see what we'd do when DB went out to feed. I figure she's really disappointed right now."

"This what you're looking for?" Rafe drew the phone from my jacket pocket and handed it to Auggie.

"Yeah. Thanks. I'm really tired," I said. "Can I lie down?"

~

Ilya

I was beginning to understand that sunlight was as essential to Corinne as food and sleep. I turned two sunlamps on for her after placing her in our bed.

"I'll order more sunlamps," James whispered behind me.

"Be discreet about it—we don't know who's watching," I said. "Come, we'll let her sleep."

~

"Hawaii?" Dr. Shaw and Colonel Hunter drank coffee with Matt Michaels in our kitchen; James and I found them there after leaving Corinne sleeping in our bedroom.

"She and I share a fascination with volcanoes," I shrugged. "We went to Hawaii after I asked her for a more hospitable spot than the top of Christ of the Andes."

"You went there first?" Director Michaels chuckled.

"Unfortunately. James?" I held up a coffee cup. He nodded, so I made two cups of coffee, passing one to him before taking a chair at the island.

"Here's the Mary clone Cori found at the wharf—I've sent Opal and Nick down to look for her, but they're traveling by conventional means and haven't arrived, yet. I doubt they'll find anything, but Nick may pick something up," Colonel Hunter shoved the cell phone across the island so I could look at the photographs.

"Definitely a Mary clone," James said. He'd taken the chair next to mine and studied the photographs with me.

"We'll have to wait until Corinne wakes to get more information," Dr. Shaw said. "I suspect there's more, anyway."

"I believe all these clones have partial information—not enough to set anyone on the proper trail," I said, handing the phone to James. "It's in Phillips' best interest to destroy the originals who know too much and only keep clones. I wonder whether any of them knew that was his plan?"

"Doubt it," Matt Michaels sipped his coffee.

I very much doubted it, too, but I kept that opinion to myself.

"I'm sending Dr. Farrell to Wales, Alaska, to look for DB," Colonel Hunter said. "He asked to go."

"That's probably a good idea," James said, handing the cell phone back to me. "That's not one of our phones," he added. "I wonder where Cori got it."

"Don't ask," I patted James' shoulder.

Why did I have the feeling that I could use that phone to call my daughter and nobody would know?

"I already have copies of the photographs—that's all I found on there," Colonel Hunter said. "You can give it back to Corinne."

"I will." I stuffed the phone in a pocket. Like the binoculars she'd given me, I imagined it worked far better than anything else currently on the market.

"We've postponed any work on the facility," Colonel Hunter began. "I wanted those windows, but bringing people in and out will just be a red flag to anyone watching. I have no idea whether we're safe here or not, but it's looking more and more like we won't be safe no matter where we go."

"Are you intending to let the Governor know that it's all right to make repairs and open the waterfront again?" Matt Michaels asked.

"I'll see that he gets the message tomorrow. In the meantime, I have eyes on Merle and his cronies. I'm interested in what they do when they get the news."

"I have some people I trust with eyes on Elliott Bay," Matt said. "I'm waiting for word—there are a few boats on the water that we haven't been able to identify."

"It makes sense that they'd be watching for DB to make his appearance. I'll bet they have cameras on all those boats, too, so they can scare the crap out of the public when DB shows up. Except he won't," James said.

"I could have them picked up, but that will tip our hand," Matt said. "I'm ordering my agents to tail them when they come off the water."

"Make it a discreet tail," I said.

"We're always that," Matt said. "Count on it."

Corinne

"Want dinner, cabbage?" Ilya woke me with a kiss. "I can't understand why you're not sunburned after sleeping beneath these lamps for four hours."

"Don't worry about that," I mumbled while stretching. "Thanks for two lamps," I blinked my eyes open.

"I'll find as many as you want," the corner of his mouth curled nicely. "I believe we've managed to flummox the enemy."

"Really? Flummox is a great word."

"The Mary clone at the wharf has escaped us, but Matt has agents tailing a few boat occupants after they came to shore. I believe they waited to record a show in the bay, and were more than disappointed when it didn't materialize."

"I think she's staying in Vancouver," I stifled a noisy yawn. "That's what I saw in her. Probably headed there, if she hasn't already arrived."

"Good information. Come, cabbage—I enlisted James' help, so we have spaghetti waiting."

"That sounds really good," I said.

"We made meatballs for the carnivores," he smiled at me again.

"I love your mouth—it's perfect," I reached up to touch it. He kissed my hand. "Come to dinner, my love. Everyone is waiting."

Marcus stared at me all through dinner. I considered sending him to Alaska to stay with DB for a few days. At least with the frenetic pace of the last two days, he hadn't gotten to torture me any. He wanted to, though—that was easy enough to see.

In my opinion, Auggie needed to find another job for Marcus. Rafe could get me through my exercises just fine. Opal and Nick were missing at the table, but Laci and her two guards had come. I recalled that Maye and Nick wanted a meeting with Rafe and me. That would have to wait.

"Spaghetti is wonderful," I sighed, giving James and Rafe the best smile I could. I was still tired, but the nap under sunlamps had helped a lot.

"Where did you learn to make this sauce—it's incredible," Laci asked Rafe.

"I had a friend who owned a restaurant in Parma," Rafe grinned. "Best sauce ever. I never get mine as good as his, though."

"This is more than good enough," Leo said. "Who has the parmesan grater?"

The gadget was passed to him.

"I'm all about the meatballs," Matt said. "They're excellent. Same teacher?"

"Yes. I've been making this for thirty years."

"They let you cook in prison?" Marcus asked, sarcasm evident in his voice.

"Marcus, I wouldn't say anything else if I were you," Auggie warned.

"I was in prison for protesting my son's murder," Ilya, accent and all, had come to the fore with a vengeance. "Baikov had him killed, because he asked too many questions. Now, would you like to know how good I am at Krav Maga?"

Marcus almost dropped his fork, he was so stunned. Yes, he was used to Rafe's American-sounding voice. This voice and accent he hadn't heard before.

"Sucks to be you right now, Marcus," I said and went back to my food.

"It does. You'll be reassigned tomorrow," Auggie growled.

You'll have to keep an eye on him, I sent to Auggie. I saw the slight nod—he understood that all too well. We didn't need another Becker on the loose, I knew that much. While Becker never had much in the brains department, Marcus just wasn't using his.

Marcus at least saw me as a more formidable target, now, so he wasn't picking on me. Instead of keeping his mouth shut, he chose to air his prejudices instead. He hadn't been briefed on the reasons Ilya was in prison; he only knew he'd been there before his escape to the U.S. and the Program.

He really didn't understand that Ilya wasn't Russian by birth, either. He should have done his homework. Now, he was getting the boot. We didn't need that sort of discord in the Program. We'd seen enough of that with Becker's intimidation tactics against me.

Marcus didn't say anything else during the rest of the meal, but he finished his food.

The schmuck.

"I think August is angry enough to strangle that boy," Laci said as she helped me clean the kitchen after dinner.

"Rafe is angry enough to strangle him," I said. "How are you doing, otherwise?" I asked. "You can go back to Seattle in a few days, I think, once they give the all clear."

"You know, I might only go back on weekends," she smiled. "I like getting my husband home every night. He says he'll spend as many weekends there as he can, so we can eat out and sightsee."

"That sounds like a great idea," I said.

"Need help?" Rafe and James were back after sending the others out the door.

"It's just about done. Besides, you cooked. We can clean," I said. "Sit down. Want some wine or something? I'm thinking about a drink."

"I'll have wine," Rafe agreed.

We offered a glass to Laci, but she wanted to follow Auggie back to their suite. I was fine with that. I needed some private time with Ilya. James took the hint and wandered toward his bedroom.

"Marcus is an idiot," I said, massaging the back of Ilya's neck. "First he picked on me, then he decided to show his ignorance." My fingers feathered through Ilya's hair. I could tell he had a headache, and the muscles were tight in his neck and shoulders.

"Let's go to bed," Ilya sighed. "I know a way to take my mind off this."

"Sounds good," I said.

The following morning, we woke to pounding on our outside door. James beat us to the door, flinging it open to find Auggie standing outside.

"Marcus managed to escape last night," he said. "I've got a search party out, but we have no idea where he is."

CHAPTER 7

Corinne

"He may be in Vancouver," I said. "If it's his intention to find the enemy, he may have better luck looking there."

"They'll take what he knows and get rid of him," Matt pointed out. "If he finds them in the first place."

"Well, I think we've already seen that Marcus doesn't bother with thinking things through," Auggie huffed.

"I don't think it's a matter of him finding them, I think it'll be them tailing him until he's caught," I said.

"Fucking fool," Rafe muttered.

"He doesn't know a great deal—they may know what he does already," Leo said.

"He knows more than they do about Corinne," Rafe said. "We don't need that. We have to find the fucker first. If he places her in danger," he clenched his fists as his face darkened with anger.

"You think he's in Vancouver?" Auggie turned to me.

"I wasn't sure you were listening, but yes, I think he may be there. It's just a train ride from here; the Mary clone was staying there, plus, you said his passport and a few other things were missing."

"How the hell did he get past the guards?" Rafe demanded.

"He told them he wanted some fresh air."

"They let him out?"

"Nobody told them not to." Auggie looked sheepish.

"I want to go after the fucker." Rafe was pissed.

"How the hell did he get to Seattle?" Leo asked.

"A car was stolen down the mountain—the owner left it unlocked. It was gone this morning. The police found it near the wharf, out of gas."

"So he walked from there to the train station, probably." So far, I hadn't used much of my talent to search for the missing Marcus. I was afraid of what I might do if I did.

"Opal and Nick are on their way back," Matt said. "We can send them after Marcus."

"I want Maye on it, too."

"I refuse to stay here," Rafe hissed. "He may put all of us in danger."

"Fine. Take Cori and see what you can do," Auggie waved a hand in dismissal. "When I tell the President about this defection, what she yells won't be pretty."

"I think he may have contacted Merle Askins," I said.

"Because he thinks that's being a loyal American, no doubt," Auggie blew out a breath. "He knows DB was removed and his general location. He knows where Farrell went. He knows too damn much," Auggie was about to have a meltdown.

"He knows Corinne is even more dangerous than she was before," Matt observed. "That means that Merle Askins probably knows, too—if Marcus contacted him, as Corinne believes."

"Then there's no way to get them to forget what they already know," Leo said.

"I still have eyes on Askins and the Joint Chiefs," Auggie said.

"We're leaving," I announced. Rafe and I disappeared.

The crisp chill of a Vancouver morning greeted us as we landed outside a nice hotel near the wharf. A cruise ship was docked nearby; passengers were departing after their cruise from Alaska.

"Why did you land us here, cabbage?" Rafe pulled me against him when I shivered—neither of us wore jackets.

"This is what I saw in the Mary clone's head—she was supposed to be here in Vancouver today—to get on a cruise ship. I think it's a way to get to Alaska without raising too much suspicion."

"She was already planning to go to Alaska?"

"Probably for reasons other than sightseeing. Alaska has a lot of open space, you know, and it borders Canada."

"You think the enemy may be in Canada?"

"It's possible. Those crazies who thought they were the four horsemen were holed up not far from here, remember? I just want Mary to lead us to her contact in this part of the world. Maybe we can get information that way. She really didn't know much—not even the name of her contact."

"Do you know who she was? Before she got the drug?"

"Something made her forget," I said. "She can't remember. She can't even remember that she was someone else. What kind of talent would that take?"

I looked up at Rafe's face—he was just as puzzled by this as I was.

He hadn't shaved, either, and wore just the beginnings of a new growth of whiskers. He looked quite good that way. "When are you going to tell Colonel Hunter that we'll be on the boat with Mary when she sails?" he asked.

"In a few minutes. It sails at four this afternoon, so we have clothes and bags to buy if we're going to be tourists."

"You're not going alone," Auggie thundered in our cell-phone conversation.

"Then who do you want to go with us?" I asked as calmly as I could. Yes, I wanted to tremble at his anger, but struggled to overcome it.

"Opal can go," I heard Matt Michaels in the background.

"I'll send Nick, Maye and Jeff," Auggie sounded defeated. "The idea is sound, I just want you to have backup in case it's needed. Matt and I can send someone else to search for Marcus."

"Then disguise the ones coming with us," I said. "I'll be there in an hour to pick them up. Make sure they have passports with them. I'll change them to reflect their disguises."

"Who the fuck can do that?" Leo asked.

"I the fuck can do that, Dr. Shaw," I said. "Stop worrying. I'll get us off the boat if anything goes wrong."

"How much did this cost?" Rafe asked as we sat on the balcony outside our cabin.

"You don't want to know," I said. "We're registered as Chuck and Wendy Scott, by the way." I held up my ship-issued ID card. "Here's yours," I handed the second one I held to him. "You have to have this to eat, drink and be merry on the boat."

"At least we have two sunlamps in the closet," he grumbled. Even in July, we'd be sailing through cloudy, misty days to reach our destination.

Maye and Opal shared a cabin on the deck below ours, while Nick shared his with Jeff, who'd been briefed by Auggie at the last minute.

All of us had watched as the Mary clone boarded the ship earlier, heading for her cabin at the back of the boat. Opal had already managed to place a discreet bug on the outside of Mary's cabin door—it would let us know whenever anyone went in or out. Opal had the bug connected to her phone, so she—and Matt at the facility—would have a visual. Matt Michaels had some very cool toys, looked like.

The thing was—we needed another bug inside her cabin. That was my job, although Rafe insisted on coming along. I discovered it was a good thing I'd shielded our presence when I transported us into the cabin in question—the bug she'd already installed would neither see nor hear us as we placed our own above her window.

"She has her own bug placed in the cabin, in case anyone comes snooping," I said, sliding into a seat at the main bar on level three. Located at the center of the ship, the bar was surrounded by rising balconies on every level up to the top of the ship.

"Want a drink?" Rafe asked, taking the seat next to mine.

"How about a mimosa?" I asked.

"Hand me your card."

I gave him my ship ID—they'd scan it before making my drink.

"MC's coming out of her cabin," Opal said softly.

"Probably headed this way," Maye said. "It's almost time for dinner."

Maye wasn't wrong. Five minutes later, our clone walked up to the bar and ordered a Manhattan.

Rafe barely glanced Mary's way before accepting our drinks from a bartender and heading back to our table.

Asked for rye whiskey in her drink. Our girl wants to take the edge off, Rafe informed me.

I can see that, I responded. Rafe and I watched as Mary gulped her drink quickly and asked for another.

"I wonder if she was an alcoholic before," Opal said softly.

"Might make sense," Nick nodded.

After downing a third drink, Mary left the bar. We waited a moment before rising and going after her. The buffet on level six was her destination. Maye rode up the elevator with her, after mentally sending the floor Mary punched before the doors closed.

Windows surrounded the buffet dining room, allowing us to watch as Western Canada slid past the ship. At least the buffet had prepared something for vegetarians—after a fashion. Mostly it was Indian and Asian selections, but I wasn't choosy when it came to food while following a target.

Mary sat by herself at a window table; we chose a larger one near the center.

"Have you ever been on a cruise before?" Opal asked me.

"No. My husband was terrified of boats and deep water, for some reason."

"I'm not," Rafe breathed against my cheek.

Does deep water turn you on? I asked.

You turn me on. I just have to look at you, he said. *I can swim,* he added.

Honey, most days, I want to crawl all over you, I responded.

I want you to.

I will. I smiled.

Finish your food. I doubt our clone is going anywhere for the next two days.

I doubted it, too. Our first stop wasn't scheduled until then—at Ketchikan.

"Says here we can see eagles in Ketchikan on one of the tours," Opal opened a brochure. "Bears, too, if we're lucky." She grinned over the top of the unfolded brochure. I wanted to laugh—she'd grown up with both those things. Opal was far older than most people could ever guess.

Notes—Colonel Hunter

"This is from the bug Corinne placed in the Mary clone's cabin," Matt set a tablet on my desk. I found myself gazing at a live transmission of her empty cabin. "Opal says this one is drinking and eating at the moment."

"So no word on Marcus," I sighed. "If Corinne didn't think it important to follow this one, I'd have asked her to stay in Vancouver to help track Marcus."

"You could have left Nick behind," Matt said.

"No, I don't want any of them out alone. If Merle and his bunch are after them, it'll be harder to take all of them on at once."

"True. I see your point."

"I still want Marcus—he can do damage to us. I've notified Farrell, so he'll watch for anyone else who's looking for DB. So far, he says he can't get radar on him."

"Then it's likely the enemy hasn't found him either. What about the other survivors that escaped the facility in Nevada? Any word?"

"Nothing. But that only means we're fighting against those who've hidden them for their own purposes."

"We still have no real idea what they're capable of doing," Matt said. "The team in Nevada only kept them alive and happy—or as happy as they could."

"While Askins received regular updates on them and we got nothing." I was still so pissed about that it gave me headaches.

"Madam President had no reason to be suspicious," Matt drummed fingers on his chair arms. "We don't know exactly what Askins and the others have planned, either; we just have well-founded hunches."

"I'm concerned about the possible connection with the Russians," I countered. "We know Baikov has likely handed out faulty advice to the President. How do we know one of his clones isn't there now, doing the same thing?"

"We don't know that for sure, but I have people on it."

"Trustworthy people?"

"The best I have in the area."

"Good. Will you keep me informed?"

"Yes."

Corinne

"She made two calls." Ilya turned my phone around so I could see the text sent by James. "He said the audio wasn't working because she had her hair dryer on. We have no idea what she said."

Somebody at the facility was keeping a constant eye on Mary while she was in her cabin. She hadn't found the bug, but took precautions anyway. Now, we were no farther along than we were before.

Ilya and I had only been awake for a few minutes; I could tell he wanted breakfast. Instead, we were dealing with the Mary clone and her indecipherable phone calls. "Stop worrying about her for the moment," I took the phone from his hand. "Let's go to breakfast. James will let us know if she leaves her cabin."

"Thank you," Ilya leaned over to kiss me before sliding off his side of the bed. Fifteen minutes later, we were on an elevator, traveling to deck six and the buffet. I went straight for the poached eggs and toast —Rafe loaded up on bacon and sausage with his eggs.

That's where Maye and Opal found us ten minutes later, sitting at a table near the port side windows, drinking coffee, eating and talking.

"Here's the latest," I pulled up the text from James and passed the phone across the table to Opal and Maye.

"So we still don't know anything," Maye sighed and handed the phone back.

"We know she's in contact with somebody," Rafe said. "We merely don't know what she said."

"We get to Ketchikan tomorrow. I wonder if she'll get off the boat," Opal said.

"We have something," Nick set his plate down at one end of the table, while Jeff took the chair at the other end.

"What?" Maye turned to Nick.

"She talked to the bartender last night about one of the bus tours in Ketchikan," he grinned. "He wanted to hook up with her, I could tell, so I asked him about her last night when I went for a beer after dinner."

"Which tour?"

"No idea—there are several buses, so there's no way to tell unless she actually books the excursion."

"Damn," Maye cursed. "We have to follow her, no matter where she goes. How are we going to do this?"

"She may be laying a false trail," Rafe bit into his last slice of bacon.

"Even worse," Opal said.

"It's what I would do," Rafe added after thinking—and chewing— for a moment.

"We'll just have to split up and stay in contact with each other," Maye said. "Corinne and I can use telepathy; the rest will have to rely on cell phones."

"I can use telepathy," Rafe grinned.

"Seriously?" Maye frowned at Rafe. "Why doesn't Colonel Hunter know this?"

"Because I haven't told him?"

"Great. Why didn't you tell us?"

"Corinne knows."

"Hey," I elbowed him—he was trying to place half the blame on me.

"So, Nick with Corinne, Opal with me, Rafe with Jeff," Maye sorted us quickly.

"I don't like that," Rafe said immediately. He wanted to stay with me.

"You outed yourself, now you pay the price," Maye pointed her fork at him. "Everybody who can do telepathy gets a non-telepathic partner."

"Dude," I nodded at Nick.

"Dudette," he grinned at me.

"Fine," Rafe breathed. *Just don't get too chummy*, he warned.

Honey, that won't happen, I replied.

Mary stayed in her cabin for the rest of the day, ordering room service for her meals and drinks. She was also drinking heavily—James let us know she ordered two bottles of expensive Scotch and consumed both by midnight.

Something was definitely going on—I just couldn't figure out what it was.

Sure, I could see things in most people. For some reason, whatever Mary was thinking or instructed to do was blocked. No matter how hard I tried, I couldn't see past that fog. Yes, I'd read a few things in her, but those weren't particularly important. The important stuff was behind a wall I couldn't penetrate.

As a casual observer, she acted nervous, too, and I couldn't explain that. She didn't recognize any of us—I'd enhanced the disguises myself.

"Nobody can get off the boat until nine tomorrow morning, after we dock," Opal said. "We'll have to watch for Mary then."

~

Notes—Colonel Hunter

"Here's the security footage—we just got this." Matt set his tablet on my desk. I watched as Marcus was shown boarding the first train of the day the morning after he'd escaped. "Train headed to Vancouver, just as we thought," Matt confirmed.

"Do you think he had contact with the Mary clone before she boarded the ship?"

"No idea. It would have taken some careful manipulation, though, if he did. After all, he had to get in touch with Askins or one of the others, and then receive instructions."

"True. She boarded the minute she could, which was shortly after two."

"There's been no sightings of Marcus after he left the train station in Vancouver, but he could be on a fishing boat for all we know. He didn't board a plane, I know that much," Matt snorted.

He'd been doing his research, I could see that. I had no idea how extensive his reach might be, but it looked impressive from where I sat. I'd come up with almost identical information, but I'd had to proceed with caution so I wouldn't alert Askins and the enemy.

My core team, after all, was on a cruise ship in Alaskan waters, their attention focused on a Mary clone.

"Anything new from the cabin bug?" Matt asked.

"Other than the clone getting drunk? No." I swiped my finger across the tablet, reviewing the security images of Marcus boarding the train in Seattle, then getting off in Vancouver and walking away.

"Fucker," I hissed, dropping a fist onto my desk with a thump. "The first sign of adversity and he runs to the opposition, ready to lick their feet."

"Corinne didn't like him from the start, did she?"

"No," I admitted. "Remind me to get rid of anybody in the future that she has a problem with. He came with such high recommendations, too."

"Probably never put to the test before," Matt said. "People behave differently when they're under fire."

"Corinne sure did. I can't believe we ever thought her weak and untalented."

"The others show their talents right away?"

"Yes. Immediately. They couldn't wait to show off what they had."

Corinne

"Cabbage?"

"Hmmm?"

"Make sure Nick doesn't put you in danger," Ilya said. We were in bed, both of us reading. There was a library on board the ship, so we'd borrowed books to read.

"That's not going to happen." I set my book down on the covers and pulled his face to mine for a kiss. "Stop worrying. You can stay in constant contact if you want."

"You should also stay in contact with me. Let me know what you are seeing, if anything seems out of place."

"I will."

"Hmmph," he mumbled against my mouth. *We will have words if you do not include me.*

What kind of words? He was still kissing me, so this was the only way I could respond.

Angry.

Then why are you kissing me if you anticipate being angry?

Just reminding you of what you stand to lose for a time should you not stay in contact.

Really? You're predicting the future? I didn't know you had it in you. He nipped my lower lip to show me he was serious. Both books were eventually kicked off the bed after he pushed me back and set about removing my pajamas.

~

She's on the move, Maye announced the following morning. Right at nine, as if she were on a schedule, our Mary clone left her cabin and headed for deck two, where passengers could disembark from the ship.

We'd separated with our respective partners inside the coffee shop on Deck three, waiting for word from those watching the feed from the bug.

We'll go first, Rafe announced. I glanced across the shop where he and Jeff sat at a table, drinking coffee and looking through the large windows at the dock outside. Ketchikan was quite pretty, actually, with houses painted in bright colors scattered up the steep hillside, which made up the majority of the small town.

We'll go last, Maye announced. *Corinne, stay with Nick—no funny stuff. Colonel Hunter's orders.*

It didn't take but a moment to realize that Maye had told Auggie what I'd done in Dublin—transporting myself in front of the Mary clone there and getting close enough for her to touch me. She could have killed me, had she suspected I might be anyone other than the Baikov clone. After my moment of consideration, I swallowed my annoyance and said *all right*.

Rafe offered a frown—he certainly agreed with Auggie—I'd gotten too close to the enemy in his opinion, too. *Fine*, I sent only to him. *I won't let them touch me again.*

Sure, I could see all that in them if I wanted, but this time around, I could shut it off easily if I wanted. Most of the time, I shut it off around those I considered allies. Marcus I'd read, but when I'd watched him before he left the facility, he was merely angry. He planned his escape later, after I hadn't bothered to monitor him. I resolved not to make that mistake again.

Going now, Rafe informed us after the Mary clone made her way down the gangway to the dock. Nick touched my arm, so I followed him off the boat seconds later.

At first, it appeared that Mary was following the crowd down a boardwalk, passing a few shops, restaurants and bars designed to draw cruise tourists. Eventually, she walked into a bar near the end of the boardwalk.

"I hope she doesn't plan to drink the whole time she's off the boat," Nick muttered beside me. We watched as Rafe and Jeff waited a few seconds before following Mary into the bar.

"I guess we get to sit at the table outside," Nick sighed. "Want anything? I'll go in and get it."

"Just a bottle of water," I said. By that time, Maye and Opal caught up with us and sat at an outside table not far away. Maye waited until Nick went into the bar before following.

"She's in there, sitting at the bar with some of the hard stuff in front of her," Nick reported, plunking a bottle of water on the scarred wooden table in front of me. He had a soda in his hand, so he set it on the table before taking his seat.

She's checking her watch, Rafe informed us.

I relayed that message to Nick.

"She's either waiting for someone or gauging her time before leaving," he shrugged.

What followed was the longest two hours of my life.

At the one-hour mark, Rafe and Jeff traded places with Maye and Opal—who sat at a different table inside the bar while Rafe paid cash for their drinks and left.

The following hour was just as boring, although the weather was nice and the day clear and sunny. We'd already heard (several times) from locals that we'd gotten ideal weather for our visit—apparently that was something unusual.

Clear and sunny in Ketchikan still meant temperatures in the low sixties, but that felt wonderful to me. As long as the sun was shining overhead, I was happy. *You're smiling*, Rafe informed me.

The sun is shining. Face it—we've had nothing but clouds the last two days.

True. I can't say I like you sleeping on that tiny sofa under a sunlamp. I'd done that for a few hours both nights—after sex. I'd gotten back in bed with him, though, for the last hour or two before sunrise.

I don't like it either, I said. *But it's necessary.*

Then I'll learn to live with it, he replied.

I love you, I said.

She's moving, Maye informed us.

Rafe and Jeff waited a few seconds before rising and following discreetly. A few seconds later, Nick nodded to me. Dumping our empty cup and bottle in the recycle bin, we followed Rafe and Jeff at a distance.

Nick was incredible at tracking someone—we were lost in a crowd twice, but both times, he grabbed my arm and led me in the proper direction. I could have done my location thing on Rafe, but with Nick beside me, it wasn't necessary.

She's seen us, Rafe sent. *It's your turn, cabbage. She's going into a souvenir shop.*

She did go into the most touristy souvenir shop she could find, crowded already with people from three tour boats, two of them lined up behind ours at the nearby docks.

"Our turn," I said softly beside Nick. He nodded and picked up the pace, heading unerringly toward the proper shop.

Mary looked at shot glasses. She looked at coffee mugs. She examined T-shirts, visors, maps, visitors' guides and everything in between.

Nick's breath caught first—he knew before we set eyes on the fucker.

Marcus walked into the shop from a second door down the way—the shop was so large it had two entrances.

Rafe, Maye, Marcus is here, I sent, attempting to avoid the urgency in my voice. Marcus didn't recognize any of us, but there was something different about him. He, like Mary, was now enveloped in a fog. Something prevented me from seeing his intentions.

"Classic," Nick breathed.

We'd watched as Marcus bumped into Mary, making her drop her cell phone. She bent to pick it up while he offered apologies.

The cell phone she tucked in her pocket wasn't the one she

dropped. Nick and I knew that immediately. I informed the rest of our team while they waited outside.

This is a way of passing information, Maye said when I let her and Rafe know. *Without sending it the traditional way,* she continued. *There'll be notes or something on the new phone, and possible notes on the one Marcus now has.*

Jeff and I will tail Marcus when he leaves, Rafe said.

He's heading for the door now, I said.

I just texted Colonel Hunter, Maye sent. *He says detain Marcus for questioning if possible.*

On it, Rafe replied. Nick and I watched as Marcus left the shop before turning our attention back to Mary. She gathered two coffee mugs, both with *Ketchikan, AK* printed on them, and headed for the checkout.

"When does the boat leave tonight?" Nick asked as we walked a discreet distance behind Maye and Opal, who'd taken up tailing Mary after she left the souvenir shop.

"Back on board by three—sailing at four, according to the schedule," I said.

Mary chose that moment to walk into a restaurant, where she ordered (no surprise) another drink and a plate of king crab.

"She'll be looped by the time she gets back to the boat," Nick said as we were led to a table near the back of the restaurant.

"There's something going on with her—I just can't figure out what it is," I said. A waiter set glasses of water in front of us and handed menus out. He took our drink order and promised to be back in a moment.

The restaurant was becoming crowded, so I figured it would be several minutes instead.

"You mean you can't just see it in her?" Nick asked. "You can anybody else."

"I know—that's what's so weird about this—it's as if there's a fog around their brain that I can't get through," I shrugged. "It's driving me nuts."

"So the enemy is doing their best to get around your talents, now."

"Looks that way," I shook my head. "This is more than confusing."

"You know they'll still try to take all of us down—that's the way this works. With us out of the way, they'll have a clear path to whatever they want."

"That means they're still scared of us," I pointed out.

"They ought to be. If they're ever face-to-face with me," Nick closed a hand into a tight fist.

"I know," I agreed. Nick still had some secrets, as did I. I think we understood one another in that way—it was to protect ourselves and potentially surprise the enemy that we held those things in reserve.

I trusted him to keep that to himself, just as he trusted me the same way. After all, I'd known those things about him from the moment I laid eyes on him the first time. I'd never told anyone what I knew and he'd eventually come to respect and trust me because of that. Handing Becker to him only solidified the deal.

"You know, most women mind their weight," Nick observed after watching Mary tear into her king crab, dipping it liberally in drawn butter before eating it. "If she eats like that all the time, she should weigh two hundred. She probably doesn't weigh more than one-twenty as it is."

"Maybe she really, really likes crab. I used to," I said. We'd already placed our order—I asked for a salad, Nick ordered salmon. After all, if you order salmon in Alaska, you're practically assured of getting good fish.

"That's enough crab to feed a bodybuilder," Nick said. "And she's still drinking."

She was—her third drink was set in front of her while we watched. Before she was finished, Mary ordered dessert and a fourth drink. At least she only ate half the tall slice of triple chocolate cake.

We have Marcus—Colonel Hunter is sending agents to pick him up, Rafe sent. At least Marcus no longer had the locating chip he'd arrived with —I'd destroyed it after mentally scanning his body. From this point on, he was off the enemy radar.

We may be late getting back to the boat, Rafe added. *We're waiting until the agents arrive.*

All right, I said. *Let me know if you need help. Mary's still drinking.*

I can't believe she wasn't staggering after she left the bar earlier, he said.

Probably had a high tolerance for it before she was made a clone, I responded.

Very possible. We'll get there before the boat sails, I promise.

Good. I hate going to bed without you.

Give Nick the information—except for that last part.

Will do.

Mary left the restaurant after finishing her drink and paying the tab, only to wander into another bar two buildings down. Maye and Opal took the watch there, while Nick and I found seats outside. A fourth cruise ship had arrived, much smaller than the three already docked. The tourist crowd in Ketchikan had just grown larger.

"I'm surprised she didn't take a bus tour after asking the bartender about it," Nick said, slipping on a pair of sunglasses.

"I think she intended to mislead anybody watching," I said. "Just in case. She hasn't behaved nervously the whole time she's been off the boat, so she either doesn't know she's being tailed or no longer cares."

"She doesn't know. I haven't seen her look behind her once," Nick said. "Anybody with anything to worry about will check their surroundings. She doesn't suspect anything."

"I hope you're right," I said.

"We just have to worry about getting that phone. Whatever information she has is probably important."

"I'd like a map to the enemy's front door," I huffed. "That's not likely to happen. How will we get the phone? I assume Colonel Hunter will have a plan?"

"There's protocol in place," Nick said. "All of which doesn't place you in danger."

"Right." I couldn't keep the sarcasm from my voice.

"Cori, you weren't military. That's why everybody looked down on you at the beginning. We assumed you were—well, worthless. We know better, now. We also know you're a primary target for the enemy and if you're lost, we're all lost. Don't blame Colonel Hunter. Not only is he protecting his best asset; he cares about you. Everybody does. Let us do our jobs around you. We've trained for that and we're good at it."

"I know." What Nick didn't say but we both knew—Madam President was terrified I'd be lost. I'd become one of her best advisors, without the promotion or the pay raise. While she and Auggie trusted my judgment of others, they didn't trust my judgment regarding myself.

Great.

"Cori, you've gone walkabout a few times—admit it. I hear you took Rafe to the top of a hundred foot statue."

"It's ninety-eight feet. Not counting the base."

"Like I said."

"Look, sometimes I need alone time. I always have—even before. I was a writer then, too. It's part of the vocation."

"We suspected as much," Nick grinned. "We just don't know who."

"I'll tell you someday. I promised Leo I would."

"See, you can call them by their first names. I say Colonel Hunter and Dr. Shaw."

"Rafe does the same."

"They won't allow anyone else to do it. From a military standpoint, it's disrespectful. From you, well, they know you care. If you started calling Colonel Hunter Colonel Hunter, he'd wonder what he did to piss you off. Leo Shaw doesn't let anyone else get away with calling him Leo."

"I feel special," I said.

"It's a compliment. They respect you more than anybody I know."

"Uh-huh. That's why Auggie told Maye to order me around."

"You scare Maye witless," Nick said, leaning forward in his chair. "She has no idea how to deal with what you can do. One minute you're in view—the next, you could be on the other side of the planet. She doesn't know how to protect that."

"Great—now you're making me feel bad."

"That's not my intention," he leaned back again, causing the wooden chair he sat on to creak as he shifted. "I'm just telling you that we're not doing any of this to make you miserable. We do it because we're worried. Colonel Hunter freaks whenever you show your independence by going off on a whim."

"You're right—I wasn't military." I turned away from him then, to check the door into the bar. *She still in there?* I asked Maye.

Yes, and still drinking.

She has to be back on the boat in half an hour, if she's going.

Copy that. Wait, she's handing the bartender cash. Get ready.

Nick and I rose after Mary walked down the street, ambling past more businesses. Following her at a discreet distance while Maye and Opal followed us, we made our way toward the line of people waiting to get back on the boat.

Everybody had to pass through a checkpoint and their belongings and purchases went through X-ray machines. I figured there wasn't anything on Mary's new phone to set it off.

Honey, she's getting back on the boat, I informed Rafe.

It'll be a while—the agents just got here, he replied. *I'll let you know when we get through the checkpoint.*

Thanks. We'll keep following her from a distance—unless she heads for her cabin.

Good. Keep me updated.

Will do.

Nick and I had little on us when we went through the checkpoint before boarding—our phones and his wallet went through the machine. Mary, still walking ahead of us, went straight to the bar on deck three.

Why wasn't I surprised?

She's in the main bar on the ship, I sent to Maye and Rafe. Nick and I took a table near the windows, where a waiter sidled up to us and took our drink orders.

"Maye and Opal are across the bar," Nick informed me when the waiter left.

"Sounds good." I didn't turn to look. Instead, I glanced briefly at Mary, who checked her watch again.

What did that mean? *Honey, you'd better hurry, it's ten till four*, I sent.

We're close, he replied.

Ten minutes passed and I hadn't heard from Rafe. I worried that he and Jeff would be left behind in Ketchikan. Sure, I could go get them, but that could cause problems later.

Mary checked her watch again before pulling out her cell phone. Fear washed over me then and I wanted to scream. I didn't. Instead, I had to act as quickly as I could to gather the four of us and transport us off the boat. It and the three ships docked behind it blew up simultaneously.

CHAPTER 8

*I*lya
　　Jeff and I had to run to get up the gangway to the checkpoint. Tossing my cell phone into the tub, it was sent through while I walked through the metal detector.

Jeff, who'd been sprinting behind me, had to take time to remove his wallet, cell phone and change from his pocket. I walked into the ship, expecting him to be behind me shortly.

I only had enough range to shield myself when the ship exploded around us. Jeff—and the crewmembers behind me—didn't make it.

Notes—Colonel Hunter
　　At least Corinne had the presence of mind to get the three others back to Seattle. She was so terrified that Rafe was dead that Shaw had to sedate her. Maye heard from Rafe half an hour after the explosions, sending a wave of relief through the facility.

Jeff was the one who didn't make it. Rafe had gone through the checkpoint ahead of Jeff, which meant that his shield wouldn't reach. Matt was receiving continuous reports on the devastation while I instructed Rafe to get to the airport where my agents were ready to take off with Marcus in tow.

We understood now that the cell phone Marcus passed to the clone had been rigged as a detonator. Somehow, divers had gotten to the hulls of four ships and planted enough explosives there to destroy all of them twice over.

Initially, Rafe asked that Corinne come for him. I'd had to tell him she was unconscious—that she was terrified he was dead so Shaw had to give her something. I think he was grateful for that, at least, although he didn't appreciate a ride in a small plane with Marcus—he wanted to break Marcus' neck for killing Jeff.

I wanted to break Marcus' neck for killing Jeff and thousands of tourists on those ships, not to mention their crews. Word was only a few were found alive—most were dead; their body parts were floating in the waters surrounding the dock, waiting for recovery teams to pick them up.

Had this been Phillips' plan to get rid of the Program? To kill all of them in the midst of thousands of others?

No wonder the clone drank everything she could get her hands on —she'd been instructed to commit suicide.

We probably wouldn't get a full body count for a day or two—the manifests would have to be examined, and there were a few—not many—who'd lagged behind and hadn't boarded the boats, yet.

They were now being questioned by authorities, when they'd had nothing to do with the explosions.

"Rafe's in the air," James informed me. "ETA around ten, local time."

"Good. I hope he's here by the time Corinne wakes."

"I thought she was going to lose it," James whispered.

"She hasn't shown any signs of PTSD until now—not that I blame her," I said. "I'd lose it if I thought Laci was dead."

"Jeff *is* dead." James sighed. This affected all of us; we'd lost enough as it was. This was one more death to add to that list—what Phillips and his cronies had to pay for. At least we knew whom to blame, now. We just couldn't find the fucker.

The other thing that bothered me just as much was he'd found a way to get things past Corinne, and neither she nor I understood that. How could that happen? "Who's with Cori?" I asked James. He was headed back to his desk.

"Dr. Shaw."

"Good."

∾

Corinne

"Rafe's on his way back. Jeff didn't make it." Those were Leo's first words to me when I opened my eyes. Yes, I'd been on the verge of another panic attack. Instead, I shoved my grief and fear away while covering my eyes with a hand.

"How?" I whispered.

He understood that I was asking about Jeff. Rafe had likely employed his shield and was bounced into the water, who knew how many miles away.

"Jeff was behind Rafe at the checkpoint. You know Rafe's shield only encompasses a few feet. He was too far ahead and couldn't save him."

"Fuck."

"Don't take the blame for this. Neither should Rafe. It's a miracle any of you survived."

"Leo, how can I not feel guilty? Maybe I should have tried harder to read Mary. Instead, I just followed her around like a lapdog, thinking she'd take us to her leader."

"Corinne, you know what we're up against. As long as our Program is alive, they know they can't take what they want. We're all that's standing between them and whatever they have planned. We've seen they have no qualms about killing—even of their own—if it suits their purpose. If the White House is the ultimate goal, well, you know as well as I that we don't need that in charge of the country."

I gave a slight nod. What Leo said made sense, but it still didn't do much to make me feel less guilty. "Is Marcus on his way back?" I asked, attempting to shove those thoughts aside.

"Yes, and Colonel Hunter says Rafe is ready to break his neck. They're on the same flight."

"I think I want to kill him, too," I said. "He thinks this is the way to be patriotic? To sign up for shit like that? He probably couldn't wait to call Askins and spill everything he knew."

"We're hoping to find that out when he gets here."

"I sure hope nobody else knows he's coming," I snapped. "I don't want somebody trying to get him away from us the same way they dealt with those cruise ships. Askins and his bunch have a lot of blood on their hands."

"Well, we know now they've been behind every attack—in a roundabout way, and that includes Montana and Georgia."

"No doubt looking for the results they achieved in Montana. That's why Askins raised his hand first when the President went looking for a place to keep those survivors."

"And why she was kept in the dark afterward, while we weren't included at all. Farrell at the least should have been pulled into the loop, but they didn't want anybody who had even a short acquaintance with morals to go anywhere near their experiment."

"You know, I think this is the first time you've ever revealed your true feelings, Leo. I'm proud of you."

"That's amusing, Corinne. Rafe should be here in an hour. If you're hungry, I'll allow you to get up."

"I want pancakes," I said.

"I'll have someone make them for you," he held up a hand. "I said get up. Not cook."

"How are Nick, Maye and Opal?" I asked as I slid off the bed.

"Shaken," Leo said. "The enemy obviously likes his surprises."

"We're lucky to be here," I said, shuffling toward the bathroom. After all, there were plenty of people who hadn't been so lucky.

"Nick said the same thing."

∽

Corinne, are you awake? Rafe sent while I examined my image in the bathroom mirror.

Honey, I can't say how happy I am to hear your voice, I said.

I don't suppose you'd come get me?

I'll be right there. Leo will have a fit, but the bathroom door is closed, so he can't have one until after the fact.

Good.

Rafe barely had time to send his one word message before I stood beside him. He'd just gotten off the small jet and stood on the tarmac of the military installation on Whidbey Island, watching two agents unloading a docile Marcus.

It was probably a wise move on Marcus' part—if he acted up in any way, Rafe would use it as an excuse to kill him.

That's how angry Rafe was. He had no desire to ride in the same vehicle on a long journey to our mountain—he wanted away from the temptation that a living Marcus presented.

"Let me tell them I'm leaving with you," Rafe leaned down to give me a hard kiss. I watched him lope toward one of the agents, who'd stepped back to allow a military police contingent to shackle Marcus before stuffing him into the backseat of an armored vehicle.

"We're good to go," he was back after a short conversation. "I had to let Colonel Hunter know, but he promised not to yell at you," Rafe offered a guilty grin.

"Of course you did. He won't yell; he'll just have Leo do it. I'm glad you're safe," I leaned into him.

"My love, you're cold," he said. "Why didn't you bring a jacket?"

"Because I wanted to see somebody really bad and didn't take time to get one from the closet."

"Then come." He led me toward a nearby guard shack. Once on the other side of it, I relocated us to the facility.

"Your pancakes are ready, and I'll hold off yelling until our session tomorrow," Leo informed me as he walked out of our kitchen. Pancakes were ready—James had a spatula in his hand as Rafe and I sat down at the kitchen island.

"Thanks for cooking," I gave James a hug when he set a plate of pancakes in front of me.

"Thanks for not being dead." He hugged both of us. Rafe grinned when James stepped away.

"I hope your pancakes are good," Rafe said.

"Come on—I can make pancakes. Not much else, but pancakes I can do."

"Marcus is in the lockup downstairs—next to the Mary clone from Dublin," Auggie said when I asked at breakfast the following morning. "He says he doesn't remember handing a cell phone off in Ketchikan."

"That's preposterous," Rafe growled. "The fucker is lying to save his ass."

"Whether he's lying or not, he's done his job. He's worthless to the enemy, now. Worthless to us, too," Auggie said. "I need more coffee."

"Auggie, do you suppose Askins and Phillips think they killed us?" I asked. "They were waiting for us to follow Clone Mary. I'm sorry I fell for that."

"Marcus played right into their plan—defecting when he did," Auggie growled. "So yes, I believe they wanted to lure us away. Who knows who might have been watching when you and Rafe first appeared in Vancouver?"

"I feel like an idiot. So many people died," I began.

"That wasn't your fault, so stop thinking it is," Rafe pulled me against him. "We wanted to follow Mary. We had other people out looking for Marcus in Vancouver. The enemy got to him first and handed him a cell phone detonator."

"This isn't the first time they've done that," Leo said. "Remember when they bombed the Mansion?"

"Yeah." I remembered, all right. Again, I hadn't seen the danger until the last moment, and people died.

"What are we going to do?" I asked, dropping my head into my arms at the kitchen island.

"Maybe we should let them think you're dead." Matt Michaels walked in.

"How will we do that and keep Madam President from going crazy?" Auggie asked. "You know they'll be watching her reaction to this news. She won't take it well if she believes it. She won't be able to hide it if she knows the truth."

"Easy. Tell her the lie in front of Askins and the Joint Chiefs. Tell her the truth later."

"That sounds horrible," I said.

"But necessary. Let them think they took you down in their well-calculated explosions. You'll be on your own to track the enemy for the most part, but with you seemingly out of the way, he may poke his head out of his shell, anyway. People are already working on their presidential runs. If he's not in the public eye soon, how will anyone know to vote for him?"

"I honestly don't give a fuck about politics. I just want the bastard dead," Rafe hissed. "What are you planning to do with the prisoners downstairs?"

I could tell he wanted to kill both of them.

"I have contacts," Matt offered. "With Corinne's help, I think we can lock them up for as long as necessary."

My help entailed disguises for Marcus and Dublin Mary. They now looked like escaped criminals that Matt assured me were dead—but nobody besides him and a handful of his agents knew that.

They'd be transferred back to their respective prisons, held in private cells and nobody would ask questions.

"We have transportation arranged to get back to D.C." Auggie said as he surveyed my work. Marcus glared at all of us from the cot inside his cell. After his capture, whenever he saw me, all he could say was "dead."

He was saying it now.

Repeatedly.

Somehow, the enemy had fucked with his head. Leo, who'd examined Marcus and asked him questions shortly after his arrival, said he'd never seen anything like it. He'd seen victims of brainwashing and mind control before, but that had always taken time to achieve.

Marcus' alteration had taken hours, at most. I still couldn't see past the fog of it, so we were no closer to an explanation than we were before.

Blood and tissue was extracted from Dublin Mary, so Richard Farrell could study it to see whether there was a way to tell who she was before, but Auggie didn't hold any hope for that—she was an exact replica of the original, fingerprints included. All I could do was consider that the drug was damned efficient in what it did.

"How much of it is left?" I turned to Auggie. "The drug?"

"Plenty. It only takes a small amount for a human, depending on their weight."

"So the Russians may have even more of it. Has anybody been able to duplicate it?"

"No, thank God."

"Are you going to report that Marcus is dead, then?"

"For now. They'll believe that—they wouldn't leave him alive if they were in our shoes."

"Good."

"Corinne, what are you going to do?"

"Make it impossible to talk about any of us or the Program," I said, lifting a hand. Auggie stared as light formed around my fingers, until it shot straight at Marcus' head.

No, he wasn't harmed. He merely had memories blocked about his time with the Program and anyone else involved, including the enemy.

I didn't want him carrying tales to fellow prisoners or prison guards. At Auggie's nod, I did the same for Dublin Mary. Let someone question them now. They wouldn't get a thing.

I turned to leave the holding cells, Auggie and Leo right behind me. "I'm no longer updating my files, Corinne," Leo informed me as we stepped inside the elevator. Auggie hit the button for the main level while Leo nodded to me. "By this time tomorrow, we'll be back in D.C., with news for Madam President. This facility will be closed and off-limits, according to the official records."

"I'm leaving necessary personnel here, to do mop up," Auggie said. "Nobody will know that James isn't directing the closing of a military facility. Don't let anyone see you, Cori. Or any of the others."

"What Colonel Hunter is saying is—don't die, Corinne. You, Rafe, Maye and Nick are all we have to fight what's coming. I'm beginning to worry that it's something worse than any of us might imagine," Leo reached out to touch my cheek.

"I'll do what I can," I said. "All of us will."

"You don't happen to have more of those cell phones—the ones we can't seem to trace or unscramble?" Auggie asked.

"You checked, huh?" I turned to him as the elevator opened on the main level. "It's borrowed technology. Nobody here knows anything about it—yet. I'll make sure everybody has one," I nodded. "Before you leave."

~

Ilya

"They won't be able to talk about us or anything connected to the Program. In fact, they don't know what it is, now." Corinne walked past me, opened the refrigerator, pulled out a bottle of orange juice and filled a glass.

"So Marcus doesn't recall what he did?" I asked.

"He didn't before. Someone or something made that happen."

"Does that make him innocent?" I was ready for an argument if she said yes.

"No. He did his part in this. He's responsible for thousands of deaths. I can't even watch this on television, Ilya. It's too horrible."

I'd seen the news—they'd broadcast images of floating bodies—at least they'd aimed their cameras at those appearing whole or mostly so. The FBI was on the scene. I figured Matt's crew and a few other agencies were there, too. So far, nobody had stepped forward to take responsibility for the bombings. Everybody referred to it as an act of terrorism anyway.

News agencies in every state had interviews with families and loved ones affected by the bombings. Tourists from other countries were also getting airtime—several countries were demanding answers from the U.S. Government for the deaths of their citizens.

I didn't envy the President or the Secretary of State—it was their job to unruffle those feathers while they desperately searched for answers.

"We're officially dead, Ilya." Corinne came to me and pressed her body against mine.

"My love," I wrapped my arms about her and spoke in my native language, "We have been dead for quite some time."

～

Corinne

James stood between Rafe and me while we watched Auggie, Laci and Leo climb into an electric cart for their trip through the tunnel. Matt's vehicle was behind theirs. He was saying goodbye to Opal, who'd elected to stay with us.

What are we going to do, Ilya? I asked.

Cabbage, we'll use everything we have to track those madmen. I'd ask you to destroy Askins and the Joint Chiefs, but that would alert the enemy and make him more than suspicious. Colonel Hunter will be watching them, as will Director Michaels.

The moment Auggie left us behind, we'd become ghosts. All we could do then is operate behind the scenes, without letting the enemy know. *If* we were lucky. If we weren't and the enemy found us, we could be just as dead as everyone would believe.

"You never told us who you were," Leo was back and standing before me.

"Oh. That." I lowered my eyes and stared at my feet. "Harriett Majors. Heard of her?"

"The queen of mystery," Leo beamed at me. "I have all her books. Most of them, I've read more than once."

"I'll sign them for you, if we live through this," I said.

"I'd like that." He walked back to the cart and climbed on. Auggie nodded to the driver and they drove away. Matt nodded to Opal and to us as he followed in their wake.

"Harriett Majors?" Rafe lifted an eyebrow while James was content to stare at me. "I had all your books. My daughter read them before she was old enough. She loved them, too."

"Huh." I turned my head away. "You have no idea how hard it was to invent everything again from scratch. I couldn't touch any of my former characters."

"You have a son," James breathed.

"Yep. He gets all my royalties, now. Last I heard, he was partying at Harvard. Still playing the *my mom was a famous author and she's dead*, card."

"The official report said you and your husband died in an accident in Wales."

"I know what the official report says. I have no idea whose remains they substituted for mine when the bodies were sent back to the States."

"I never wished I could tell somebody I met somebody famous so much," James breathed.

"Stop treating me like a celebrity," I said. "I'm just Corinne, now."

"Who has three pen names," Rafe reminded me.

"Yeah. Well, I have more important stuff to do, now." I turned and walked toward the elevator.

Ilya's arms folded around my shoulders, his chin rested atop my head and he sighed as we both stared out our window at Puget Sound, far in the distance. Surprisingly, the day was clear and sunny. Auggie, Leo and Matt chose a good day to fly out of Seattle.

"They'll set up a meeting with the President and the others," I said.

"When they get back. Auggie's planning to tell them that they had to make sure we were among the dead before reporting it. The Program will officially close—at least our part of it. I'll be interested to see whether they decide to scrap it or try again."

"I hope they bury that filth where nobody will ever find it," Rafe breathed against my hair. "It is causing too much trouble in the wrong hands."

"Would you like to place a memorial—for Jeff—in Ketchikan?"

"Yes. He was a faithful soldier, who died in the line of duty. I wish to take the others, too. We will pay our respects."

"All right."

Nobody would have recognized us. We looked like a group of schoolchildren, dropping a wreath into the waters an hour later. Opal stood beside Nick, who hugged Maye as she wept. James gripped my left hand, Rafe my right as we watched the wreath float away.

"From these honored dead we take increased devotion to that cause for which they gave the last full measure of devotion," Rafe quoted. He'd memorized the *Gettysburg Address*. His words were poetic and heartfelt.

"That we here highly resolve that these dead shall not have died in vain," Opal added.

"Goodbye, Jeff," I said. "May your next life be a happy one."

Ilya

"James, we know that Marcus likely reached someone in Vancouver," I said once we were back at the facility.

"Stands to reason," he said. "He got that phone somewhere between Vancouver and Ketchikan."

"Then, Mary conveniently shows up not far from where we are, just as Corinne suspected she would, effectively distracting us from chasing after Marcus."

"True."

"Can you find information on when her ticket was purchased? Were we targeted all along, as Corinne believes? Was Mary waiting for us to spot her in Seattle? Did Marcus have some hidden instruction that Corinne may have missed when he joined the Program? I know she didn't like him from the first. Colonel Hunter should have been more attentive and let him go immediately."

"I'll dig into this," James promised. "I just need my laptop."

He was in our kitchen following the return from Ketchikan, waiting for us to tell him what we wanted him to do.

"Hide your tracks," I called out as he ambled toward his bedroom.

"I will." He waved a hand as he walked away.

"I hope we don't walk into another trap," Corinne murmured. "What do you want for dinner?"

Notes—Colonel Hunter

"We're closing the facility in Washington State," I said. Matt Michaels and I sat in the Oval Office with Madam President, Merle Askins and the Joint Chiefs.

We'd already informed her that everyone left in the Program—Maye, Jeff, Nick, Corinne and Rafe—were dead in the Ketchikan ship bombings. Madam President looked ready to cry. The others appeared stone-faced. I'm sure Corinne might have read their satisfaction at what they were hearing, however.

"We waited until we had proof," Matt slid a file folder onto her desk. "It's all there, DNA evidence, photographs of what remains we could find," he shrugged. "I lost one of mine in the bombings, too."

Matt was so efficient it was frightening. It was his idea to present proof—he figured Merle would be quite interested in that.

"We can't even mourn their deaths," the President murmured, placing her hand on the file folder.

"That happens every time we lose an agent," Merle Askins said, his voice stiff. "They all know the risks."

"You're speaking of my friends," Madam President snapped.

"Of course. If you'll excuse me, I have an agency to run." Merle Askins rose from his chair.

"Colonel Hunter, do you need time away?" the President turned to me.

"I'd like a few days," I nodded. "I'll make sure all the records are stored safely after that, Madam President."

"Thank you."

Matt and I walked out behind the Joint Chiefs, none of whom said anything to either of us. I preferred it that way. I just hoped the President wouldn't hate me when I informed her that what we'd told her had been an elaborate lie.

Corinne

"I can stay a while—Colonel Hunter has approved leave for me after I officially close this facility," James informed me at breakfast two days after Auggie and Matt Michaels left. "I got the information on Mary's cruise ticket," he added.

"What did you find?" Rafe asked immediately.

"The ticket was bought the day before Cori saw her in Seattle, down by the wharf."

"So they did plan this." I didn't feel good about falling for their ruse. They'd left just enough unclouded information in Mary's mind to lure me in.

"When will all the remaining personnel be gone?" Rafe directed his question at James while gripping my fingers in his. *Not your fault*, he assured me. I wished I could believe that.

"Four days," James shrugged. "Colonel Hunter is sending them to Alaska to help Dr. Farrell when they leave here."

"Has Dr. Farrell contacted anyone?" I asked.

"Colonel Hunter gets regular e-mail updates. So far, no sightings of DB. It'll help when the personnel from here arrive to help. He only has two assistants right now."

"Sightings of Mary or Baikov?" Rafe asked.

"None to report."

"Do you suppose the enemy is breathing a sigh of relief before plotting his next move?" I asked Rafe.

"Possibly. They may be waiting to make sure we don't make further appearances."

"That's comforting."

"They may make a foray up the mountain, to check this facility after James locks it behind him," Rafe said.

"You know, maybe we should visit Dublin again."

"I suggest Alaska," James shrugged. "I've never been," he added. "We're supposed to fly into Anchorage to meet Dr. Farrell. Colonel Hunter said I could stay as long as I wanted before going back to D.C."

"Anchorage?" I chewed my lower lip and blinked at Rafe.

"I can keep you warm," he shrugged. "I've been. The city isn't large, but the wilderness outside it is beautiful."

"I see more sunlamps in my immediate future," I grumbled. "Who's going to tell the others?"

"Wait, I'm getting something," James tapped his tablet. He'd gotten a message from Opal.

Got this just now from Matt. Take a look and pass on to Corinne and Rafe, Opal had written.

Below, in a short, clipped message from Matt, were two photographs taken by locals near Juneau. *Bigfoot walking his monkey,* the caption read.

"Oh no," I sighed. Two of our escaped fifteen had been photographed.

CHAPTER 9

*C*orinne

"They're baiting us, to see whether we're still alive," Opal said. "Matt thinks the same thing."

"So we ignore this?" Nick sounded flabbergasted.

"For now. There's no indication that they're dangerous, and Bigfoot sightings are reported several times a year," Opal said. "If they ate somebody, then we could look into it. Carefully."

"At least they sent out those closely resembling something already here," Rafe observed. "If some of the others were photographed, we could have trouble."

"Do you think they still plan to discredit the President over the Program? She wasn't the one who started it."

"She's the one who allowed the sixteen to be kept alive," Rafe said. "There are still fifteen left."

"Who have to be killed or captured by normal means, or they'll suspect we're still in business," James said.

"I think Matt may have some friends who can help," Opal mused, staring at the images again.

"Fascinating idea," I said. Opal turned a bright smile in my direction.

"You thinking what I'm thinking?" Nick lifted an eyebrow at Opal. "Maybe."

"I may have friends who might help, too."

"Shall we plot and plan?" Opal asked.

"Sure. I'll make calls if you will."

"What the hell are they talking about?" Maye asked as the two of them walked out of the room together.

"It's better if you don't know—at least for now," I said.

"I think we should find a place to stay in Alaska," Rafe said, attempting to divert Maye's attention. "We need something large enough, but hidden as well as we can manage."

"How about one of those fish camps?" I asked. "Some of those things are really nice and look more like fancy hunting lodges."

"Are you prepared for wilderness living?" Rafe asked.

"No. I'm just making suggestions."

"I'll contact Dr. Farrell. He may have ideas," James offered.

"Anchorage, since you can get us in and out if necessary," James informed me at dinner. "Colonel Hunter worries that Dr. Farrell may be watched, so we shouldn't be together. That means he won't be meeting us there—he'll stay where he is. Besides, we'll be close enough if Bigfoot shows up again and causes problems."

"Where in Anchorage?" Rafe asked.

"Just outside, actually. We'll have some land between us and the neighbors."

"Not looking forward to snowfall measured in yards this winter," Maye said.

"Anchorage isn't that bad," Rafe grinned. "I found good restaurants the last time I was there."

"When was that?" Nick asked.

"Thirty years ago."

Nick opened his mouth to respond. "No, wait," I held up a hand. "I have to slap my forehead and say duh, first."

"Things may have changed," Nick ducked his head to hide the grin.
"Or not." Rafe chuckled.

Three days later, we stood outside my suite at the Pilchuck facility—
all of us, with bags and personal items gathered about us. The other
personnel had already left to join Dr. Farrell in Wales, Alaska. We
were ready to go to Anchorage.

I'd already sealed off this portion of the facility—even if Merle and
his followers came knocking, they'd never find this part. Maye looked
uncomfortable at being locked inside what now appeared to be a
shallow cave, but I was ready to take her out of those confines.

"Ready?" I asked.

"More than ready," Maye studied her boots.

"We're gone."

Notes—Colonel Hunter

"We're good," I said, flopping onto a chair in Shaw's new office.
That was code between us—Leo would understand that what
remained of the Program had just arrived in Anchorage.

Shaw nodded—he'd gotten the message from Corinne, just as I
had. It amazed me that she could insert the words straight into our
heads, when we were as telepathic as two stumps.

I just wished we could send messages back. Even with the phones
she'd given us, I worried that Askins and the others were watching us
too closely. It made me want to visit Alaska, just to dodge that
scrutiny.

I'd be followed, so that was out of the question. Instead, Laci was
attempting to settle into her life again in the Capital's shadow, while
Shaw and I worried about our charges.

"Want lunch?" Leo rose and nodded to me.

"Yeah. What sounds good?"

"Philly cheese steaks?"

"Sure."

~

Corinne

It was breakfast time, where we were. Auggie and Leo were about to have lunch. They were about to have company.

Disguised company.

We looked like a group of middle managers from a nearby office building as we wandered into The Sandwich Line, a popular lunch destination in Silver Spring.

Leo, we're here, I sent. Long, communal tables were scattered throughout the small shop, which served hot and cold sandwiches. *Nick's guarding the table at the back—he's wearing the gray suit coat.*

I watched as Leo nudged Auggie as they stood in line, waiting to order.

Cabbage, what are you getting? I don't see anything on the menu you might want, Rafe informed me. We now stood at the back of the line, but it was moving efficiently. Names would be called whenever an order was ready, so all we had to do was order for Nick and ourselves, then sit down to wait. *I'll have a toasted sub with everything except meat on it*, I responded to Rafe's question.

"How the hell?" Auggie stared at us as we took seats across the table. He and Leo saw us as we were—I found I could manage that. Everybody else saw men in suits.

"Anybody trying to listen will only get the conversation around us," I shrugged.

"How's the place in Anchorage?"

"I feel like I'm in a *Bonanza* episode," Opal said.

"Logs. Big logs," Nick grinned. "I like it."

"You would," Maye frowned at him.

"I need you hooked up," Auggie said to me. "I want updates on what Askins is plotting, or what he knows. You can tell me that, I assume."

"I can tell you that—as much as I can see in him," I said.

"Good. You're sure those phones we have can't be compromised?"

"Yes."

"Good. I'll start sending stuff to you. Feel free to let me know what you think—in the same way you set up lunch."

"I can do that," I said. "Are Nelda and Ray still watching Laci?"

"Yes. They're on the job," Auggie said. "We both feel better about that."

"I want to know if Askins ever leaves town," Rafe said. "Are we prepared to follow him? Are his calls monitored?"

"Matt is working on both those things," Auggie said. "We just can't be seen together very often, you understand."

"I'll be watching to see if any politicians start making a stir about running for the White House," I said.

"Are you saying that this one could already be in office?" Leo breathed.

"It makes sense," I shrugged. "Somebody doesn't run for the Presidency after appearing from nowhere. Auggie, can you get me photographs of all Members of Congress, Governors and big city mayors?"

"I'll do that," James said.

"Current photographs, James," I turned to him.

"Why are you asking for current photographs, now?" Leo was curious.

"Because I want to know whether our enemy is now wearing a disguise and posing as a legitimately-elected politician. I won't know that from an old photograph."

"Holy, fucking hell," Auggie muttered.

"In fact, make sure all photographs sent to me from now on are current. If he's hiding behind somebody else's face, I want to know."

"Anything new on the fifteen?" Opal asked.

"No new sightings, but that could change. We have people—and dogs—in the Juneau area, but so far, nothing has turned up," Auggie replied. "Tracks end in water, that kind of thing."

"So, other than looking at politicians, our hands are tied," Maye huffed.

"For now. We have to lead them to believe you're dead," Leo pointed out. "Don't forget you're all in danger if they learn otherwise."

～

Merle Askins' Office

"Sir." A tablet was set in front of the CIA Director.

"Hunter and Shaw went to lunch?" Askins watched the video.

"You asked that they be followed—this is all we have."

"Look at that jerk in the gray suit at the end," Askins snickered. "Bet they're sorry they didn't get their sandwiches to go. Shaw and Hunter are just sitting there, grimacing while the idiots at their table are laughing and joking."

"Want to retain these images?" Askins' assistant asked.

"Hell no. Don't bring me more of the same, either. If it doesn't look useful, trash it."

"I will, sir."

～

Corinne

"Home again, home again." I studied the kitchen after we landed in it. A shopping trip to the grocery store was in order—I'd brought what we had from the facility, but supplies had run low before we left. I'd also traded appliances—the ones in our new home weren't up to my (or Rafe's) standards.

"Want to make a list?" Rafe asked, pulling the phone I'd given him out of a pocket.

"Yeah. Put milk and bread on there first."

～

"How did you create a bank account for all of us with our new IDs?" Rafe asked as we browsed the produce aisle later.

"It was easy," I shrugged. "I didn't want Auggie connected to anything like that—we could be found out. I had the money stashed in a private account, which I don't care to name, so I just created accounts for all of us. Everybody gets a credit card to match their ID, which is connected to their new bank accounts. End of story."

"Under what pseudonym?" Rafe demanded quietly.

"Not under a pseudonym. Under a Swiss bank account, registered to Harriett Majors, which only I and my husband knew about," I snapped. "I pulled the money out and redistributed it. Congratulations—you now have a million or two at your disposal."

"What about the others?"

"They only have a few hundred thousand to spend. I love you the most," I shook a bunch of celery at him.

He rubbed his forehead, but I didn't miss the slight curl at the edge of his mouth. "Are you going to beat me with that celery or will it go into the soup tonight?" he dropped his hand and grinned.

"Soup," I said.

"Very good. Onions next on the list, cabbage."

The Range Rover we'd inherited with the log cabin was filled with groceries when we got back. Grateful that there'd been a freezer in the garage for extra storage, we unpacked with help from Nick and Opal.

Although it was made of logs, the house looked as if a wealthy family had built and owned it at one time—it had five bedrooms, an entry, living area, media room, large kitchen with pantry, and six bathrooms. It also had several fireplaces and two wood burning stoves —in case the power went off, I suppose.

We now owned it—utilizing James' technical expertise, I'd bought it, Range Rover included, from someone looking to leave Alaska before cold weather set in.

Still, we needed at least one more vehicle. "Who wants to buy another truck?" I asked, once all the groceries were put away.

"I wouldn't mind," James grinned.

"I'll come with you," Nick offered.

"Get something useful," I called out as they headed for the back door and the Range Rover.

"They'll come home with a Corvette," Rafe said.

"I sure hope not," I said. "It'll be snowed over until spring if they do that."

～

"Another sighting—different ones, this time," James handed a tablet to me while Rafe and I cooked dinner later. He and Nick had come back earlier with a four-wheel-drive SUV, which warranted a hug for James. I might have hugged Nick, too, but Ilya was watching.

"There isn't a single thing on the planet—even in mythology—that looks like that one," I sighed, pointing to one of the creatures. To me, it looked as if a giant capybara mated with an alligator. The head and long tail—all alligator. In between—capybara.

The whole animal stood around five feet tall at the shoulders and looked meaner than a rattlesnake. Its partner was smaller and looked more like the other one's dinner.

"What the hell are they doing—out for walkies?" Nick asked, peering over my shoulder.

"I think they're still trying to draw us out, testing whether Auggie was telling the truth," I said. "Any damage?"

"Nothing reported," James said. "The tabloids are going crazy with this, and I gotta tell you, some of them may be closer to the truth than most people believe."

"Any finger pointing at the President?" Opal asked after joining the crowd.

"Not yet. I figure it's only a matter of time."

"Where, this time?"

"Outside Sitka," James said.

"That means they're definitely in Alaska somewhere," Rafe wiped his hands on a kitchen towel before lifting the tablet from my fingers.

"We can't go after them—for obvious reasons," Maye said.

Opal lifted an eyebrow at Nick, who shrugged.

"How long will it be, you think, before they begin to believe we're really dead?" James pointed his question at Rafe.

"If it were me, I'd wait at least a month and place as much temptation to draw them out as I possibly could."

"What sort of temptation, honey?" I asked.

"I don't want to frighten you," he said, setting his hands on my shoulders.

"More people are going to die, aren't they?" I whispered.

"It's likely," he said.

"Cabbage, wake up, my love."

"Huh? What's wrong?"

I was still trying to get used to the hours the sun kept in Anchorage. I knew something was wrong, just from Ilya's voice.

After wrapping me in a robe, he herded me toward the media room, where the others were already gathered, watching the early morning news.

"To recap," the D.C. journalist announced, "The White House and the Secretary of Defense have been tied to an experimental program, which went terribly wrong. Classified documents were passed to a New York Gazette reporter, who published the story this morning. There has been no comment from the President on these allegations, and the Secretary of Defense has refused requests for an interview."

"Three guesses who released those documents," Maye huffed.

"The photographs taken recently of those survivors from Montana were printed with the article in the newspaper," James said. "Only they're not labeled as such. The whole thing is listed as experiments on animals that went wrong. They're saying the animals escaped and could be dangerous."

"And it gets better," I mumbled. "How is Askins going to dance away from that? He was in charge of that part."

"He may have photographs of us at the Nevada facility," James hung his head. "From the security cameras they have, there."

"So we get tied to that shit while he stays squeaky clean?" I snapped. Yes, I needed coffee. And sunshine. I had no idea how quickly I'd get either.

"We're dead, remember. I wonder what they'll say about that? You notice nothing was said about human experiments, instigated by former President Phillips."

"Are they expecting us to prove the lie by coming out and defending ourselves?" Nick asked. "To spell out why we were in Nevada to begin with?"

"This is completely fucked up," Opal sighed.

"Auggie will be forced to resign," I said. "Because all this is top secret. He can't say what all of us are or can do, or what the Program really is. Merle Askins is a dick, and he's using the usual scare tactics to freak out the population. They'll expect monsters under beds and in closets. For real."

"All they'll have to do is hand over photographs of DB," Nick said. "And then say they don't know where he is, now. Which is true."

"Better yet, they only have to produce photographs of DB in the Bering Strait, and everybody will go batshit," Opal said.

"You know, that's probably what they're letting the others out for," Maye observed. "They're looking for signs of DB."

"Too bad he doesn't look like a dolphin," Opal offered.

"Too bad they all don't look like dolphins," Nick agreed. "Everybody loves dolphins."

"Maybe Merle Askins should be a dolphin. I'd like him better that way," I said. "By the way, who all knows where Richard Farrell and the facility staff are? What I really mean is—are they in danger because of this?"

"I'm not sure anyone else knows," James began.

"Right. If he's using a phone or e-mail, somebody knows," Maye snapped. That threw me back for a moment—Maye *liked* Richard. Since I'd shut off reading those around me, I hadn't realized that, yet.

"Maybe we should get you there—in disguise," I said.

"What?" At least three people threw that question at me, all of whom were not Maye.

"Hey, nobody will know it's her," I said, attempting to defend myself.

"Colonel Hunter will object," James began.

"Colonel Hunter is in enough hot water," I said. "Richard Farrell may need somebody who can kick ass," I added. "If Merle Askins is looking for DB, too, what are the odds he's looking for Dr. Farrell first?"

"We should consult with Colonel Hunter," Maye said. I could see the hope in her eyes, however, and had no desire to kill it.

"I have an idea," Nick said. "Why don't you disguise him and bring him here? Let one of his guards take his place."

"That may be a death sentence," Rafe pointed out.

"At least they'll be alert to the fact that they're in danger," Maye said. "They can request more troops—that's standard and has nothing to do with us."

"Let me think about this," I held up a hand. After all, I'd be involved if we went forward with that idea.

"Cori, I know you can send him a mental message—you've done that before," Nick turned to me. "At least let him know he may be in danger."

"I can do that much," I agreed. "Richard is more than trustworthy, and I'd pull him away from there now, if I thought I could get away with it."

Dr. Richard Farrell

Private Journal

"The sighting turned out to be a whale," the radio crackled at my elbow.

"Understood," I held the button down to reply. "Keep looking in the area."

"Yes, sir."

I released the button with a sigh. I sat in the back office in a small building in Wales, Alaska, wondering how things had come to this. I'd gotten word from Leo Shaw that information on the supposed animal experimentation done by the Program had been leaked to the media.

A photograph of the team sent to the facility in Nevada to investigate the disappearance of the creatures was included in a follow-up article, which clearly showed me as a member of that group.

Oddly enough, none of those stationed at the Nevada facility were shown anywhere. Clearly, the public now believed that the Secretary of Defense, a noted scientist and several others were involved in this illicit experimentation.

I wanted to laugh, but the situation was far too serious.

I wondered, too, who would come looking for me first—the media or the enemy.

Our research facility was spare and rough—only a few comforts had been hurriedly provided as it hadn't been used in several years. The personnel I had with me were more accustomed to assisting with research rather than carrying rifles and guarding anyone.

Richard? Corinne's voice floated into my mind. *We think you're in danger. I know you're alone right now—I just wanted to give you a heads up to lock the door—I'll be there in two minutes.*

My sudden movement sent the metal chair scraping across the bare, concrete floor as I slid off it. The lock was forced shut as quickly as I could manage it.

Corinne

I couldn't convince Ilya that I would be fine going alone, so he went with me. Richard was waiting for us when we arrived.

"What can we do?" Richard asked the moment we materialized inside his tiny office.

"Isn't this below your pay grade?" I looked around me—there was nothing comfortable about this place, including his office chair.

"Scientists are often the last ones considered where comfort is concerned," Richard offered a smile. "Tell me there's a way you can get me out of here without causing a fuss."

"I have a way, but you may not like it," I said.

Actually, the Ukrainian mountain had suggested it, and the idea was a sound one.

"What's that?"

"You're about to have a heart attack," I shrugged. "A small plane will arrive to carry you out of here to a hospital. Sadly, you won't make it. You'll be dead like the rest of us."

"Not in the literal sense, I hope." His words were dry.

"I hope not, too. Rafe says he can fly the plane, so we'll be your disguised medical personnel."

"What about the body—when you get me to a hospital?"

"I'll take care of it," I said.

"When?"

"How about before dinner? Say—seven or so?"

"Sure."

Notes—Colonel Hunter

If Corinne hadn't sent a mental message, I'd believe what I was watching on television. Dr. Richard Farrell, the scientist everybody was currently vilifying in the media, was dead of a heart attack, according to physicians in Nome, Alaska.

He'd been flown from Wales to Nome for treatment after suffering the attack, and was now dead.

According to the physicians and the media, anyway.

Corinne let me know that Richard was now safe in Anchorage, in disguise like the rest of them.

If this were real, I'd think that common decency would keep the media off his back, now that he was supposedly dead.

Nothing was farther from the truth. The background the Program had carefully built for Dr. Farrell was being tested—to its limits. I was grateful we'd built a background for someone who should have been dead years ago from natural causes.

Whatever Corinne had done to provide a replacement body for Dr. Farrell had worked flawlessly—extensive tests were run to make sure of his identity. Dr. Richard Farrell was now officially dead.

It made me wish I could do the same—I couldn't walk outside my office or drive up to my house without the media crowding around and asking questions while shoving microphones in my face.

Madam President—naturally—had to distance herself. It was planned, too, that my resignation as Secretary of Defense would come the following week. In the interim, I would be hounded to death by people asking questions about something I hadn't been involved in.

Did Askins expect me to point fingers in his direction? I figured he had a defense carefully planned that excluded him and the Joint Chiefs from any blame in the matter. After all, there were no photographs made available showing him leaving the Nevada facility.

Laci now spoke with Shaw several times a day. I'd thought our marriage was finally back to what it should be—this threatened it all over again. This time, I wouldn't get Laci back if she decided to leave me.

Under the circumstances, it was understandable.

～

Merle Askins' Office

"That's one down for sure," Merle studied the newly-acquired autopsy report, photographs included. "His outer body looked younger than the internal organs. I always wondered about that."

"What about the rest?" His assistant asked.

"Oh, we still have something planned. If that doesn't draw them out, nothing will."

"So we can be assured they're dead, if they fail to respond?"

"One in particular, and without a doubt."

～

Ilya

"Where are they—Maye and Dr. Farrell?" I asked. Dinner was long over, the kitchen cleaned and everything put away. I'd built a fire in the fireplace inside our suite while Corinne dressed in warm fleece.

"They're out spooning," she said.

"Spooning?"

"They haven't gotten to the forking part, yet. They're still discussing spooning."

"How old are you again?" I grinned at her.

"Younger than you," she swatted my arm before dropping onto the thick rug before the fireplace.

"Is this an invitation?" I asked, reaching for her outstretched hand.

"What else would it be?"

"Excellent." I dropped to the rug beside her.

"Want some wine?" she asked.

"I don't need it," I leaned in to kiss her neck. "I have what I need."

"Me, too." She pulled my face up for a kiss.

Perhaps if we had gone to bed instead of making love, or perhaps if our timing had been different, something might have been done. As it was, when the deed was accomplished in a city far from where we were, Corinne went into shock. Dr. Farrell, thankfully, was available, or she might have left all of us behind.

CHAPTER 10

otes—Colonel Hunter
    I'd gotten a coded message from James while I watched the news the following morning. Every crawler on every station said the same thing—Darin Majors, Jr., shot by unknown assailant at his apartment in Cambridge, MA.

Every newscaster was having a field day with the fact that Darin Majors, the only child of noted author, Harriett Majors, and Darin Majors, Sr., a prominent Atlanta attorney, was now dead.

You'd think that Harriett Majors was dead all over again. I remembered news of her death, more than six years earlier. I'd believed the information disseminated then—that she and her husband were killed in a car accident in Wales.

I wanted to laugh bitterly. Richard Farrell, noted scientist, had been in Wales, Alaska, when he'd supposedly suffered his heart attack. Both he and Harriett were still alive.

Darin—Sr. and Jr.—were the ones dead.

James' cryptic message informed me that Corinne was suffering in some way; he just couldn't elaborate. He'd called her Tippy, she was a stray cat he'd found, and was now receiving veterinary care.

At least Richard Farrell was there to take care of her. I had no idea what this would do to her in the long term—both her husband and son, now dead, likely due to the same source.

This was their last ditch effort to prove the lie we'd told.

Instead, they'd killed an innocent man. After reflecting on thousands of deaths in Ketchikan, one more would mean nothing to them.

What was their end game? Phillips had control of the U.S. before. Wasn't that enough?

Let Tippy know you love her, my text read. *Sometimes that helps as much as medicine.*

I will. The vet has her on an IV right now. I hope she makes it.

Ilya

She wouldn't wake. At times, I thought it a blessing, as the fucking media wouldn't drop the news about her son. Harriett Majors' last dust jacket photograph was shown continuously, next to a yearbook photo of her son.

Police had no suspects and few leads on the shooter—the best they had was someone out walking his dog who reported a shadowy figure slipping between buildings not long after the body was discovered.

There was no description—it was too dark to get useful information.

Those of us in Alaska knew who was behind this killing, however. They'd attempted to draw Corinne out one last time.

They'd sacrificed her son to continue playing their game.

Would they reveal their agenda openly, now? Would Corinne come back to us to help wage that battle?

I felt lost again. I did convince Farrell to set sunlamps about our bed, however. They were now on constantly while we waited—and hoped—for her recovery.

Private Journal

   Dr. Richard Farrell

Although Corinne's vitals were marginally normal, it's as if we were back to the point after she'd been shot in D.C. She was so deeply entrenched in her unconscious that nobody could pull her out.

Was she mourning or dying? I couldn't tell. An IV was the best I could do for her—we didn't have the necessary equipment to do more than that. Rafe admitted they were asleep after sex when the murder took place—she was likely worn out after a long day of rescuing me.

It was no surprise that the enemy would target someone she cared about. They'd caught her unaware, this time. I had no idea what she'd have done if she'd been aware.

Maye's arm slipped around my waist as I stood at the bedside and studied Corinne. Maye's affection had come as a surprise—yes, I felt something for her, but imagined that she'd refuse any advances.

I was wrong—and gratefully so.

"We won't make it without her," Maye said. "Six years ago, I never thought I'd be saying those words."

"What if we're forced to go on without her?" I asked, kissing Maye's temple gently.

"I guess we'll go down fighting," she said simply.

Notes—Colonel Hunter

"For now, you're still my Secretary of Defense," Madam President snapped. I'd attempted to submit my resignation, but she'd refused it. "Look, I know Farrell's death hit you hard so close to the others, but we have a new problem."

"What's that?"

"This." She pushed a tablet across her desk. "I got this from Matt Michaels this morning. Want to speculate on why it came from him instead of Askins? Our people in Cuba are still trying to wrap their heads around this."

"This has to be a joke," I said, flipping through the report and the photographs included.

"It's not. They're filling up an airfield in a remote area."

Russian fighter planes and bombers were lined up on cracked tarmac, with grass growing between those cracks. "This one hasn't been used in a while," I said.

"No, it's used—they just don't have the money to repair or replace it. Until now, unless Matt and I miss our guess. We really haven't seen anything like this, though, since Grenada in 1983. We may have to close the embassy there if this escalates."

"I knew they were landing at Latin American bases, but this? This is preposterous. Any word from the Cuban or Russian Ambassadors?" I understood the Grenada reference—that had been named *Operation Urgent Fury*. It lasted less than two months. I worried that this wouldn't be so easily contained.

"Neither are returning my calls at the moment," the President answered my question. "If we ever needed Corinne's help," she rose and paced behind her desk. I rose with her—and watched her agitated journey as it turned toward the window behind her.

"That's not possible. I wish it were otherwise," I said. With Corinne's current condition, it might always be that way, too. Madam President still thought them dead—all of them. For now, she could be close to correct regarding Corinne.

"Get with Matt and the Secretary of State. Find out as much as you can. Is this just posturing, or is there a real threat in this?"

"I'll do everything in my power, Madam President," I said and strode from the Oval Office.

~

Ilya

Darin Majors, Jr. was buried two weeks after his murder, following an autopsy. Relatives on his father's side made the arrangements, and buried him near his parents' graves in Atlanta. There were no known relatives on his mother's side—she'd been adopted as an infant after someone left her at a hospital. Her adoptive parents were also dead, for at least twenty years.

Corinne still hadn't wakened, although Farrell was surprised that her body wasn't wasting away. The sunlamps were still on and standing about her bed; I refused to allow the others to turn them off.

Farrell was surprised, too, that her skin failed to burn. At least he'd learned to listen to me when I said she never suffered any effects from spending hours beneath the lamps. In fact—she didn't even show a tan.

"It's over, my love. He rests near his father's grave," I touched Corinne's hand, folding it into mine.

"I know." She opened her eyes, then.

I didn't ask her where she'd been. "I'm glad to hear your voice," I said instead.

Corinne

Everybody gave me space, except for Ilya and Richard. Ilya wanted to hold me; Richard wanted to examine every inch of me.

Both of those things happened.

It kept my mind off the obvious. I had to stay away from that, just to keep my sanity and the world safe.

"Flowers, cabbage. I found them at the grocery store." Ilya brought in a vase filled with a mixed bouquet.

"Those are nice. You went out to find some, didn't you?"

"Yes. This is better than having a florist deliver. We don't want to draw attention."

"Thank you, honey." I kissed him, took the flowers and set them on the kitchen island. He'd found me there when he got back, having coffee and staring into space.

The others had gone out for lunch at a local pizza restaurant. "I heard from Katya," he said, taking the chair beside mine. "She says that the underground is reporting sightings of Baikov in Russia. This coincides with the idiotic show they're making of crowding South

American air bases with planes and recklessly flying missions just outside U.S. air space."

"Bastards."

"I have better terms," he shrugged.

"The underground, huh?" I said, bumping his shoulder with mine.

"It has to be hidden. Many of them are on Russian hit lists."

"So Katya and her husband are doing what they can to undermine Baikov and the President? Do you think that was the reason the Baikov and Mary clones were in Ireland?"

"I think that, yes, and the underground is doing everything it can to stop them," Ilya huffed. "I told Katya to be careful. We know what the enemy is capable of, and somehow, he has his hands on any incarnations of Baikov that may appear."

"True. Do you think this is so he can come riding in on a white horse and save the country from the big, bad Russians?"

"That is one possibility, yes."

"Idiots."

"He seems to be quite persuasive," Ilya observed. "The enemy. You recall those—idiots—who thought they would bring about the apocalypse?"

"The ones responsible for Wyoming and Georgia?"

"Yes."

"You don't have far to go to persuade idiots of what they want to hear to start with," I snorted. "The four horsemen? Seriously? A prime example of having more money than sense."

"And a devious way to get supporters for any opposition out of the way."

"You know, I never thought of it in those terms, but you're right— their empires broke apart overnight and everybody is still arguing over who gets what. I'm sure any politician who received money before is crying in his breakfast cereal over the current lack of funding."

"Too many politicians and elections are purchased, nowadays," Ilya said. "No matter where they are. Too many are willing to make fools of themselves, just to align their views with those of their sponsors."

"And let's face it; none of them are going to win the smartest person on the planet award, anyway."

"Is there such a thing?" He wrapped his arms about me before leaning his chin on my shoulder.

"Nah. Besides, if there were, somebody with a ton of money would just buy it, anyway. Everything's for sale, you know."

"Not love. Not real love," he murmured before kissing my temple. "That is a gift. An unexpected and wondrous gift."

"Well, there's one thing not for sale, then," I sighed. "Thank you—for being here for me."

"You are welcome." His mouth claimed mine.

Notes—Colonel Hunter

I brushed my teeth while watching the morning news on the small television screen in the bathroom. So far, nothing untoward had occurred. I had a meeting with Matt Michaels and the Secretary of State at nine, so I'd forced myself out of bed early to get some research done before going into the meeting armed with information.

My cell phone rang as I rinsed my mouth.

"Hunter here," I barked. I recognized the phone number—someone from the White House was calling. Had Madam President changed her mind about accepting my resignation?

"Sir, there's been an incident in Colombia." I recognized Secretary of State Marshall's chief of staff—Gerard usually made calls on the SOS's behalf.

"Tell me," I lifted a towel and wiped my face.

"A British airliner has been shot down over the jungles," Gerard said. "The Colombian government is blaming it on rebels, but we have other suspicions."

"You think the Russians are involved." It wasn't a question.

"We are concerned, yes. The Brits are requesting assistance—they want a specialized crew to investigate and recover bodies. They're also calling for the Colombians to hunt down these rebels and bring them to justice."

"No survivors, I take it?"

"No, sir. All two hundred eighty-one dead, including the crew."

"Tell the British Ambassador I'll call him within an hour."

"Yes, sir. The Secretary is on the phone with him, now."

"Good. We'll do everything we can."

"Thank you, sir."

"I thought there was a vast reduction in Colombian rebel activity," I said.

"This may be a smokescreen for what's really going on," Matt suggested.

Secretary of State Marshall sat listening to both of us as we shared our thoughts on the plane crash.

"I'd like to say you're both right, but we don't know for sure," Chuck Marshall leaned back in his chair with a shrug. "I want a team put together to work with the Colombians and the Brits," he added. "So we can have the truth on this."

"Agreed," Matt said. "I think we can put something together. Don't you?" He turned toward me.

"Yeah. Give me a few hours. We'll have somebody to send."

Corinne

"I'm supposed to go back to D.C. and do my job," James informed us. "The rest of you—Colonel Hunter wants you to go to Colombia as disguised civilian contract employees. He wants you to make that happen, Cori."

"I can do that," I said.

"Then, you'll join the team he and Matt Michaels are sending down there to investigate the crash."

"What is he planning to tell them about us?"

"That you're very talented ex-military, hired through a private contractor. Matt already has information on all of you. You'll have to fly out of Chicago—they don't want any red flags to pop up. You understand the importance of staying incognito."

"Honey, I think we all understand that," I sighed.

"Good. Cori, he says if you find anything, then all of you have to figure out a way to prove it by logical means. People will be watching, so we have to do it this way."

"I think I can do that," I agreed. The others, their eyes turning in my direction, nodded.

"Good. You'll get dossiers on who you're supposed to be. You know the drill. Follow protocol unless Cori thinks you're in danger."

"How are you getting home?" Maye asked.

"I'm on a private jet to Seattle, and then on a commercial flight from there, just like it's supposed to be. Matt arranged for the private jet, so that won't be traced. He also said to tell Opal to be careful."

"Huh," she snorted. I wanted to laugh. It was a joke between them —I could see that easily enough.

"Here's the address in Chicago," he handed a slip of paper to Rafe. "Go there first; you'll find your dossiers and everything else you'll need, including appropriate clothing and plane tickets. There's a van there, too, for you to drive to the airport. Don't worry about picking it up later—somebody else will do that."

"So, we have IDs waiting, and I'm just making us look like those IDs?" I asked.

"That's the plan."

"Sounds fine, then."

"Good. I'll get a cab to the airport, I need to be there in an hour," James said. "Don't contact us until after you get to Chicago, and use your new covers when you do."

The location in Chicago was a business address—one used in the past by Director Michaels for his agents. Inside a meeting room we found bags, file folders, plane tickets and anything else we'd need for the trip to Colombia.

"Efficient," Rafe proclaimed as he studied his dossier.

"I'm a former medic," Richard turned his photograph around so I could look.

"You look like you're four feet tall," Maye frowned at the photo.

"Five-six," he corrected her with a smile. "What, you don't date shorter men?"

"I'd date you any day," she whispered. He laughed.

By the time I was finished disguising everybody, including matching their height and weight, I felt tired. At least our flights weren't until the following morning, so I spent several hours beneath the sunlamps Matt had thoughtfully supplied.

"I have to get used to this," Ilya nuzzled my cheek while we dressed early the following morning. I understood what he was saying—I was Latina and a former Marine, according to my dossier, and was the member of the team responsible for any necessary translations.

The language I could do. The Marine part? I hoped nobody asked me to arm wrestle.

Ilya, on the other hand, was now blond with cloudy blue eyes, slightly shorter and packed with muscles. I guess I could get him to do my arm wrestling.

Renata Jimenez and Trey Henson. What a couple.

"Ready?" he asked.

"I'm ready, Trey."

"I hate that name already."

"You're not Trey material—the normal you, that is."

"I'm glad you see it that way."

"Please keep your comments about Renata to yourself," I warned.

"I would not demean you or Renata," he gave me his most innocent expression.

"Good, because Renata would retaliate."

He snickered. "Come on, blond boy," I took his arm and steered him toward the door. "Let's go to the airport."

One of Matt's investigators met us at the airport in Bogotá and drove us away in an armored van. "Step carefully around Captain Finch," Lieutenant Nathan Cross said as he drove us through the streets of the city.

Captain Finch was the commander of the investigative team Matt and Auggie had assembled—we'd gotten their dossiers, too. I understood one thing from Nathan's words—Finch had no love for private contractors, even if they were ex-military. Perhaps Maye should teach him a lesson.

"We're not here to cause trouble," Opal said. She was blonde, too, and somewhat shorter than she normally was.

"I guess what I'm saying is this—just stay out of his way. Everybody will be happier."

"We're here to do a job," Rafe snapped. "Perhaps it would be better if he stayed out of our way."

Honey, I can send him to Bora Bora if he messes with us, I sent.

I will not get into a pissing contest with someone suffering from ego issues, Ilya's words were a growl in my head.

"I don't believe we'll be stepping on anyone's toes," Richard offered. "You're here to investigate the crash site. We're here to track the ones responsible."

"We're supposed to provide information on what type of missile or bomb was used," Nathan began.

"We will welcome any information. However, I believe we may be able to get work done while waiting for it," Richard responded.

"You have leads?" He sounded surprised.

"We have some information. If Captain Finch needs anything, then have him send someone to me. I'll be happy to share what I have."

"Then I'm asking now," Nathan said.

"We may have coordinates for the missile," Maye said. "From satellite images. We'll investigate that first, while you're working at the crash site."

"Ground missile, like they're saying?" Nathan was more than curious.

"That's the information we currently have," she replied. "Our first priority is to check that site, to see whether we can determine who may have fired it."

"Wow—this is more intense than I thought it would be," Nathan shook his head. "Look, we're quartered outside Bogotá, on the eastern edge of San Cristobal. You'll be in the building next to ours. Supplies and vehicles are provided—you're responsible for your own meals."

"Not a problem," Rafe said.

The crash site was in Chingaza National Park, not far from a glacial lake. Part of the Andes, Chingaza was natural and beautiful— except for the burned area where nearly three hundred people died. In San Cristobal, we'd be stationed as close as we could be while still within sight of civilization.

"When are you going out?" Nathan pulled into a driveway located between two concrete buildings.

"Tomorrow—we have some planning to do and connections to be made," Richard said.

"Good enough, I'll let Captain Finch know."

"You do that," Rafe said.

"I've seen worse," Rafe said as he surveyed the kitchen. Saltillo tile covered the floors, more tile covered the counters, the stove was small and looked as if it were twenty years old or more, the refrigerator almost as old.

"The window is filthy," Opal said, attempting to peer through it.

"It's pointed toward the other building—the filth may turn into a blessing," Rafe said.

"Nah, I want to see this Finch guy if he decides to visit," Opal said.

"He'd better bring everybody he has," Nick growled. "Anybody who makes that kind of snap judgment needs his ass kicked."

"I'll let you be in charge of ass-kicking, then," I said. "My solution is to send him to Bora Bora."

"Bora Bora is too good for an asshole," Maye said. "I've been there."

"Panama?"

"Better, but still too good for assholes."

"Siberia," Rafe said.

"Bingo," Opal touched her nose.

As if on cue, the asshole knocked on our door. Nathan, following in Captain Francis Finch's wake, looked apologetic as Finch stormed into our kitchen.

"What's this I hear about you having possible missile coordinates?" he demanded.

"Well, hello to you, too," Opal said, lifting an eyebrow at Finch.

Finch looked to be a welterweight in mixed martial arts, with buzzed dark hair, green eyes and a nose that had been broken a time or two. The scowl he wore was extra, strictly for our benefit.

"You know, someone three miles away may not have heard you. Would you like to repeat that—louder, this time?" Nick asked. "It's classified information—we're allowed to share it with you and your team, nobody else."

"Then show me."

I wanted to tell him to ask nicely. I didn't. Instead, Richard pulled the satellite images up on his tablet and handed it to Finch.

"Here," Richard pointed out the light that flared on the surface, and the time stamp on the image. "The plane was destroyed right after," he said, pulling up the following images.

"I see it," Finch grumbled, going back to the first image, and then to the second. "I'd like to send Lieutenant Cross with you tomorrow, when you go to this site."

"If he wants to come," Richard shrugged. "We may end up spending at least one night in the wilderness—this is up a mountainside and may take time to get there."

"I'll come prepared," Nathan promised. I could tell he was more excited to be coming with us than staying with Captain Finch. Oddly enough, I felt the same way.

"We need to check the climbing equipment," Rafe nodded to Nick.

"I'll get on it," Nick said.

I knew what they were thinking—that Nathan Cross would slow them down. I hoped that wasn't the case. We had to be on guard, however, and make sure everyone stayed in character.

"What time should I be here tomorrow?" Nathan asked.

"Oh-six-hundred," Nick said.

"I expect a full report." Finch turned and stomped out the door.

"I think he can expect a full bag of dog shit," Nick muttered. Opal snickered.

Nathan wanted to smile but held it back. "I'll be here," he said and followed Finch out the door.

"I think he was offended by our uniforms," I said. We had a video conversation going with Auggie and Matt.

"Khaki is not what he's upset about," Auggie snapped. "He says you were rude."

"So he heard the dog shit comment?" I asked.

"What dog shit comment?"

"Okay, pretend you didn't hear that," I said. "How were we rude? I don't recall being rude."

"He says one of the men complained about the loudness of his voice."

"Oh, that," I said. "If he'd bothered to allow us to introduce ourselves, then he'd know who to blame for that," I added. "And he was loud. Blustery. Also rude and offensive."

"He's effective," Matt offered. "Just do the best you can to work around him. I hear Lieutenant Cross is going with you in the morning?"

"That's right," Rafe sat beside me and nodded. "I hope he doesn't slow us down."

"Just stick to protocol. I'm not sure whether you'll find anything useful, but you'll know what to do," Auggie nodded to me.

"I do."

"Good. Keep me apprised."

"Yes, sir." Rafe ended the video call.

"I hate khaki already," I mumbled. Rafe laughed.

Finch is effective, like Matt says, but his methods aren't always the best, I responded to Maye's mental question over dinner. *I read in Lieutenant Cross that Finch manages to annoy or alienate anybody he meets.*

What did you see in him? she asked.

He thinks he's God's gift to the world, and everybody should bow first and then get out of his way.

He's not short enough to have a Napoleon complex, Rafe supplied.

There may be a whole new complex named after him, Maye said.

That won't feed his ego or anything, I pointed out.

"Ahem. Will somebody pass the tortillas?" Opal interrupted.

Maye laughed. I hadn't seen her laugh or smile so much in the entire time I'd known her. Richard was working miracles, in my opinion. It helped, too, that she and Nick were beginning to see me as a real member of the team.

"I like this—being able to share meals with all of you," I said. It helped with the pain in my heart—after recent events, some things would never be the same again.

"Well said," Nick held up his glass of beer.

Auggie, I'm thinking of you, I sent to him. *Stay tough.*

Notes—Colonel Hunter

So many times, I wished there were a way to respond to Corinne's telepathy. I would have thanked her for her words—Matt and I received fresh news of more creature sightings, this time in northeastern Washington State.

It made me think Askins was intending to check the facility we'd abandoned inside Pilchuck. At this point, I wanted him to look. James had taken photos before they left—Corinne didn't leave anything to chance. The facility looked gutted—just as it should. It amazed me that she could accomplish what she did, but that was just part of the changes she'd experienced.

We were fortunate to have her on our side. Without her, Askins and Phillips would likely have taken over. They could still do it, but with Corinne, we had a fighting chance, at least.

Corinne

I was asleep when the wards I'd left inside the Pilchuck facility were tripped. They weren't shielded when they walked into the place —perhaps they didn't think it necessary. The creatures (most of them, anyway) and their handlers had moved in, lock, stock and furry barrel.

Auggie, James, Leo, I sent to them. *I'm sorry to wake you, but Askins just moved his band of bogies into the Pilchuck facility.*

CHAPTER 11

*N*otes—*Colonel Hunter*

"You can speak freely—we're not bugged here," Matt said.

Here was inside his office in Silver Spring.

"Our opponent has taken over the facility at Pilchuck," I said. "Without paying a pet deposit."

"That confirms that he knew we were there," Matt said, drumming his fingers on his desk for a moment. "Any word on DB?"

"None. I don't know where he was placed, but nobody has seen anything."

"I think they really want him," Matt said. "To prove their point. The others aren't giants and can probably be contained once we find them."

"You think they want him to attack a coastal city?" I asked.

"I think they've been watching too many monster movies," Matt huffed. "Don't get me wrong—I'm glad they don't seem to have many original thoughts."

"That would be frightening," I agreed.

"You think they imagine that they're hidden well enough at the facility? That we won't suspect they're there?"

"We have no reason to—we abandoned the place and left nothing useful behind. For all anyone knows, it's just an empty shell."

"Or, if they think we know, they're just rubbing our faces in it," I said.

"I'll put somebody on that," Matt said. "Did Corinne block the tunnel leading out of there?"

"Yes. I asked James to set explosives, but she had a better way."

"How did she block it?"

"The entire thing looks like it imploded. Completely filled with big rocks, now. They'll have a hell of a time getting through that mess."

"Good. Very good. When will the team arrive at the launch site?"

"Later today if we're lucky," I said.

"You'll let me know?"

"Of course."

~

Ilya

Lieutenant Cross arrived ten minutes before the scheduled time, so Corinne offered him a cup of coffee. He accepted and watched as the rest of us loaded our gear. We had two large military vehicles to carry us into Chingaza, where the roads were less than hospitable much of the time.

Our targeted area was in a mountainous region, which would likely require the climbing equipment Nick and I loaded into the back of each vehicle. I worried for Corinne—she'd never done anything like this in her life. I think Nick and I were prepared to carry her if she couldn't make it on her own.

"Do you prefer Nathan or Lieutenant Cross?" Corinne asked before loading into the truck with me.

"Nathan's fine—I almost feel like a civilian right now," he grinned at her.

"Awesome. Want to ride with Trey and me, Nathan?"

"I'd be happy to."

~

Corinne

The drive was a long, tedious one, across narrow, grassy tracks at times, as we followed the GPS coordinates we'd been given. Our vehicles roared, growled and whined as we drove slowly along, while the rough roads shook or swayed all of us in our seats.

With only a brief stop at midday for a quick meal we'd packed ourselves, we were on our way again. After a while, we had to leave the trucks behind and backpack the rest of the way. Our arrival below the sharp, rocky peak that was our destination occurred before three that afternoon.

"Experienced climbers could get up there without much equipment, but we're taking no chances," Rafe said, slinging a pack and a coil of rope about his shoulders. Nick did the same and both went up together.

Once they had everything in place, the ropes were lowered and Maye went up the first one, with Richard almost behind her on the second. Then, Opal and Nathan went up. I was left to go up alone.

You can do this, cabbage, Rafe sent.

I think I'll use a little of what I have to help, I said and grabbed the rope. At least we had leather gloves—I didn't want burns on my palms if I slid down. Following the path the others used, I worked my way up the rocky cliff, balancing myself with power. Yes, if I hadn't had it, I might have fallen—twice. Instead, I came up in a semi-professional manner, Rafe grinned and we were off to find the launch point.

~

Notes—Colonel Hunter

"They're close," James pointed out the GPS signal in Chingaza. I could see the pinging signal the vehicles sent, and then that of the search party, not far away. Six miles away, I could also see the signal at the crash site.

"Keep me informed," I said.

"Yes, sir."

It was nice to have James back. I almost felt normal again.

Ilya

Here, Corinne informed me. She stood on the scuffed, rocky surface, where hundreds of hikers and backpackers had likely stood before, on a flat surface with a very good view of the lake below.

But this is not where the light appeared—that is still farther in, I argued.

I don't know what that light was, but this is where the rocket was launched, she insisted.

Maybe we ought to take a look, then, I agreed. Her mental voice had sounded worried and that, in turn, worried me.

Yes. Come, now, I turned and followed the others. Nick had taken the lead—he was using his hypersensitive nose to detect scents. He was careful not to disturb any evidence; I understood that, too.

Barely a hundred yards away, and halfway down the peak on the opposite side, lay the coordinates. Nick knew it first, but as it didn't hold as much horror for him as it did for Corinne, he warned us, first.

Notes—Colonel Hunter

I didn't have enough words to describe what I saw in the images sent by Nick. Sixteen bodies, hacked apart by a machete or something similar, were strewn about the site. Two of them looked as if they'd been blown apart by a blast, first.

The bloom of light we'd seen—this was it. We'd never caught the actual launch with the satellite images we had. The bodies looked to be locals—what remained of their clothing supported that theory.

Auggie, these were hired locally, Corinne sent. *I feel sick*, she added. Then, she sent names—of the dead. There was no identification found amid the carnage, but she knew their names. Forcing my hand to steady, I wrote them down to send to Matt. We could coordinate with the local police to get missing persons leads, along with a forensics team up the mountain to collect and catalogue the remains.

Get down the mountain, I sent an e-mail back to Nick. *Let the local police handle this.*

Will do, he responded.

I was on the phone to Matt seconds later, and was connected to Bogotá police shortly after that. Police were dispatched already when the signal from our group went dead.

Corinne

When the rocket hit the launch site, we were already at our vehicles—I'd been forced to move us when I received my usual last-minute warning. The problem was, our vehicles were no longer safe, either. I could either use what I had to make them safe or I could do my other usual and get us the hell out of there.

Nathan was already hyperventilating after we watched half the mountain we were just on get blasted to bits. *Want me to disarm the bombs they've planted on our trucks?* I asked Maye and Rafe. *Or do you want me to get us out of here?*

Disarm the bombs, they both said.

It took just a moment. I left the disarmed explosives where they were, however, so Nick and the others could examine them—maybe they could be identified. Whatever had been left on that mountain, including the bodies, was now blasted or incinerated.

The local police wouldn't find much—if anything.

Auggie, somebody just blew up the mountain top and strapped explosives to the underside of our trucks, I reported. *Nick says he's lost contact with you,* I added as we climbed hurriedly into the vehicles and took off.

Nathan was still in a daze of some sort, so Opal had taken charge of him. I'm sure whoever had blown up the mountain and then attempted to bomb our vehicles were expecting us to be dead already or explode after we drove away.

Not until an hour later—when that hadn't happened—did they

think to get on our trail. Two helicopters could be heard in the distance, and I knew, whether anyone else did or not—they were tailing us, with more missiles to deliver.

"Cabbage, what are you doing?" Ilya hissed.

"I've never fired one of these before," I said, as the rocket launcher appeared in my arms. "Give me a minute to download the instructions," I added while attempting to juggle the heavy weapon. I'd pulled in the biggest one I could find at such short notice.

"Download? What the hell are you talking about? Opal," he huffed, "put that boy down and help Corinne."

"I got this," Opal patted a dazed Nathan's shoulder and took the rocket launcher from my arms. It was just as well; I was handling it awkwardly and I knew it. I also wasn't relishing the idea of shooting down two helicopters, even if they intended to kill us.

I ended up hanging onto Opal so she wouldn't fall through the window as she leaned farther out than was safe and fired the first rocket at an approaching helicopter.

Everybody heard it explode seconds later.

"I need another rocket," Opal shouted at me.

"It's in there, just fire," I shouted back over the truck's roar. The remaining helicopter fired its rockets at us; Opal fired at them at the same time. I had to disarm the ones aimed at us while they were flying toward us. Opal hit her target; the helicopter exploded in a fireball behind us as its disarmed missiles hit the back of our truck with a huge, metallic clank. The truck careened and fishtailed from the impact, tossing up clouds of dirt and mud; Rafe braked and manhandled the steering wheel, trying to keep the vehicle on the road after we'd been hit.

The canvas cover on the back of the truck was now in shreds, with strips of cloth flapping noisily behind us as Rafe righted the vehicle and hit the gas. I'm sure he was mentally telling Maye ahead of us to drive faster; he had no desire for more helicopters to show up.

By the time we neared the entrance to the park, we met the police on their way up. Thankfully, some of ours had been dispatched with them. Poor Nathan Cross was having a breakdown in the back seat, so Richard and I went to tend him.

~

Notes—Colonel Hunter

"These photographs of the area are all we have—this site was bombed shortly after our people got there." I handed the tablet with the images pulled up to Madam President.

"What about your people?"

"Barely got away," I said. "They found bombs on their vehicles; they disarmed those and drove away, only to be attacked by two helicopters before they could get out of the park."

"Then what?"

"Luckily, they had a rocket launcher with them," I said. That was true—but they hadn't started out with one. Corinne had seen to that; Opal had fired the weapon, bringing down both helicopters. Corinne also made sure the rockets fired at them didn't explode—both landed in the back of their truck. I didn't mention the damage to the vehicle from that impact—the President looked worried enough as it was.

Those unexploded rockets and the bombs attached to the trucks were given to Captain Finch later, so he and his team could determine their origin.

To say Finch wasn't happy would be putting it mildly. His Lieutenant—Nathan Cross—hadn't recalled much of what happened. Richard, posing as a medic for the group, said it was possibly due to the shock waves from the first blast. He said Lieutenant Cross had been closest to it and was knocked down, hitting his head.

He had bruises and swelling, that much was true. I just hoped the enemy didn't become suspicious over their miraculous survival.

"Where are they now?" Madam President asked, handing the tablet back to me. "Your people?"

"Back in San Cristobal, but they may be in danger, staying there. The police are still asking questions, and they have their experts swarming over the helicopter wreckage. I'm worried the Secretary of

State may have to get involved to get them out of the country again. They're refusing to let them investigate further, until they resolve this mess."

"Which could take a while," Madam President sighed. "Go ahead, get Chuck Marshall involved. If the locals don't want them to investigate further, then we'll pull them out."

"Thank you, Madam President."

The call from Matt Michaels came not long after I left the White House. "What do you have?" I asked.

"The rocket shells are old and pretty battered—they look like leftovers from World War II," he said.

"Somebody sold old warheads? No wonder these didn't explode," I snapped.

"No, that's not it," he said. "The outer shells are probably that. What's inside is another story."

"What did they put in there?" I stopped walking for a moment.

"Newer technology," Matt said. "We haven't identified it, yet. Hell—my team hasn't seen anything like it before."

"Nothing to tie it to the Russians?"

"Not yet. We're working on that. Any word on getting yours out of there?"

"I have to see Chuck Marshall about that—the locals are still trying to make some connection to them for all this, when they were the ones attacked."

"If Chuck doesn't have any luck at this, let me know. I may have a trick or two up my sleeve."

He and I were dancing around the fact that Corinne had already played as much of her hand as it was safe to play—we didn't need them disappearing into thin air. "I'll take anything, as long as it doesn't land us in hot water," I agreed.

Corinne

Since Nathan had been a member of our party, Finch instructed him to stay with us until the locals were done with their investigation. From what I'd seen already, that could take a while.

It made me wonder, too, how long it would take the enemy to bribe or coerce the locals into giving them our information. They knew where we were, after all.

Since we couldn't leave the country and had been advised to stay close to our quarters by an angry Captain Finch, I turned my attention to Merle Askins and the Joint Chiefs. There had to be a way to implicate them instead of Auggie, but so far, I didn't know what that was.

Rafe found me on the back porch three mornings after our narrow escape in Chingaza, soaking up sunlight and pondering Merle Askins' ability to always slip away from any blame.

"Cabbage," he leaned down to kiss me.

"Hi, honey," I said. "I told Auggie that Nathan's bruising actually came from banging around in the back seat of the truck."

"Good." Another cheap, wooden chair scraped across the porch as he drew it beside mine and sat. "Coffee," Opal walked through the back door and handed a mug of coffee to each of us.

"Thanks." I held my mug up with a smile before drinking.

"How are we going to get out of here?" Rafe asked.

"Matt has some ideas," Opal shrugged. "We just have to take Nathan with us."

"I like Nathan. Poor guy," I said.

"Yeah, he's stuck with us, now," Opal agreed and settled cross-legged on the wooden planks of the porch.

"I hope Matt acts quickly. I have no desire to talk to the local police again," Rafe said. "Their questioning tactics are idiotic at best."

"They're not even looking for anyone else—they're saying those helicopters fired on us at the launch site. There were no helicopters anywhere around—we'd have heard them. That missile came from somewhere else," Opal huffed.

"They didn't want their evidence found," Rafe said.

"Or they wanted to kill whoever came looking for it," I offered.

"Finch says his team didn't recognize the technology inside those old shell casings they fired at us," Opal said.

"Yeah." I hunched my shoulders uncomfortably. Things were moving quickly, now, and I didn't like the direction they were going.

"What do you know, cabbage?" Rafe asked.

"I can't tell you. Not here," I said. "I just don't like any of this. It makes me uncomfortable."

"I hear that," Opal agreed.

"At least they're letting Finch's crew continue their investigation of the crash site," Rafe said. "While they continue to glare in our direction, as if it's our fault."

"Get inside," I lifted my hands and stretched before standing. "Now."

We walked into our ugly, concrete housing as if we were going in for breakfast, before shutting the door and locking it behind us. Rafe and I exchanged glances just before those surrounding our building opened fire with machine guns.

"We're dead again," I said, brushing plaster dust off my sleeves. We stood in Auggie's office in D.C. while he stared at us in shock.

"What about bodies left behind?" he whispered.

"Taken care of," I shrugged. The others stood around me, most of them adapting to the idea that they were still alive instead of cut to pieces inside a poorly-constructed building in San Cristobal.

Poor Nathan didn't understand at all.

"Welcome to the Program," Auggie told him. "I'll have my assistant fill you in."

James explained to Nathan (as well as he could) about the Program and why he was now considered a part of it. I'd given the okay to

Auggie, so he felt comfortable making the addition. I had an ulterior motive in the addition, but that I kept to myself.

"Where will you go?" Auggie asked us while James had his meeting (and lunch) with Nathan.

"I think we should go back to Seattle—there are plenty of suitable places around Granite Falls," I said.

"We can keep an eye on the mountain from there," Rafe agreed.

"Opal and I can pose as hunters if those things get out," Nick had a light in his eyes.

"You really want to go back there? I have no objections, but," Auggie began.

"I think we should," I said. "Vancouver isn't far away. It won't prevent us from taking day trips there and maybe tracking down what we didn't look for before."

"You think somebody's there, don't you?"

"Maybe. Right now, it's all we have," I said. "If you need more help with that British crash, let me know."

"I'm hoping to keep you out of it past this point," Auggie sighed. "Finch has enough information, and as you know—we can't identify the technology used. That means we can't tie it to the Russians or anybody else for now."

"Hold that thought," I said. "Maybe we can get to the bottom of this eventually."

"I sure as hell hope so." Auggie wasn't happy, that much was clear. "They're hauling bodies out of that building in San Cristobal right now. As you said, you're all dead. Again."

"I'm tired of dying," Richard pointed out. Maye touched his arm in sympathy.

"You're arranging this?" Auggie asked, turning back to me.

"Yeah, I guess I am."

"Get the information to James as discreetly as possible."

"I will."

"Cori?" Auggie added.

"Huh?"

"Don't die for real, all right?"

"I'll do my best."

~

Merle Askins' Office

"I think we have a clear path, now," Merle said, handing the flash drive to his assistant. "Those in Bogotá died like any other human would. Bodies are being shipped back to the states, but we have the necessary information, on that," he nodded at the flash drive. "You know where to send it."

"I do," his assistant agreed. "Will you be out the rest of the day, sir?"

"Yes. I hate seeing a doctor," Merle rumbled.

"You've had that cough for three weeks and it isn't improving. You probably need antibiotics," his assistant pointed out.

"Probably. I'll be back tomorrow morning. Knowing for sure we've gotten rid of any effective opposition is worth a few thousand lives, don't you think?"

"Of course, sir."

~

Corinne

"I like this better than what we had in Alaska," Opal said.

"I had to do some upgrades," I admitted. The outside of the house looked just as it did four hours before we took over as renters. The inside was as luxurious as I could make it, given the time I'd had.

Rent was less than four thousand per month, and the owner lived out of state. That was fine by me—James had set this up for us and paid six months' rent using the bank account I'd created for him under an alias.

Everything was fine—and unless the owner pissed me off somehow, he would benefit from our inhabiting his large, split-cedar home.

"When will we begin our search in Vancouver?" Rafe asked.

"How about tomorrow?" I asked. "Weather is supposed to be nice tomorrow."

"That sounds fine. We can get used to our new kitchen in the meantime."

~

Ilya

For dinner, I made a coulibiac—salmon pie—while Corinne cooked vegetable potpie for herself. "I've heard of you." Nathan watched as I placed the salmon pie in the oven to bake.

"Done your research on Russian spies, I take it," I said, attempting to ignore the interruption.

"I know you're from Ukraine," he said. "And I know that you can pound me into dirt if you wanted to. I just wanted to thank you—and Corinne—for saving my ass in Colombia."

"Then you're welcome. Corinne has faith in you, and that is generally a very good thing. For you."

"Who knew the Blacksmith liked to cook?" Nathan wandered away. I snorted a laugh.

"Is there enough room in the oven for my potpie?" Corinne set her smaller pie on the stove.

"I will make room," I told her, stealing a kiss.

~

Corinne

"If we go to the library in Vancouver, we can meet there later to come back home," Nick suggested. We were discussing our game plan after breakfast the following morning.

"That sounds just as good as anything else," Richard agreed.

"Library sounds good," I said. "It's centrally located and any cab can get you there with no fuss. Nathan, do you want to go or would you rather stay here?"

"I think I'd like to go," he said.

"Then you come with Nick and me," Opal said. "We'll keep you out of trouble."

Nathan gave Opal a wide grin and nodded.

"Do you have any cash?" I asked.

"I only have the clothes James gave me," he shrugged.

"Okay." I handed cash over. "That's in case you want a soda or something."

"Thanks."

"Ready?"

At everybody's nod, I transported them to the library in Vancouver, which (on the outside) resembled the Coliseum. A rectangular building lay inside the colonnade, so we landed between the two. Making sure we were shielded from view until nobody could see us appear from nothing, we agreed to meet later at a designated time.

"I like this," Ilya whispered against my hair as we took off down the street. The day was sunny and warm while we walked in sunlight. The shadows were cooler, but we stayed in the sun as often as possible.

"You look good in sunglasses," I said, smiling at him. He did—he wore aviators, a bomber jacket, black jeans and boots. I felt young at that moment, as if we'd been sent on vacation for a day.

Granted we were looking for traces of the enemy, but that didn't mean we couldn't enjoy the day and the company.

"Where do you want to look first—in a coffee shop?" He grinned.

"Nothing wrong with that," I said and leaned into him.

We found a Starbucks just a few blocks away. "I'm buying," Ilya smiled and handed the cashier his credit card.

I really didn't care who paid—I just wanted a latte. If it made Ilya smile to buy me coffee, then he could buy me coffee anytime.

By the time we walked out of the coffee shop, however, we had to turn back to business quickly.

Although we were disguised so that nobody would recognize us, we watched as a Baikov clone walked past us on the sidewalk.

Dressed casually in jeans, a polo and boots, Baikov could have been anyone on the street that day. *What the fuck is he doing here?* Ilya sent as we settled in to tail him.

Maybe he was here before—with the Mary clone, I said. *They were paired in Dublin, maybe there are other pairs elsewhere. Too bad this Mary blew herself up. Wonder if they're sending another Mary to replace the first?*

We will follow this one. Make us invisible, cabbage. I do not want them to see us coming.

Honey, they'll never know we were here, I said, putting up the shield he requested. We tracked Baikov's latest incarnation as he walked purposely down sidewalks, crossed streets and passed shops with barely a glance.

This one—I hadn't seen much in the brief glance I'd gotten of his face. What I knew is that he'd been to a business not far from the Starbucks where we'd stopped, and now was on his way elsewhere.

Tour buses passed now and then, while curious tourists peered out at the people and buildings of Vancouver. I knew many visitors took tours of the city before boarding a boat or leaving Vancouver. We watched as our clone waited at a bus stop and stepped onto a tour bus when it stopped at a designated spot to let tourists on and off.

We need to be on that bus, Ilya kissed my temple.

You got it, honey, I replied and transported us onto an empty seat at the back with nobody the wiser.

We were now tourists, just like all the others on the bus, who were using their cell phones or cameras to snap photographs as we went along. When we arrived at Stanley Park, which had nature trails and gardens, Baikov stepped off the bus.

Ilya and I left the same way we'd gotten on—I moved us.

Looking both ways as the bus engine rumbled into gear and pulled away, Baikov walked toward a trail leading into a rose garden nearby.

Ilya and I, still invisible to anyone around us, followed from a safe distance.

The roses were beautiful when we arrived, and their scent filled the air on a beautiful Vancouver day. Baikov, with little regard for his surroundings, walked up to Hal Prentice—the one posing as the former President of the United States.

CHAPTER 12

*C*orinne

　　　Secret Service agents were posted discreetly throughout the rose garden while Hal had his conversation with a Baikov clone. Ilya and I watched and listened nearby; neither suspected how close we were—or were aware that we were there to begin with.

I was grateful.

"They are dead," Baikov's clone reported. "The ones in Colombia—also dead. Not the same ones of course—forensics bears this out."

"Then our few losses were worth it—to destroy the Program in the U.S.," Hal said.

"Our experiments were much more successful," Baikov agreed. "While there was moderate success with those created in the U.S., they were not equal to what we created."

"We've seen that evidence for ourselves," Hal agreed. "We remain committed to the plan, one-hundred percent."

"As do we."

"Do you have more information on the break-in?" Hal switched topics quickly, leaving me puzzled as to what *the plan* actually was.

"Nothing yet. We inventoried everything carefully—nothing was taken."

"Whoever it was likely didn't know what they'd found and left, looking for more lucrative contraband."

"We concur, and steps have been taken to protect the new facility. Everything was moved afterward, you understand."

"Of course. My condolences on the loss of your lover. She was instrumental in bringing the U.S. Program down, and we will honor her memory."

"I thank you. Perhaps you will see fit to provide a replacement?"

"We will consider it—if you remain faithful."

"You have my promise."

"Good. Return to Seattle tomorrow. Take the rest of the day for yourself," Hal instructed.

"Thank you."

Baikov turned to walk away while Hal went in the opposite direction. His agents gathered about him then, and herded him toward a waiting car.

What should we do? I asked Ilya.

You follow Prentice, he said quickly. *I will track Baikov.*

Notes—Colonel Hunter

Auggie, I'm following Hal Prentice, Corinne's voice settled into my head. *Rafe is following another Baikov clone. They met in a park in Vancouver, had a few words and then went their separate ways.*

Never in my life did I wish for Corinne's gift so badly.

She was tailing one enemy while Ilya tailed another.

I wanted to shout. Or swear. Probably both. I settled for swearing, which brought James at a run.

"They're in Vancouver," I said. "Corinne and Rafe had to split up to track two different people." I shook my head, as if that would effectively relieve my worry or solve the problem.

"Colonel Hunter, just relax. We have to wait this out," James advised.

"I know that, dammit. And I don't want to relax."

Corinne

Ilya, he's boarding a helicopter, I sent.

Corinne, do not follow that bastard—we can find him easily enough later. Do you hear me? Do not follow him!

Honey, calm down, I returned. *He's on his way to Toronto—I saw that much.*

Good. I am tracking this Baikov duplicate. Meet me at the coffee shop—I believe he is heading back that way.

Okay. I'll wait there for you.

He is boarding another bus—I will follow.

Forty minutes later, I watched as Baikov's clone walked past the coffee shop as if he had nothing to do with murder and mayhem. Not far behind Ilya strolled, feigning interest in his surroundings like any tourist. I could see past his disguise, since I'd created it. Anyone else saw a shorter, brown-haired man who wouldn't stand out in a crowd.

I only intend to see where he goes, Ilya answered my questioned as he passed the coffee shop without a second glance.

Let me know if you want me to come get you, I said.

I will.

Twenty minutes later, he did just that. We now had the address of a condo, where the Mary clone and the Baikov clone had likely spent their short time together, before she was ordered to commit suicide, taking four cruise ships filled with passengers with her.

I figured Auggie was having a panic attack by the time I got back to him with the address and the news that I hadn't followed Hal Prentice to Toronto.

My cell phone rang shortly after I sent my mental message. No surprise—James was on the line.

"I'm in a secure place," he said. "Colonel Hunter says he'll have someone watching the condo soon."

"I think the target is going to Seattle tomorrow," I said. "That's what we overheard, anyway."

"All right. We've had word through Matt Michaels' office that the Russians are increasing their fly-bys and flirting dangerously with U.S. airspace," James said. "There's a meeting on the Hill tomorrow to discuss this with the Russian Ambassador. Matt spoke with the Ukrainian Ambassador earlier today, but I haven't heard what they talked about."

"He's probably glad that Russia is annoying us, now, instead of harassing Ukraine constantly," I said.

"And trying to kill them," James added.

"Yeah. We've seen too much of that lately," I agreed.

∼

Merle Askins' Office

CIA Director Merle Askins picked up the phone reluctantly. His assistant informed him that the doctor's office was on the line.

"Askins here," he barked, as if that would stave off bad news.

"Merle, it's Doctor Warner," his doctor said. "I'm afraid I have bad news—it's lung cancer. We need to run more tests to see how far it's spread, or whether we can contain it with surgery."

"When?"

"Tomorrow if possible. We don't want to wait on this—you understand."

"I do."

"I have the number of a counselor who specializes in this sort of thing," Doctor Warner offered.

"Not needed." Askins hung up the phone, stood and swept everything off his desk in one, angry motion.

∼

Corinne

"Unless they have an alternative method of getting to Pilchuck, they'll have to drive past us," Richard said as he and I stood at the kitchen window, with its view of Mountain Loop Highway.

"I'll know when he goes past," I said, sipping the club soda in my hand.

"I'm impressed that you and Ilya came up with the same information on the rented condo that Nick and Opal found," Richard smiled. "Good Scotch," he lifted his glass and drank.

"Nick and Opal are special," I said. "As are you and Maye. It's just a different kind of special."

"We had a nice day in Vancouver," he smiled as he lifted his glass again.

"I got to see the Rose Garden at Stanley Park," I shrugged. "While we watched Hal Prentice, posing as former President Phillips, trade secrets with a Baikov clone."

"They just referred to it as the plan?" Richard turned toward me, curiosity in his gaze.

"Yeah. I couldn't see past the fog in both of them to determine what the plan actually is. As for the break-in they talked about, somebody probably found their secret stash, didn't know what it was and took off."

"The plan could be anything from stealing a secret recipe for fried chicken to Armageddon."

"I'm more worried about the Armageddon thing," I said.

"Me, too. As for their stash, well, we didn't know where it was to begin with, so we're no more in the dark now, after they moved it."

"I still can't figure out what they intend to do with all the furred, fanged and scaled folks on the mountain."

"I'm worried about what they intend to do with DB if they find him."

I snickered and choked on my club soda. Richard thoughtfully patted my back until I cleared my throat.

"What did you do?" he asked. He smiled as he said it.

"DB is now roughly the size of a large tuna," I shrugged. "Unless they recalibrate their search criteria, they're not going to find him."

"So my crew in Alaska is just a front?"

"Yeah. Sorry for the wild goose chase."

"Brilliant." His smile grew wider.

"As long as we're still looking for him," I added, "They'll continue to look and waste their resources doing it. Whatever they were hoping to do with him, well, they're still hoping."

"One arm of their plan has withered," Richard nodded. "What's for dinner?"

∼

Dinner was grilled steaks and vegetables on an outdoor grill beside the heated pool. Rafe and Nick handled the steaks while Opal and I skewered vegetable kebabs.

"Nice work on locating the condo," I said.

"I was going to say the same thing about Hal and Baikov," she laughed.

"I thought about getting on that helicopter with Hal," I said. "Just to see where he went."

"I would not allow it," Rafe said, taking skewers from my hands to place on the grill. "I would have to follow, and I would be angry when I caught up with you again." Ilya was out in force, accent and everything. Opal snickered.

"Do not frown at me, cabbage," he said. "We are together. Of course I will be angry if you are in danger."

"Just remember you said that," I said, pointing a finger at him.

"The angry part?" He sounded surprised.

"No, the together part."

"I will never forget that," he huffed.

"Okay."

∼

The Baikov clone drove past the house before noon the following day. "He's on his way up the mountain," I informed Ilya, who sat nearby in our suite while I watched current news on a tablet with earphones in my ears, so I wouldn't disturb Ilya's reading.

"Good. All the mice in one trap," he said.

"Not all. I'd feel better if they were in one trap. The big rat is still out there somewhere."

"This I know," he agreed. "I want his throat in my hands."

"Honey, that may be too close for my liking," I responded. "Just shoot him from a distance, all right?"

"Whatever you want."

"That's what I want, if I can't get to him first."

"You don't think he might be bullet-proof?" Nathan asked.

"If he were bullet-proof, I think we'd have seen him before now," Ilya growled. "A vulnerable man hides. He has a weakness."

"I think Corinne terrified him," Nick observed. "You see he did his damnedest to get her out of the way? The rest of us were just icing on the cake."

"Thanks for the vote of confidence," I told Nick. "I just don't like the fact that he felt comfortable killing so many people just to get to me."

"That's why it's prudent to stay dead until he declares himself," Maye said.

"I'm beginning to wonder when that will be," Richard broke in. "We have no idea who else he may target—now that he has discredited Colonel Hunter. Word has it that the President is searching for Hunter's replacement—according to the media."

Ilya had some choice words to say in his native language, which expressed his feelings on the sensationalism-hungry media succinctly. I ducked my head to hide my smile. He didn't miss it, though. Pulling my face up with a finger under my chin, he kissed me decisively.

What did he say? Maye asked.

He called them sphincter-sucking deviants, I replied.

Remind me not to make him mad, she struggled to hide a smile.

"Opal and I may do some hunting tonight," Nick announced. "Up the mountain."

"But what if," Maye began.

"They won't recognize us," Opal said.

"It's time to show you," Nick agreed. "Don't be shocked—these are my favorite jeans, he said, unbuttoning them and letting them drop before coming out of his T-shirt.

"He has to get naked?" Nathan asked.

"Just hold on," I touched Nathan's shoulder. It happened in a blink. Nick's underwear was torn to shreds and dropped beneath the huge wolf he'd become.

Opal, with a huge grin, also changed.

A huge version of a velociraptor continued to grin at all of us.

CHAPTER 13

orinne

"That explains a lot," Maye breathed, her eyes wide with wonder. Nick stood as tall as her shoulder as he stretched and yawned before lolling his tongue in a wolfish version of a chuckle.

You knew this? Ilya's voice sounded in my head. He didn't appear to be happy.

Their secret to tell, not mine, I replied. *If they meet up with anybody tonight that's on the enemy list, it'll suck to be them—the enemy, that is.*

What if they are in trouble? Ilya asked.

"I'll know," I said aloud.

"Cori will know," Opal was back to herself. "Just have your weapons ready if she says we're in trouble."

"What weapons will I have, cabbage?"

"Whatever you want," I shrugged. "Just tell me and it's yours."

"Just remember that a loaded rocket launcher weighs almost as much as she does," Opal said. "In case that's on your list."

"I can handle my cabbage easily; however a rocket launcher is not on my wish list."

"Let's eat before we talk big guns," I said.

"Good idea," Nick said, becoming human again and lifting his jeans off the ground. Clothed or naked, he had nothing to be ashamed of.

~

Ilya

I wanted to be furious with Corinne for not telling me about Opal and Nick. After thinking it over, however, I appreciated her willingness to protect them, because she also protected me with the fiercest loyalty.

It helped, too, that she provided our small compound with enough weapons to fend off most attacks—I worried that the creatures at the mountaintop would be set on us, should the enemy learn how close we were.

While I didn't ask for a rocket launcher, Opal did. Corinne equipped all of us who were able to handle weapons expertly, including Richard Farrell.

The last thing she gave me I hadn't asked for—it was a type of pistol I'd never seen before.

It appeared before her instead of in her hands, like all the other weapons.

"Reach out and take it," she told me. I lifted it from whatever energy held it in mid-air. "It will only fire for you, now," she said, visibly relaxing.

"What is this? Something experimental?" I asked, looking the weapon over.

"No. It's alien technology."

"Where are the bullets?"

"There aren't any. It's solar powered and fires blasts. Be careful—it'll bring down a helicopter with no trouble."

"If I shoot a person?"

"There won't be much left," she explained.

"Very nice," I handled the weapon with new respect.

"I suggest using it as a last resort. If it falls into any hands except yours and they attempt to use it, it will explode, taking them with it."

"Impressive."

"Anybody trying to take it apart will be met with the same results," she warned.

"I like this." I turned the weapon in my hand. There were markings on the barrel that I couldn't read. I wondered whether she could read them before deciding I didn't want an answer to that question.

"You still mad?" she asked, her face tilted upward to mine.

"No." I leaned in to kiss her. "You did the right thing."

"Good. You can go play target practice now, if you want," she said.

"I have a better idea," I mumbled, setting the gun aside and reaching for her.

"I was hoping you would," she responded dryly.

Corinne

"My cabbage is feeling neglected?" Ilya breathed against my neck.

"Um-hmm," I sighed as he nibbled sensitive skin. "I thought you were leaving me for a pistol."

"Never." His fingers tickled my ribs gently as he pulled the hem of my T upward. "Do not suggest such a thing again. It was only a mild flirtation."

"Mild? Your hands were all over it."

He bit back a laugh. "Come," he pulled me toward our bed.

Notes—Colonel Hunter

"Look—they're using too much power," James set his tablet in front of me. We were at the office late, deciphering information Matt's team in Bogotá had sent, complete with specs on the rockets my team handed over before their untimely faked deaths.

Too, the squatters at the Seattle facility were drawing more power than appeared normal as they settled into their new hiding place.

Corinne sent information earlier when the Baikov clone made his trip up the mountain.

Whatever the plan was that Prentice and Baikov discussed, it wasn't hinted at anywhere. The technology used in the Colombian rockets was also a mystery—nobody had seen anything like it.

A few theories swam through my head, but I didn't know how to search for information without alerting Askins and his cronies. Resolving to ask Matt about it, I studied the graphs on James' tablet.

"Who knows what they're doing and the taxpayers are picking up the tab," I grumbled, comparing charts on the power usage while we'd been in residence to that of the ones now using the facility.

Theirs was higher, for some reason.

"James," I said, lifting my gaze to him. "I want to talk to Corinne tomorrow. I know she can get in there without being seen. I need to know what these fuckers are doing."

"I'll make sure the call is safe and you're not disturbed," he promised.

∽

Corinne

Opal and Nick's hunting party had no results, but I think they enjoyed letting their alter egos out for a stretch. Nick certainly appeared happier when they returned after midnight.

"No scents?" Ilya asked the proper question as Nick foraged in the fridge for leftover food.

"Nothing," Opal answered for him as he handed her a container of leftover steak. Apparently, the shift in their bodies required extra sustenance. Ilya and I made sure the food was heated, fresh bread toasted and drinks supplied as both settled at the kitchen island to eat.

"So they're staying inside for now," Ilya took a seat at the island. He and I had risen after our lovemaking session, just so we'd be available when Nick and Opal returned.

"I can't imagine that the creatures aren't feeling cooped up," Nick said, stuffing a large piece of steak in his mouth and chewing.

"I felt cooped up and I'm not like them," I said.

"You had a way out," Ilya observed. "I admit I was not happy about that."

"Coolest way to travel," Nick said, washing down steak with a bottle of imported beer. "I don't like flying much. Corinne getting me somewhere? Works for me."

"How does it work—do you know?" Ilya asked. I was surprised he hadn't asked before.

"Do you have a dollar?" I asked.

"Why do you need a dollar?" he rummaged in his pockets for money before handing me a crumpled five. "Will this work?"

"Yeah," I said, laying the five on the island and smoothing it out as best I could. "Now," I said, "here's where I am." I tapped the left end of the bill. "This is where I want to go," I tapped the right end. "This is how I get there." I folded the bill in half so that both ends were together.

"Fuck me," Nick breathed.

"Looks like it takes power and talent to do that," Opal observed.

I shrugged at her, not wanting to explain more than I had already. Ilya took the five from my hand and unfolded it, then folded it again.

"Does it stay folded?" he asked.

"No, that would cause problems," I said. "I'm only folding the minutest amount of space possible. A pinpoint, at most, and it springs back immediately."

"This falls into the next to impossible category," he muttered.

"Honey, look at us," I said. "All of us fall into that category."

"Truth," Nick pointed his fork in my direction.

"What's on tap for tomorrow?" Opal asked, cutting another piece of steak into a manageable bite.

"I think Auggie will call and ask me to get into the facility," I said. "Just so he can see what's going on."

"You're not going without me," Ilya growled.

"Honey, I think that's a given," I said.

❧

Auggie's call came at eight local time the following morning. I was barely awake and sipping coffee when my cell phone rang.

"Hi, Auggie," I said after putting the call on speaker.

"Cori."

"Yeah."

"What I called to say," he began, "I want you to take Ilya with you, mind, but I need to see what's going on inside that facility. I know he can shield you while you're in there, so remain invisible, see what's going on and report your findings to me. Take cell-phone photographs if you can."

"I can handle that," I said.

"Good. How soon can you go?"

"As soon as she has breakfast," Ilya growled over my shoulder.

"Good morning, Rafe," James called out.

"James, we've missed our adopted son," Ilya laughed. "Corinne misses cooking for you."

"Oh, man, I wish I was there," James whined.

"James," Auggie barked.

"Bye," James said, his voice sounding wistful.

"Get back to me ASAP," Auggie said. "I want anything you can get."

"We will," I promised. "After breakfast."

After Auggie hung up, I brought in sunlamps and worked and ate under them.

"Ready?" Ilya asked after I'd dressed properly and brushed my teeth.

"Yeah. I'll take care of this—if they have equipment that can sense body heat or anything, well, I can shield that and any noise we make."

"Then I'll take photographs and keep you out of trouble," he said.

"Okay." Taking his arm, I folded space between our house and the facility on Mount Pilchuck.

Notes—Colonel Hunter

"You're not going to like this," Matt said, dropping a folder onto my desk. He'd shown up unannounced shortly after I'd ended my conversation with Corinne and Rafe.

"What is that?"

"Information from the UFO crash," he said. "You have no idea what I had to go through to get this without alerting anybody."

"What is this?" I opened the folder and stared at mechanical drawings. It looked like a machine with many parts missing.

"I think they improved on those specs to build the weapons used in Colombia," Matt replied.

"Are you telling me that this is from our side, while the Russians may have had better information?"

"Likely a whole weapon—or mostly whole, rather than the bits and pieces we found," he nodded.

"Was any of this ever pursued here?" I asked, setting the first page aside and staring at another incomplete drawing on the second.

"I didn't dig that deep—I didn't have much time," Matt said. "It's possible, but there wasn't enough found to work with, or we'd have it already."

"How big was this—or what they found in Colombia?"

"Less than a two-inch square," he said. "That was enough to destroy that airliner and not leave much to search through."

"What sort of information did you give the Brits?" I asked.

"I told them we're still working to identify the weapon, which is basically true. And that we're still trying to separate and identify remains. Not an easy job at any time, but worse, now."

"What did you tell Madam President?"

"What I told the Brits."

"Yeah—I said the same thing about the weapon, but didn't have any information on the remains."

"I have other information," Matt said, examining his fingernails for a moment.

"What's that?"

"I have it on very good authority that Askins has lung cancer. Don't know how bad it is, yet—we're waiting on test results."

"Holy shit," I breathed. "Is that true?"

"Yeah. Chances are, though, that he'll maneuver one of his cronies into that spot if he has to step down."

"I know he stopped smoking ten or twelve years ago, but this," I shook my head in disbelief.

"It happens," Matt said. "In this case, perhaps karma intervened."

"Couldn't happen to a nicer guy," I joked.

Corinne

Ilya cursed in several languages at what we saw. They'd taken our facility and turned it into a lab, where they were cloning the creatures they had as quickly as they could.

I wanted to curse, too, but followed my instincts and went to the pool that had never been completely filled during our stay.

Ilya's cursing stopped then—we were both at a loss for words.

DB's clone swam happily in that huge pool, but it wouldn't contain him for long. Already he filled a third of it and was still growing.

All they needed to do this, after all, was blood from the original creature pumped into a human with the same blood type. *Et voilà—* another clone was made. I felt ill.

Honey, I sent, *what should we do?*

We must confer with Colonel Hunter. His words were accompanied by a mental sigh.

I understood that sigh all too well. I wanted to find their stash of creature blood and destroy it. I wanted to turn the mountain into dust. I wanted former President Phillips deader than a doornail.

If I did the first two things, it would put Phillips on alert, letting him know we were still alive, because we still didn't know where the bastard was. Whatever or whoever was hiding him was also on my list.

Let's get out of here, I said and folded space.

Half an hour later, Auggie and James sat at our island, eating a sandwich and staring at the photographs Ilya had taken. I hadn't felt safe sending these through even the securest methods. Therefore, I brought both of them here for an hour so they could see for themselves what was happening only a few miles away.

"It makes sense that they'd take samples from all of those creatures," Opal said. "I just didn't expect them to make more—not like this."

"This pisses me off," Auggie grunted, staring at the image of DB Jr., swimming in his newly filled pool.

Nick said, "If you don't have a clone, get one."

"Cori," Auggie turned to me, "Do you think these clones know that they're clones?"

"Some of them do," I said. "The Baikov clone in Vancouver didn't have a clue that he was, although he knew his lover was a Mary clone."

"So this Baikov thinks he's the original?"

"That's what I understood," I said.

"What's the difference, then? Why would some know and some not?"

"Somebody is deciding that for them, I suppose," Richard offered.

"What about the ones who realize they're clones?" James asked. "Do they remember who they were before?"

"Some of the original creatures did—and still do," I said. "Remember, DB recalled who he was for a while, and that held him back from eating his handlers, I think. When the animal began to take over more, he remembered less and less. I think that's the case with the others, unless things happen like Richard said and somebody, somewhere, decides differently. The ones who remember, well, I can see that in them. The trouble is, not many of them remember. That fog over their brains has caused me problems all along."

"What about these?" Auggie pointed to the photograph of the dining area where at least fifty men ate a meal while Ilya and I wandered through, unseen and unremarked.

"Probably candidates for cloning," Ilya huffed.

"What are we going to do?" Maye asked.

"I have to consult with Matt, but let's face it, if we build up a military presence here, it'll tip our hand."

"Build it up elsewhere and let Corinne bring them in if needed," Opal suggested.

"Not a bad idea—I'll put that on the table," Auggie agreed.

"I'd like to stop their cloning before the fifty here get turned into creatures," I said.

"You have any suggestions?"

"I may have something, conveniently attributed to Mother Nature," I said. "With some help, you understand."

"How dangerous?" Auggie asked.

"Not as dangerous as setting creatures loose in Seattle," I said. "Especially not as dangerous as letting DB Jr. out to play in Elliott Bay."

"When?"

"Two-three days, maybe."

"The less I know, the better off I'll be, I'm sure," Auggie stated baldly. "Take us back to D.C., Corinne, and plan carefully. You know what's at stake."

"Yeah. I know that, all right."

My plan was in place, but had to be postponed; another plane was shot down—this time in Argentine airspace.

The plane—Australian, this time, had flown from Sydney and was scheduled to land in Buenos Aires. It didn't quite make it.

Again, all on board perished.

Matt transferred most of his team in Colombia to Argentina, leaving only a few behind to continue working the first crash site while they set up the investigation into the second.

Understandably, we received a call from Auggie, asking us to go, only under cover and invisible when we went to launch sites.

That's how we ended up in Buenos Aires an hour after Auggie's call.

This time, nobody could blame anything on Colombian rebels. Argentina was in complete confusion as to what had happened, and at first considered that the plane had developed some sort of mechanical problem.

The media ran wild with speculation while Colombia denied any involvement on news programs from pole to pole and sea to sea.

"We won't be staying here long," I said, after we checked into a hotel as tourists.

I intended to get us back to Seattle once we gathered available information and sent it to Auggie. I didn't want to leave the clone factory alone for long—I worried that they'd suddenly release their army on an unsuspecting population and things would get worse in a hurry.

Nick had information from James, with possible coordinates for the launch site. The information had come from a satellite feed, just like before. This time, I was concerned because the last one was a definite convenience—for those who'd tried to kill us.

Too afraid to speculate about sources of information and the hands it had passed through on its way to Auggie, we gathered in Maye and Richard's suite and worked out our plan.

"You can hide us from all eyes?" Richard asked.

"We hid from those at the facility," I said. "I'll have to make a bubble shield so even your footsteps won't impact the ground, but yes—nobody will know we're there."

"Will I be able to use my nose?" Nick asked.

"Yes. We're invisible from the outside. You'll still get scents because we're not blocking the air."

"I'm not sure how you do that, but I trust you," Opal said.

"Cool."

"This says the launch site is in the Andes, west of Mendoza. That's more than seven hundred fifty miles," Richard studied Nick's tablet.

"They're testing their devices with propulsion and guidance," Maye offered. "Something that small and with that big a punch—that's genius."

"Matt's team may not find much if they've gotten away from those antique metal shells," Nick nodded.

"Let's go—at least we won't be climbing this time," I sighed.

Mount Aconcagua was easily accessible from the north, or by using my method. Landing at a spot more than twenty-thousand feet up, the snow remained undisturbed as we looked about the launch site. I was glad we didn't disturb anything—the snow told a grisly tale of its own.

Blood spatter and spray surrounded us; the body of the man responsible lay a few feet away from the launcher. Little more than a metal tube with a firing mechanism, the launcher remained anchored on the side of the mountain.

It wasn't difficult to determine that the person responsible for the launch had then used the gun lying near his body to commit suicide.

Yes, he was dressed as a local.

Ilya recognized him, however, even with a sizeable hole in his right temple. He wasn't happy with the knowledge, I could see that easily.

"Leonid Dubov," he muttered softly. I nodded—I'd seen the same thing. Leonid was in his fifties at least, although he looked to be fit enough to be where he was. I could see Ilya was troubled by the fact he'd taken his own life.

"He would never have done this," Ilya muttered.

"I've got pictures," Nick said. "Can you get us to the other side of the body so I can get that, too?"

"Sure." I moved us around. He recorded additional images. "Don't touch anything," I said. "It's all booby-trapped beneath the snow."

"Including the body?"

"Yeah. Once his body temperature dropped far enough, it enabled an explosive planted inside it," I said. "If you move the body now, it detonates."

"Clever," Richard said. "Is anyone watching?"

"I wouldn't be surprised. If we touch anything here, somebody will know."

"Then let's take these photographs back to Buenos Aires," Nick said.

"Sure." I transported us back to Maye and Richard's suite.

Notes—Colonel Hunter

Everything's booby-trapped, Corinne reported. *I'll come for you in an hour so you can take a look at what we found.*

True to her word, she arrived in my office in an hour and hauled me to Seattle. James knew to keep anyone else out of my office while I was gone.

"What the hell?" I gazed at the photographs Nick handed to me. "Who is this guy?" I asked.

"Funny you should ask," Rafe responded.

Corinne

"He was a thorn in the President's side in Russia. Leonid disagreed with most everything Baikov or President Zoran did. He would not do this for anything, yet there he was, on the side of that mountain," Ilya explained.

"Corinne, did he really do this?" Auggie turned to me.

"Yeah. I saw a fog in him like I've seen in others. Somebody else was behind that, and I believe Ilya when he says this guy wouldn't do that. Someone forced him to do it."

"So they take out an enemy and implicate him in a terrible crime at the same time," Auggie shook his head in confusion.

"And they want to take out anybody who finds the evidence, and destroy it at the same time."

"What are we going to do with it, then?" Auggie asked.

"I think I know," I said.

"What?"

"There's a pile of rock and snow higher up. All we need is an avalanche," I shrugged.

"How do we make one without alerting them," Auggie began. "Oh," he said.

"Already done. If they're recording the site, they'll see the snow begin to slide and watch it hit the site in seconds, detonating their devices. You should have a report in ten minutes. Maybe less," I said.

"Damn," Auggie rubbed his forehead.

"Ready to go back?" I asked.

"Yeah."

∾

Notes—Colonel Hunter

"We just had a report of an explosion on Aconcagua," Matt said the minute I answered my cell phone.

"I see. Any other activity?"

"Should we be watching for it?"

"I think so."

"I'll put someone on it." Matt didn't bother saying good-bye—he was already barking orders at someone when the line went dead.

∾

Corinne

"You knew him, didn't you?" I let my hand wander gently down Ilya's back.

"I did. He was the one that told me who murdered my son."

"A friend, then?"

"Of sorts—yes. I trusted him."

"Everything is so fucked up." I sat beside Ilya on the glider by our heated pool.

"I don't feel like cooking tonight, cabbage."

"I'll cook," I said.

"No, I want to take my cabbage to dinner."

"Where would you like to go?"

"Dublin?"

"It shall be so," I said and transported us away from the compound.

~

"I told Maye we were going out to eat," I said as Ilya pulled a chair out for me at his daughter's hotel restaurant.

"Good. They won't shoot us when we get back, then."

"I hope you're right."

"The soup is good," he smiled and shook out my napkin for me.

"Then I'll have soup."

The broccoli-stilton soup was wonderful, as it turns out. As was the pasta primavera. I was full and sipping the last of my wine when Ilya took the glass from my fingers and set it aside.

"Cabbage," he said, taking both my hands.

"What, honey?" I asked.

"I want to marry you."

Several questions ran through my mind; one of them was—why? He already had me—mind, body and spirit. "Are you sure?" I asked.

"More than anything." He wore a nervous smile, suddenly, and I realized how much this meant to him.

"Then yes—I'll marry you anywhere and anyway," I said.

"Good. Very good. I will buy a ring soon. You will help."

"Okay," I said. "Just let me know."

He couldn't pay fast enough to get us out of there so I could take us home. Once we were back at the compound, I was undressed and in bed with him as quickly as he could make it happen.

~

Ilya

"What's wrong?" I asked. I woke to find Corinne sitting up in bed, arms wrapped around her knees and staring at the bedroom wall.

"Some of the creatures were moved last night," she said.

"Do you know where?" I was sitting beside her quickly.

"Out of the country," she said. "And into Iraq."

I cursed and slid off the bed. "Cabbage, we must inform Colonel Hunter. If those terrorists have creatures at their command, what might they do?"

We were more than familiar with the videos splashed across the Internet—none of which Corinne could watch—where soldiers, civilians and volunteers were beheaded with regularity.

We were back to the rogues there, and their funding, which had to come from somewhere.

We were back to stolen crowns and who knew what else.

"I think we should get dressed and go tell Auggie in person."

"Then come," I held out my hand and pulled her off the bed.

Corinne

I warned Auggie that we were on the way—I knew he was in his office early. James was there, too, and he locked the door behind him the moment Rafe and I appeared.

"They moved some of the creatures last night," I began. "They're on their way to Iraq to join the insurgency."

I'd never seen anger overcome Colonel August Hunter so swiftly. He had Matt Michaels on the phone almost as fast, and Matt was on his way in less than five minutes.

"James, bring coffee and anything else you can find," Auggie snapped. "They haven't had breakfast, yet."

Rafe and I heard other news from Matt after he arrived and accepted a cup of coffee from James. "The insurgents are either killing locals or paying them off to do whatever they want and take whatever they want," Matt said. "It's leaking into surrounding countries, too, as you might imagine."

"Because they have unlimited funding," Rafe nodded.

"That makes sense, and we know now who's behind this, I think.

My question is why?" Auggie growled. "That part of it makes no sense at all."

"We have to figure this out," Matt said. "Before we find ourselves in a situation we can't handle."

"If those creatures are seen in Iraq, Auggie, they'll try to charge you with treason."

"Because we're the only ones they can tie this to," Matt stood to pace. "This is untenable."

I was beginning to realize that Matt was included in this attack, and he'd recognized it before I did. In fact, Auggie was just a steppingstone to get to Matt Michaels. Both were targets, just as the Program had been, but Matt was important in ways that even I couldn't explain.

"Corinne?" Auggie lifted his head, turning dark eyes on me. I understood what he was asking.

"You know they'll realize I'm still alive if I do that," I began.

"I think we can deal with that," Matt sighed.

"No," I said. "You'll be signing death warrants if you do that." He was thinking of placing agents in likely spots, all of them looking like me. They'd be easy targets.

"You think we can't handle weapons and give them backup?" Matt asked, his forehead creasing with worry. He knew, just as I did, that this would place valuable lives in danger.

"It'll make them think we have clones of you," Auggie breathed. "That's genius."

"Feel free to clone me," Rafe said. "Seemingly, anyway."

"That might work; they know you're together—or were," Matt agreed.

"I can't believe you're serious about this," I said. "They'll come out, guns blazing."

"Maybe that's what we need—a direct confrontation," Auggie sighed. "We can have people in place ahead of time, watching for any activity. We already have surveillance on Askins and his buddies."

"You know the bodies will pile up," I warned.

"Corinne," Auggie said. "Destroy those creatures in Iraq. That's a command."

"Where have you been?" Maye demanded when Ilya and I arrived in the compound kitchen two hours later.

"Starting World War Three," I said.

CHAPTER 14

erle Askins' Office

"What the hell are you saying—they're all dead?"

"Including the ones at the Seattle facility."

"Holy fucking hell," Askins snapped. "She's alive. This is impossible. Have you notified?"

"Hell yes," came through his cell phone. "You're not dealing with a moron, here. I've notified everybody involved."

"I'll start the hunt immediately."

"I think that's prudent."

Merle Askins shrieked when the creature's body landed in his office, breaking furniture with a resounding crack and scraping artwork from the walls while glass shards tinkled to the floor. All this occurred while the huge, scaly body pinned him against a window that threatened to break. Dropping the cell phone from numb fingers, Askins realized the dark-scaled creature was quite wet as well as very dead.

She'd killed their prize in its pool and then dumped it in his office. He screamed for his assistant before realizing that nobody could get in or out—the creature filled every bit of space in the room.

~

Notes—Colonel Hunter

Madam President was late returning from a meeting—Matt and I sat in the Oval Office, expecting a tongue-lashing when we informed her that Corinne was alive.

"Gentlemen," Madam President swept in. We rose and nodded respectfully to her. "What do you have for me?" She sat behind her desk, indicating that we should sit, too.

"We have a confession to make," Matt began.

"What confession is that?"

"Well, we lied. For a good cause, you understand."

"Let's hear it." I could tell she wasn't happy with whatever meeting she'd gone to, so we were walking into a landmine.

"Corinne is alive," Matt said. "As are Rafe, Maye and Nick. Jeff is the only one who died in Ketchikan."

I didn't expect what happened. I expected a drubbing. Instead, she blinked away tears and her hand trembled as it covered her mouth.

"Please say this is true," she whispered.

"It's true. I can probably get them here if you want to see for yourself."

"No—keep them safe," she said.

"There's more," Matt admitted. "We were forced to bring Corinne out of hiding this morning, because they sent twenty creatures to Iraq, to join the insurgents."

"They're dead?"

"All of them. Including the cloning farm they set up in the Seattle facility shortly after we left it behind."

Madam President considered that information for a moment. "Will they be able to make more elsewhere?"

"We don't know. Corinne destroyed everything at the facility, so they won't be able to do it there again."

"Where is she? Never mind—I can't say what I don't know," Madam President held up a hand.

"She'll move if it's warranted," I said. "We have another plan to put in place, but we need your permission, first."

"Tell me," she said, pulling a tissue from a desk drawer and dabbing her eyes.

~

Corinne

"Everything inside the mountain facility is destroyed or useless, including the drug they had there," I said. Everybody was eating lunch while we had our impromptu meeting around the kitchen island.

"Anybody left alive?"

"I left a few humans alive, but all the creatures are dead."

"Which humans?"

"The ones that didn't have fogged brains," I said. "There were only five of those; they worked the computer system and didn't know what was going on above their heads."

My cell phone rang. Auggie was calling.

"Corinne, do you know anything about a creature landing in Merle Askins' office?" he barked at me.

"Uh, yeah."

"Nice work."

I savored the compliment for a moment before I spoke. "Thanks. It'll take chain saws and a small army to get it out of there."

"Even better."

"I sent information to the newspapers," I said.

"What sort of information?"

"Showing his department spending taxpayer funds for experiments, as well as photographs of those experiments. One of those photographs eerily matches what just landed in his office."

"Corinne?"

"Yes, Auggie?"

"Remind me never to piss you off again."

"Good plan."

"Thank you."

"You know this'll piss the enemy off and he'll come after us soon?" I said.

"We know. Madam President also knows. She gave Matt permission to substitute his agents for you and the others."

"We're aware of that. I can send information about the plane used to transport creatures to Iraq—ordered by Askins."

"Go ahead."

"Done."

"That fast?"

"Yeah."

Merle Askins' public shaming began that evening, on every news channel, which included images of the effort spent to remove a huge, dead creature from his office and the plan to blame everything on Secretary of Defense August Hunter.

Askins' office came back the following day, begging for sympathy because the CIA Director was dying of cancer. That and his guards kept Askins away from public scrutiny. By the third day, he'd resigned his position while waiting for the Justice Department to file charges against him.

We still had the Joint Chiefs, who were separating themselves from the fray as quickly as they could. The media attention was drawn away, however, when two airliners were shot down, one over Ukraine, the other in Spain.

We weren't involved in those investigations, but information was shared and the method turned out to be the same—tiny missiles, fired from far away, were responsible.

"They've released their findings to the media," Opal said at breakfast three days after the crashes. "I heard from Matt a few minutes ago. He says they're ready to run with it."

"Anything different about these?" I asked.

"Not so far. I think everybody's afraid to fly, now. Those flights were selected randomly—or that's the current theory."

"I'm surprised they're not targeting military flights," Ilya set a cup of coffee in front of Opal.

"Don't jinx it," Opal warned. "Right now, anybody who flies is a target."

"They don't have to target airplanes," I pointed out. "They can target anything."

"You had to make it worse, didn't you?" Opal grimaced.

"I'm not the one with the tiny rockets," I said.

"Tiny rockets," Nick sang the words to *Tiny Bubbles* as he walked into the kitchen.

"Don't start," I held up a hand. Nick laughed.

We watched the special report from the White House later that evening, as information was disseminated. It clarified what the media had reported as truth, when most of that had been wild speculation.

"This is the size of the bomb, which has some sort of guidance and propulsion system," Madam President's Press Secretary reported, holding up a rough copy of the rocket used in all the airline bombings. "We don't know where these were made or who is responsible for firing them, but we have put every airline and every military installation on notice—that anything they fly can be in danger. We've estimated the range of these things to be at least a thousand miles or more."

"What's to keep them from bombing ships or anything else?" A reporter in the crowd asked.

"We don't know whether anything is preventing that. There's a theory that they're letting us know how well these things work—after all, it's much more difficult to hit a moving target."

"How hard do you think it is to create these things? Are you willing to release the specs?" Another journalist asked.

"No idea," he said. "We don't have technology to match what little we've found, and we will not release any information—you'll have to wait until it's declassified."

That resulted in general grumbling.

"Is there any discernable pattern to the bombings?" A third journalist asked.

"We don't have any theories yet—so far, it seems random. It appears they want to make an enemy of everyone."

"Bingo," I said, pointing my finger at the Press Secretary.

"Huh?" Maye turned to me.

"I think that's what they're after—they want to be everybody's enemy," I said. "For whatever reason."

"They haven't hit the same country twice," Nick agreed.

"Perhaps we should alert Colonel Hunter to that fact," Richard said.

"I'll make the call," Nick held up his cell and walked out of the media room.

Notes—Colonel Hunter

"They may target the countries they haven't hit, yet," Nick said. "So far, the same country hasn't been hit twice."

"True—we can put them on alert without sharing that information with the media," I agreed.

"Colonel Hunter, do you think we should move? Maye and I are concerned for the safety of all involved."

"I've thought the same thing," I said. "We have a plan to plant decoys, but if the enemy locates the real thing, all that planning will be a waste and we'll be in trouble."

"That's my thinking," Nick agreed.

"Any suggestions?" I asked.

"I may know a place. Opal is in agreement."

"Then run it past Corinne and get back with me."

"Yes, sir."

~

Corinne

"We think we should move." I was reading on the patio when Opal and Nick approached me.

"I was thinking about that. Sort of. What do you have in mind?" I studied both of them, realizing quickly they'd come to the same conclusion.

"I know people who have a vacation home on the Gulf Coast of Texas," Opal said. "I can borrow it with their permission and no questions asked."

"With a water view?"

"The best they have to offer."

"Sounds fine," I shrugged. "When?"

"Tonight?"

"Is it big enough for all of us?"

"With room left over."

Opal has a nice smile, when she chooses to offer one.

"One place is just as good as another," I agreed. We were coming to the part where we'd be in danger, no matter where we were. If moving made them feel more comfortable, then we'd move.

"You tell Rafe, we'll tell the others," Nick grinned.

"Leave me with the hard job, huh?"

"Goes without saying."

"What goes without saying?" Ilya walked in. He hadn't bothered to sound like Rafe around the others in days. He felt comfortable being himself, I think.

"That you're the hard sell," I said. "We're moving. To the Gulf Coast. It'll make them feel better," I nodded to Nick and Opal.

"What about you?" He sat down beside me, his dark eyes wandering my face, attempting to read my preferences.

"It doesn't matter where we are," I said. "Plus, we've probably been here long enough."

"Then we'll move," Ilya slapped his knee as if that were the last word on the matter.

"You don't have to pack anything—I can take it with us. How's the kitchen where we're going?" I asked Opal.

"Everything you'd want and more."

"Outstanding."

~

"You have rich friends," I said the moment we landed in the huge beach house. With three levels and more than six thousand square feet, it had to cost in the millions.

"I call dibs on the first-floor bedroom," Nick said. I wasn't surprised; it was next to the state-of-the-art workout room.

Richard, Maye and Nathan took the suites on the second floor, leaving the top floor master suite to Ilya and me.

A half-moon hung low over the water as I walked onto the large deck behind the house. Darkness had fallen earlier, but moonlight glittered on the waters of the gulf behind the massive house.

"This is nice," Ilya breathed against my neck as he leaned in to place a warm kiss. "I haven't seen you use the sunlamps much lately. Are you all right?" He pulled away, concern in his eyes.

"I've developed a way around that," I said. "I can't explain it—it's sort of complicated."

"As long as you are all right," he said and tilted my chin. His mouth met mine in a demanding kiss.

"I'm fine," I said, after he broke the lingering connection.

"If we were alone, I'd make a bed here in the moonlight and we would make love," he said.

"That sounds nice," I breathed. "Really nice."

"Will you take us to bed?" he breathed against my mouth.

He didn't have to ask twice.

~

French and German airliners were shot down the following day. Somehow, I felt the enemy was rushing his plans after he learned I was still alive. That's why I took Ilya with me when I paid Merle Askins a visit in D.C.

He was cleaning out his desk to make room for whomever took his place. His assistant almost screamed when Ilya and I appeared inside the office and blew the door shut with power. Evidence of the creature's temporary occupation of the space was everywhere—the new Director would be forced to redecorate.

"Don't scream again," Ilya cautioned Merle's assistant, holding up a hand. "You won't like my reaction if you do."

"Are you threatening us?" Merle snapped.

"Seriously? I wouldn't bother to threaten you—I'd just make you dead, Merle," I deadpanned.

He backed up against the window, hoping, I'm sure, that the cavalry would gallop in to rescue his sorry ass.

"I came to make an offer," I said. "Come clean about your real boss, and I'll cure your cancer."

"My real boss was the President," he began.

"Which one?" I asked sweetly.

"What?" he sputtered.

"You know what I'm talking about, so stop pretending. Tell me what he looks like now and I'll fix your lungs. No worries."

I saw the fear come over him, then. He wanted to live, but the horror of what his boss might do to him was greater. Fortunately, I was able to read that in him—there was no fog on his brain. At least not yet. He knew Hal Prentice was posing as the former President. He knew the real former President was behind Hal Prentice's masquerade. He didn't know much past that, but a confession would call out the enemy, at least. Askins wasn't willing to cooperate because he was terrified.

"Fine," I tossed up a hand. "Just remember that I offered." Ilya and I disappeared.

We heard from Auggie and Matt Michaels later the same day. Hours earlier, a technician in Matt's employ had found a tiny chip in one of the rockets I'd deactivated in Colombia.

It had a code on it.

I had to pick both of them up at Auggie's office, but that wasn't a problem. "We think we've found where these things are manufactured, or at least some of their components," Auggie said as Ilya set glasses of iced tea in front of him and Matt. "We traced the chip back to a factory in Russia, but that's not where they're making the rockets. We had to do some careful maneuvering, but the chips were delivered to a building on the Russian-Ukrainian border. We believe they're transporting the chips underground to manufacture the rockets elsewhere."

"Where is that?" I asked.

"Here," Auggie pulled up a map on his tablet. I stared in dismay at a map of Chernobyl.

Ilya cursed in Ukrainian over my shoulder. "They're doing it there, because people are kept away from the area," Matt explained. "For obvious reasons."

"My son was questioning activity there when he was killed," Ilya snapped, the accent heavy in his voice. "By Baikov."

"And they likely laid low for a while afterward," Auggie nodded.

"I do not want my cabbage anywhere near that place," Ilya exploded.

"I wasn't suggesting that," Auggie said. "Calm down, I think we may be able to get someone else in there. Photographs are all we need."

"Let me guess—you have someone watching satellite feeds, now?" I asked.

"Yes. Is that a problem?" Matt turned to me.

"Who is it?"

"Don't worry, this isn't the same one who watched the South American feeds—we're keeping an eye on him already."

"Good. Have fun getting your photographs," I said. "I really don't want to go to Chernobyl."

"You think they're using the underground site near Chernobyl-2, don't you?" Ilya breathed.

"Yes. Know anything about the Russian Woodpecker?" Matt's left eyebrow lifted.

"Hmmph. I laugh at American conspiracy theories."

I looked from Ilya to Matt and then back again. What I understood from all that I wouldn't want to say. Not in public, anyway.

"There was a tunnel from that facility into Russia," Ilya confirmed. "It was reported to be blocked when Ukraine became independent."

"Ukraine doesn't realize it's being used again," Matt said.

"Corinne?" Auggie gave me a pointed look.

"Hey, don't look at me," I raised both hands in surrender.

"Who are you sending in there?" Ilya asked. "I warn you, if they are caught, it will not go well."

"I'm sending Opal," Matt said.

"Are you sure?" I asked Opal for the third time.

"I can get in and out," she said. "No problem."

"Can you speak Russian?" Ilya asked.

"I can say *nyet*," she laughed.

"Look, I'll know if you're in trouble," I said.

"Cori, stop worrying about me," she leaned forward and hugged me. "You have enough on your plate. Let me do my thing."

"All right."

"I still do not like this," Ilya crossed arms tightly over his chest.

"You could come, too," Opal pointed out. "And bring Corinne, because she can haul your stubborn ass out of there when it needs to go."

"Honey, let's go," I said, allowing my shoulders to droop. "I don't want anybody in more danger than they're already in."

"In and out," Ilya commanded. "When I say leave, we leave, you understand?" My face was in his hands as his eyes locked on mine.

"Okay," I squeaked.

"Good. Come, I will make sure you dress appropriately."

~

Appropriate dress was all black with black athletic shoes. Apparently, Ilya conveniently failed to remember that we hadn't been seen when we visited the facility outside Seattle.

Opal was dressed in black, just like we were, when we met in the kitchen again. "Don't be detected," Matt warned. "Any sign of it, you get the hell out."

"Sure thing. I'd salute, but that just seems silly," I said.

That's when I saw the dimple in Matt's cheek for the first time. "Come on, you know you want to laugh," I said.

He choked trying not to laugh.

"Now you know what I've had to deal with for years," Auggie told Matt.

"You poor thing. I'll buy you ice cream when I get back," I teased.

Matt burst out laughing.

"Cori," Auggie warned.

"Yeah."

~

I saw the actual Russian Woodpecker when we arrived where Ilya directed. It was a huge metal frame, stretching far into the night and towering above the trees that grew around the base.

Fact and fiction of conspiracy theories aside, it was used during the cold war to detect any missiles lobbed in Russia's direction. The metal frame of it stood as a testament to the nuclear standoff. I realized that base-jumping tourists now leapt (foolishly) off the thing at times, but that was their reason for being there, not mine.

Want inside the underground facility or in the tunnel leading into it? I sent to Ilya and Opal.

Tunnel, Ilya responded.

Tunnel it is, I replied and moved us there.

You sure we can't be seen? Opal's mindspeech made me want to laugh. *I know you knew*, she said. *Thanks for keeping my secrets.*

I told you I would, I said. *Come on, we'll be moving in a bubble—you won't need to walk. I don't want to put pressure on anything.*

Only a small part of the underground facility was actually in use, and that turned out to be the part closest to the tunnel. The rest was blocked off, with a thick wall between it and what was accessible aboveground. Ukraine was harboring the enemy without anyone being aware.

Passing computer stations and technicians dressed in plain black uniforms with no insignia, we eventually reached the manufacturing room.

Idly, I read a notice written in Russian hanging on the wall, concerning the safe handling of all components.

Piled at the end of a long assembly line was a rack of tiny rockets. The rack stood six feet high and twenty feet long, and was nearly full of the small explosives. Ilya snapped photographs inside the silence and invisibility of our bubble, while Opal and I watched the placement of three more rockets on the rack.

Calculating mentally, I realized there were enough rockets there to destroy thousands of targets. I shivered.

Out now, cabbage, Ilya said.

I got us the hell out of there.

"There's a reason they're doing it there," Opal said when Matt asked after studying the photographs. "It takes the blame from Russian shoulders and places it on Ukraine instead, in case anybody finds out."

"This is impossible," Auggie rumbled, looking from one photograph to another.

"You see this," Ilya tapped one of the photographs.

"What is it?" Auggie asked.

"This measures the radiation levels there. See—the indicator shows it is safe enough, although the level is still somewhat high."

"So they're monitoring the radiation from Chernobyl, still," Matt said. "Probably a wise decision. That gauge is huge, though. We've got tiny ones that probably work better."

"Seventies technology," Ilya explained. "They tapped into what was already there, as long as it was still working."

"I swear I saw a floppy disk being used in the computer room," Opal said.

Auggie huffed a humorless laugh. "Leftovers from the nuclear standoff. Most of the technology from that time period is still in use for the nuclear weapons program."

"Yours and theirs," Ilya confirmed.

"Watch out, your spyness is showing," I said.

"Internet," Ilya said. "See for yourself."

"Well, now we have to figure out how to tie this to the right people," Auggie said, rising and stretching. "Need to check in with the President first, though. What can we do about all those rockets in the meantime?"

He'd pointed his question at Matt.

I answered. "Already taken care of," I said. "They'll look live when they're sent out. They'll go dead before they reach their target."

"Like the ones fired at us in Colombia?" Opal's eyes gleamed with amusement.

"Yeah."

CHAPTER 15

*C*orinne

"Watch out, your coolness is showing," Opal grinned at me.

"Nah—the cool part will be figuring out how to move that mess from Ukraine back to Russia and send the blame where it belongs."

"I worry that this is only a temporary fix—we're still no closer to finding the mastermind in all this," Matt observed.

"You are correct," Ilya agreed.

"I'm concerned about the ultimate purpose of it," Auggie said.

"Me, too," I rubbed Auggie's back.

"We should probably get back," Matt said. "Before somebody comes looking for us."

"Okay," I said.

"You may consider bringing James and Shaw for a short visit," Auggie said. "I think they're feeling left out."

"I can do that," I shrugged. "When?"

"Tomorrow? They'll need time to pack."

"All right. I'll be there tomorrow at noon. They can have lunch here."

"Corinne," Auggie began, "I don't want you to do anything foolish, or anything without letting me know, first. I have a report that you showed up in Askins' office and made threats."

"I offered to cure his cancer if he gave up his boss," I said. "I never heard of that being a threat before."

"You can do that?" Auggie frowned.

"Richard could do that," I flung out a hand. "If Askins wants to die with that much blood on his hands, then so be it. I made the offer. It still stands. He hands over his boss and everybody's happy. He gets to live longer, too."

"Corinne, the public is already wondering—and rightly so—how a huge creature was lodged so tightly into Askins' office that it took a butcher job to get it out of there."

"I hope they're wondering why Askins was making creatures to begin with," I huffed.

"Look, I didn't intend to start a fight," Auggie held up a hand. "I just don't want information leaked on what you can do. It can be twisted to work against us."

"You think I don't know that?" I snapped. "People have died in plane crashes recently, Auggie. Maybe it's time to let the enemy know what he's really up against."

"Corinne," Rafe hissed, gripping my arm. "You will stop this immediately. We do not need disagreement among us now."

"Fine. Tell Leo and James I'll be there tomorrow," I said and stalked away.

"Corinne," Auggie barked. "You have to take us back. Now."

I did, but I wasn't happy about it.

At all.

Notes—Colonel Hunter

"I think she's tired of everybody second-guessing every move she makes," Matt said the moment Corinne disappeared and we found ourselves inside my office. "Look at it this way—Askins likely knows now that she can find him. He's seen enough to know she can kill him without thinking very hard about it. If he's closely connected to the enemy, well, it may draw his attention away from shooting down airplanes."

"If she finds the enemy, he knows she can kill him, too," I sighed. "He's hiding from her—you can bet on it."

"We spoiled his plans in the Middle East—or Corinne did. I have satellite images of dead creatures being unloaded from the plane Askins sent. Except for the one that landed in Askins' office, they sent the worst of the lot."

"I'm sure they wanted to tie those things to us—or to me directly, and that would have brought on a war with every country in the region." The thought had just hit me—likely Corinne had seen it long before I had. She'd neutralized the problem before it became a problem.

"She was protecting you just as much as she was protecting the country," Matt blew out a breath. "I guess we ought to find a way not to fight with her. In the meantime, I think I can put some of my agents around the entrance to that tunnel, to watch for the next load of rockets going out of there. Once we have those images, we can call the Russians to account."

"Good. Let's hope we can take care of that part and keep Corinne out of it."

"I'll keep you posted," Matt nodded and walked out of my office.

Corinne

I was still fuming when I picked up James and Leo the following day. Not just at Auggie, but at Ilya, too, who'd used the Rafe persona to castigate me in front of everybody.

"Hello, Corinne," Auggie said the moment I arrived in his office. I didn't speak to him. Instead, I hauled James and Leo out of there quickly, without asking if they were ready.

Yeah, I was pissed and rude at the same time.

"Want to talk about this?" Leo asked the moment we landed in the huge beach house.

"Honey, I'm so mad right now, I don't want to talk to anybody," I said, patting his shoulder instead of apologizing. "I'll get over it," I said. "Make yourselves at home." I disappeared again, defying anyone to send mindspeech to determine where I'd gone.

~

I hadn't been to a bookstore in more than a year. Settling at a café table inside the Corpus Christi chain store, I sipped a latte and looked around at the shelves of books. My books used to be on those shelves. Some of them still might be—the mass-market versions, anyway.

Gone were the days of hard-cover releases and book signings. Nowadays, I released my work mostly in e-book format, with quality paper sales a faint afterthought. I hadn't written anything in weeks, too, because of the mess and intrigue surrounding a former U.S. President and his flunkies.

I'd lost myself, somewhere amid the list of crises that threatened all of us. After receiving the drug a second time, there'd been no period of adjustment for me, like there'd been the first time.

I'd been forced to hit the ground running, while those around me continued to question every move and decision I made.

Yes, I realized every relationship had its bumps and potholes, including relationships with friends. Auggie and I had our share of those. When he thought I was useless, he'd tolerated me. Chastised me at times, when his non-military charge chose to do things differently.

Brushing tears away, I lifted my latte and transported myself to the beach house.

~

Ilya

She reappeared, took a seat at one of the round, wood tables on the deck and drank coffee from a bookstore coffee shop. There was a flowerbed at the front of the house. I went there first before approaching Corinne.

Corinne

A pink hibiscus bloom was set carefully in front of me as I wiped more tears away. My coffee cup was dry—I'd finished my drink. Ilya took the chair across from mine, settling on the wooden seat, which creaked slightly beneath his weight.

Dark eyes searched my face—I figured I looked horrible after crying for half an hour.

"I love you," he said. "I beg you to never forget that, even when I am being an ass."

"I know," I quavered, covering my mouth with a hand to hide the trembling of my lower lip. Fresh tears fell, so I turned my head away.

"Here, now." He rose and came to me; I watched as he knelt beside my chair and wiped more tears from my cheeks with his thumb. "It hurts my heart to see my cabbage cry."

That's when my arms went around his neck and I sobbed.

Ilya

Dr. Shaw followed me as I carried Corinne toward the stairs. She still wept against my shoulder.

"No drugs," I said. Shaw silently nodded his understanding.

Corinne

"Hush, my heart," Ilya murmured against my hair as I was placed on the bed. "There is no need for this."

"Corinne, Colonel Hunter regrets his words," Leo Shaw sat on the chair beside the bed. "I know they upset you anyway."

He was right—words can never be taken back, and harsh words are remembered the longest.

"Here," Ilya sat on the edge of the bed and pulled me up so I could lean into him. His arms wound around me, holding me tight against him. "You're shaking, my love," he whispered. "Are you cold?"

"No," I shook my head.

"Panic attack," Leo murmured.

He was right—I hadn't been able to stop this one. The hurt and the panic had bubbled up and I hadn't been able to force them down.

"Breathe with me," Ilya coaxed. "Long breaths. In—and out."

"Let me know if you need anything," Leo said softly and left our bedroom.

~

Notes—Colonel Hunter

"I'm not sure how to reduce her stress," Leo Shaw said over the phone. I was more than grateful for the cell phones Corinne had given all of us—even Matt had attempted to trace them and was unsuccessful.

This conversation needed to be kept private; Corinne had experienced a meltdown. I was responsible and said as much. "You're not totally responsible," Shaw informed me. "I think you were the tipping point. Too many factors weighed into this, I believe, and while she has been able to manage this on her own up to a point, it eventually overloaded her."

"I still feel responsible," I said.

"Stop worrying about it—this will pass. You've had some disagreements in the past, this is no different. Besides, she didn't grieve as she should have for her son. As I said; too many factors."

"We have to find this bastard before he finds her," I hissed.

"I agree. The death toll is staggering as it is."

"At least we know he has a big connection to Russia—that has been proven time and again. I have no idea how many Baikov clones there are, but rest assured he's controlling them, and likely the Soviet President through them."

"It's possible your theory is correct—that he wants to destroy the peace between countries and then appear the hero by taking back the White House and forging peace again."

"This is a fucking sick way to do it," I said.

"It wouldn't be the first time a leader has murdered to further his personal goals."

"History is full of that," I agreed. "I worry that we'll never get past it."

"I hope we survive it—both on a personal and global level."

"Is it professional to call him a fucked up, sick bastard?"

"If there isn't a code for that in the diagnosis manual, there should be," Leo affirmed with a chuckle.

Corinne

I woke next to Ilya late the following morning. He was sitting in bed, scrolling through the cell phone I'd given him.

"Research?" I croaked. My throat fell raw from weeping and then falling asleep, so I held out a hand and *Pulled* in a bottle of water.

"A talent I wish we all had," Ilya said, setting the phone aside and taking the bottle to remove the cap.

"The cool thing is I can recycle the bottle using power," I said after drinking nearly half the contents.

"You can?" He offered a gentle smile.

"Why do you think you haven't had to empty the trash in a while?"

"You've recycled all of it?" Now he sounded surprised.

"Yeah. We each give back in our own way," I teased.

"Feeling better, then?"

"Yeah. I was tired and stressed."

"I understand. Cabbage?"

"What, honey?"

"I want to buy your ring. There are jewelry stores in Corpus Christi. I desire to take you to one."

"Which one?"

"This one." He lifted the phone and showed me the online advertisement.

"That's in a mall," I said, before realizing he already knew that.

"This is the one I want," he insisted.

"Okay. Let me get dressed."

I shouldn't have been surprised that we weren't able to leave the house without taking everybody with us.

I also wasn't surprised that James and Nathan had spent the night together. I'd understood they could be a good match—fortunately, they'd seen it, too.

I landed us in a dim hallway away from any security cameras or eyes that might see, and we walked into the mall from there. "Meet in that hallway in two hours," Leo commanded. He was the ranking officer, after all.

Ilya steered me toward the jewelry store, first thing, while the others fanned out to shop or look around. Opal and Nick headed for a popular Chinese restaurant near the center of the mall. James and Nathan walked toward the trendy electronics store, while Richard and Maye had no particular direction and strolled away, holding hands.

"They should be shopping for rings, too," Ilya breathed against my ear as he steered me on a steady course toward the jewelry store.

"Up to them," I replied and worked to match his long-legged stride.

There's a reason the jewelry stores place their engagement rings and wedding bands in an easy-to-discover spot. Ilya zoned in on them as if he had radar.

"Tell me what you like, cabbage," he said as we leaned over the long, glass case and peered at all sorts of diamonds.

I sighed when one of them caught my eye. "I'd like to see that one," Rafe pointed to the one I couldn't look past.

"A good choice," the salesclerk said, unlocking the case and pulling the ring from its velvet nest. "Two and a half carat oval diamond, surrounded by smaller diamonds with more falling halfway down the band." He set it on a convenient black velvet pad so we could see the brilliance of the cut.

My breath caught when I saw the price—thirty-eight thousand dollars. "Try it on," Rafe smiled, reaching for my hand and placing the ring on my finger.

"We'll size it for free, with a lifetime of free cleaning and mounting checks," the salesclerk beamed.

Holy shit, Ilya, I sent to him.

Worth every penny, he shot back. "We'll take it," he nodded to the clerk. "With the matching band and a man's wedding ring."

He ended up selecting a band for himself that had diamonds spaced about the wide ring made of gold and platinum. The total? More than fifty thousand.

He didn't blink when he handed over the credit card I'd given him, either.

I'd have spent more, he informed me as he signed the slip. *But this is what my cabbage wanted.*

"Do you want those sized? We can have them ready in a week," the clerk offered.

"We'll bring them back. For now, I'd like to take them with us," Ilya said.

We watched as the rings were boxed up, tied with ribbons and placed in a pretty, white bag with the store's logo on the front. We walked out seconds later. In all, we'd spent less than twenty minutes in the store.

"Will you transport us to Vegas? I want to get married today," Ilya said, taking me by surprise as we strolled through the mall.

"Can we get that done in an hour and a half?" I blinked up at him, feeling nervous, suddenly.

"Come—take us there and we will see."

〜

I trembled slightly as I said my vows, but they were said. Ilya kissed me nicely at the end, too. The moment the license was signed and witnessed by two chapel employees, we left Las Vegas behind and landed in the dim hallway with five minutes to spare.

I'd had to size the rings using power, but they fit.

The others found us kissing in the hall when they arrived a few minutes later.

"Did you?" Leo began.

"License," Ilya handed the folded paper to Leo.

"Holy shit," James crowed after looking over Leo's shoulder at our proof of marriage. "Congratulations."

"If you're wondering, Rafe is registered at guns-n-bombs-r-us," I said.

Nick snorted a laugh.

"Nice ring," Opal grinned.

"Yeah."

〜

Notes—Colonel Hunter

"We have something," Matt laid a folder on my desk. He'd shown up unannounced and scared my temporary assistant so badly the man could only stutter as he ushered Director Michaels into my office.

"Close the door, Corporal," I motioned for my assistant to do just that.

"Yessir," he couldn't leave my office quickly enough.

"What's this?" I opened the folder to look. Photographs were inside, taken with a Telephoto lens.

"They're taking the rockets through the tunnel," Matt smiled. "You can see for yourself—those crates contain their weapons."

"Crates don't mean anything," I began.

"No, but keep looking."

Matt had done a thorough job. Whoever he'd had on this

assignment was more than good—they had photographs of the crates going into trucks, the trucks driving to a facility ten miles away on Russian soil, and then the same crates unloaded onto a dock leading underground.

The last photo was the best—somehow, an agent infiltrated the facility and snapped photographs of the crates as they were unloaded, revealing the rockets meant for shooting down planes.

"We need to see the President. Now," I stood and slapped the folder shut.

"Already have an appointment."

"When?"

"When we get there."

~

Ilya

The order came from Colonel Hunter as Corinne and I had a late lunch on the beach house deck—we had to get to D.C. as quickly as possible.

~

Notes—Colonel Hunter

I'd directed them to the ugly building in Arlington. They'd stay there until word came from Matt or me. Meanwhile, Matt put the plan to work to pose agents as Corinne and Rafe—I felt he was taking a big chance doing so, but I didn't argue the point.

Things had gone from a crawl to a gallop in the space of a few hours. Madam President already had a call in to the Russian Ambassador, demanding his presence at the White House.

Two of Matt's lookalikes would be there with us when that meeting took place. Matt intended to photograph the Ambassador leaving the White House, accompanied by those same lookalikes.

It was our way of cloning, when nothing could be farther from the truth. I hoped the enemy wouldn't realize it, however.

We were gambling, Matt and I, and I hoped we wouldn't be caught with a losing hand.

"What is the meaning of this?" the Russian Ambassador demanded the moment he was ushered into the Oval Office.

"Sit down," Madam President ordered. "There's something we'd like to get to the bottom of, and you're the first rung on that ladder."

The Ambassador looked from the President to me, then to Matt and the two agents, both of whom closely resembled Corinne and Rafe. He swallowed with difficulty. The corner of Matt's mouth curled.

∾

Corinne

"Matt got photographs of the rocket shipment into Russia," Opal said. "Plus he managed to infiltrate the storage facility, too. Undeniable proof. I can't wait to see how the Ambassador dances around this."

"I'd like to see how he'd dance around all the Baikovs we've killed off, with more probably waiting in the wings," I said. "Not to mention all the Marys and Beckers and who knew what that scaly woman was."

"Good point," Opal agreed. "At least we haven't found any more with those metal contraptions hooked to their spines."

"An unfortunate piece of equipment," Leo said. "The last I heard, ours were working on a similar model."

"Leo, did you intend to spoil my day?" I turned to him, then. "Those things are an abomination all the way around."

"Corinne, I never intend to spoil your day," he said. "Do you feel better?"

"Yeah."

"Except for the argument over her last name," Ilya said.

"Honey," I sighed.

"We will discuss this later," he nodded. Somehow, I had the feeling that he'd end up getting his way, like he usually did.

We were considering what take-out to order when more

information came from Matt and Auggie—while they'd grilled the Russian Ambassador at the White House, Matt received word from an undercover operative in Iraq.

A shipment of tiny rockets had arrived in Mosul, after traveling a roundabout route over land and water to get them there.

None of these were the ones I'd deactivated in Russia.

The insurgents now had two large crates of tiny rockets that they could fire at will to destroy whatever they wanted.

Notes—Colonel Hunter

"I swear this must be the work of criminals—the Kremlin had nothing to do with this," the Russian Ambassador blustered. We needed the real Corinne and fast, to see whether she could determine the truth or lie of his statements.

I'll admit, Matt had instructed the Corinne lookalike very well; she stood with her arms crossed, gazing angrily at the Ambassador.

"I'll be back in a moment," I held up my cell as if I were receiving a call. Striding out of the Oval Office as quickly as seemed prudent, I made a call to Leo Shaw the moment I was down a hall and alone.

"We need Corinne in the Oval Office," I said as softly as I could. "She just has to come in invisibly. I need to know whether the Russian Ambassador is telling the truth."

"We're here," Corinne and Rafe appeared beside me before Leo could give an answer.

"Never mind," I said and ended the call. "Invisible, now," I hissed at Corinne.

"We are invisible. And soundproofed. You're not," she pointed a finger accusingly at me. "Lead the way. We'll be right behind you."

Corinne

Ilya and I floated invisibly behind Auggie as he walked into the

Oval Office. Madam President glanced his way quickly before turning back to the Russian Ambassador, who was sweating.

He was lying, too—I think Matt had already figured that out. Something bothered me about his demeanor as well.

I made a mental note to scan everybody from then on—I barely had time to get everybody out of there, including the Secret Service agents standing guard outside the door. The Russian Ambassador exploded, taking the Oval Office and everything in it with him.

CHAPTER 16

otes—Colonel Hunter

Richard Farrell studied the metal device attached to what was left of the Ambassador's spine. The President wouldn't be pleased to learn that another device had found its way into the White House. At least she was alive to be angry about it.

The media had already begun its speculation, with a leak from somewhere reporting that the Russian Ambassador had been summoned to the White House just before the Oval Office was destroyed by a bomb.

The President was obligated to appear at a short press conference after that information was revealed, confirming that her agents had gotten her out of the Oval Office when they realized the Ambassador was wired with a bomb.

That didn't alter the fact that we still had to deal with the insurgency in Iraq, who now had small, deadly rockets at their disposal. I didn't have time to speak with Corinne or any of the others about that—we'd been too busy taking care of the President and the aftermath of the bombing.

Matt had been on his cell phone constantly after the explosion, attempting to get his field agents to follow the rockets in Iraq. Ever since this terrorist offshoot had sprung up years ago, we'd made inroads off and on, only to see it surge back, just as strong or stronger.

It didn't help that people from other countries kept signing up with the rebels, either, and that in itself was impossible to stop.

I had no doubt as to whom they'd target—anybody who fought or stood against them would be bombed into oblivion.

"Want a ride to Arlington?" Matt shut off his phone and looked at me.

"Richard?" I turned to Dr. Farrell.

"I wouldn't mind a ride—I've done as much as I can do, here," he nodded.

"Good. Let's go," I said. "I want to talk to Corinne and Rafe."

Ilya

"This is where the shipment of rockets was seen," Matt pointed to a spot on the map of Iraq. "I have someone there who sent the information, but we can't blow his cover or he's dead—you understand?"

I did—the merest whisper of suspicion in this group and you'd die —death was their main purpose. They didn't veil their actions behind religion—they'd gotten so far away from any tenets of their religion that they no longer bothered to claim it.

"What do you want us to do?" I asked. I assumed they wanted me to be involved, somehow. Corinne stood next to me, studying the map while Matt and I spoke. Iraq was the last place I wanted Corinne to be. I'd thought Chernobyl the worst, until this was placed before us.

"Pictures?" Corinne asked, surprising me for a moment.

"Huh? Oh." Light dawned in Matt Michaels' eyes. "Yes, I think I can arrange that."

"It may convince them to attack sooner," Colonel Hunter pointed out.

"Nothing will stop them from attacking. Sooner or later, does it really matter?" Matt asked.

"Not with these," I said. "Their only concern for life is for their own."

"I'll have images in an hour," Matt said, lifting the cell phone Corinne had given him and placing a call.

"Come, cabbage," I breathed against her temple. "Sit with me for a while. I need to have you close to me."

~

Notes—Colonel Hunter

"There are no innocent lives to be concerned about," I said as photograph after photograph was loaded onto a tablet for Corinne. "She'd recognize them anyway, if there were."

"That is an outstanding gift," Matt said. "I think it's extremely unusual, even in her current race."

"Current race?" A chill passed through me at Matt's words.

"She's not human. I hope you realize that," he said. "Nick isn't human, either. Maye is the closest to being human. Rafe's talent for shielding is certainly not human."

"Fuck," I scrubbed my face with a hand. "I never really thought of that, before."

"The evidence has been in front of you all along. That's what the drug does. Why it created a dinosaur from another planet, and creatures you've never seen before. Why so many died. That drug was never meant to be given to humans. It's why we have an enemy to fight, now."

"Because somebody decided it might be fun to try," I sighed.

"For whatever reason," Matt confirmed. "Richard may be the one to ask about that."

"Maybe, when this is all past us," I said. "This is the hand we have to play now, before more innocent lives are taken."

"Very true," Matt confirmed. "Almost done, here. Will it be a problem that we have more than four hundred in this initial round?"

"No. I've seen her do this before," I shrugged. "No innocent lives, remember?"

"I remember."

~

Corinne

In for a penny, in for a pound. That old saying went through my mind regularly as Rafe held me. We stared out a window of the ugly building in Arlington, while I contemplated the task before me.

Just making people dead wouldn't be enough. There had to be something else—something that would make those who remained fear for their own lives. I had to dig into the past to determine what might work.

"Ready?" Auggie's voice was soft as he interrupted us.

"Yeah," I sighed. Ilya loosened his arms—I accepted the tablet Auggie handed me. "Dead," I sighed at the first photograph. "Dead," I spoke to the second.

~

"Corinne? Cori?" Auggie snapped his fingers in front of my face. I had no idea how long I'd been catatonic, but it must have been a while. Leo sat with Ilya on the other side of the room; Ilya looked ready to either fall apart or kill somebody.

"They can't fire the rockets," I said, blinking to bring Auggie's face into focus.

"Why?" He knelt beside me, concern in his expression as he asked the question.

"One of the people I made dead knew where they were," I shrugged weakly. "I deactivated all of them, including the propulsion system. They won't work, now."

"Where were you?" Auggie asked. "You've been out of it for more than two hours."

"Killing is a terrible thing, Auggie," I said. "Nobody should do it."

"It was necessary, cabbage," Ilya sat beside me.

"I know. I still hate doing it."

"We have word," Matt strode into the room, waving the cell phone I'd given him. "The insurgents are so angry that the rockets won't work, they've declared jihad against Russia."

"Who are they blaming for the deaths?" Auggie rose and asked.

"They don't know who to blame, and they're afraid to place blame, most likely," Matt said. "Here's an image of the note pinned to every dead man."

"I can't read that," Auggie said. "It looks like Arabic."

"It is. It says, and I'm paraphrasing, *this death was deserved. Carry on in this one's footsteps and you will receive the same.*"

"Corinne?" Auggie turned to me. I shrugged again.

"I didn't kill three," I said. "But I gave them a warning."

"What was the warning?" Matt asked.

"I told them in mindspeech that they were marked," I replied. "I figure they're trying to get the hell away from the others now. After all, I saw plenty of others after reading each one before he died. I have just about the entire insurgent army inside my memory, now."

"Holy fucking hell," Auggie swore.

"I'd prefer not to kill them," I said. "But I could."

"Matt?" Opal walked into the room.

"What is it?" We both knew, just from the tone of Opal's voice, that something had happened.

"The Kremlin was hit by two rockets," Opal said. "Seven are dead and the Russian President is having a meltdown."

"Good," Ilya muttered.

Notes—Colonel Hunter

"Am I to understand that the Kremlin has been harboring insurgent leaders?" Madam President demanded.

We'd had to meet in another wing of the White House while the Oval Office underwent repairs. Her questions should have been posed to the Russian Ambassador, who was still just as dead as he was before. Russian President Zoran hadn't named a replacement—his state house had been hit, just as ours had been.

He still claimed he knew nothing about the bomb his Ambassador wore. We were hesitant to call him out on the device attached to the Ambassador's spine. He'd refused a video call, preferring a normal telephone conversation with Madam President instead, after the Kremlin was hit.

"Perhaps it's time to stop the lies," Madam President said. "We found the cache of rockets used to bring down those planes. That warehouse is on Russian soil, President Zoran. We also followed another shipment of those weapons as it traveled a convoluted route, only to arrive in Iraq. Can you explain that?"

"Those responsible are outlaws. I beg you to forgive my government—the signs of this illegal activity were certainly missed. We had no knowledge of it."

"Then what do you want us to do? Are you going to shut down that operation? I have no idea what the UN may say about this—those rockets killed hundreds of citizens from several countries. I believe those countries will be quite angry if we release the information we have."

"Yes, of course—I have already taken steps to shut this down and capture those responsible," he said.

"What about the insurgents who did their best to destroy the Kremlin?"

"We were working on a peace treaty, so they would not attack us," Zoran whined. "Instead, they turn on us without letting us explain."

I wanted to express my disbelief at this point—Zoran was lying, that was easy enough to see. Madam President wasn't buying it, either, but diplomacy is a dance at best, and often a downright hostile one.

"Perhaps we could meet soon and work out a peace of our own," Madam President said.

"Yes. Please. If you will agree to help defend us against these insurgents, then I will agree to meet with members of all countries affected by those terrible weapons and we will discuss peace and full disclosure."

I had to cover my mouth to keep the words behind my teeth. I had no idea what the fucker really wanted, but full disclosure wasn't one of them. I wanted information on his version of the Program. I doubted that would be forthcoming.

"Very well. Decide on a date and I'll see about bringing the others on board. We can meet at Camp David or the White House if you prefer."

"Yes, that sounds quite good," Zoran agreed. "I will let you know soon. But please, any assistance you might provide against these insurgents will be most appreciated."

"I'll see what we can do," Madam President said dryly and ended the call.

"He's lying," I almost exploded.

"I agree," Matt said. "But what does he really want?"

"I say we call his bluff and find out," Madam President said. "Matt, are you still tracking Askins? I've asked the Justice Department to hold off charging him, in case he leads us in the enemy's direction."

"I've had his phone tapped for a while, but he's not using that one to contact anybody except his doctor and other people who don't matter."

"Does he have what you have? I have to say, this cell phone is amazing," she held up the one Matt had given to her—it was one of the phones Corinne had given to us before we left Seattle.

"I hope he doesn't have anything like that," Matt said. "But he's hiding his tracks somehow—you can bet on that. He hasn't spoken to the Joint Chiefs, either, not since Corinne sent the package to his office."

"Anything from them?" the President asked.

"Nothing. They're so squeaky clean it hurts to look at them."

"I just want the bastard to come out of hiding," the President fumed.

"We gave that a shot—letting him believe Corinne was dead. Too bad we couldn't let that continue," Matt said. "It would have been worse, though, to let those creatures loose in Iraq."

"It would have been too bad to allow them to fire those weapons wherever and whenever," the President nodded. "We know he has ties to whatever faction is in Russia, developing those weapons. I worry that those in the Kremlin are in this up to their eyebrows. I just want to know what the hell he intends to get from all this."

"I think we'd all like to get that answer," I said. "If Corinne can't see it, you know where that leaves the rest of us."

"I do."

Corinne

"Matt says the Russian President is begging for a meeting, so he can claim that criminals are behind the weapons manufacturing in Ukraine and Russia, leaving his hands clean and preventing the insurgents from blowing up more of the Kremlin," Opal said as she slid onto a barstool at the kitchen island.

Since we occupied the ugly building in Arlington, I'd made a few improvements in the ugly kitchen. Now it wasn't ugly, and actually had updated décor and appliances.

"So he wants everybody to believe he had nothing to do with the Russian version of the Program," I muttered, handing Opal a cup of hot tea.

"Looks that way. I wouldn't want every other country in the world looking at me as a target, for blowing up their airplanes," she shrugged.

"So he wants to bring them together so they can applaud his song and dance routine?" I asked.

"Yeah. He's a piece of crap," she said, sipping her tea.

"I've only seen him once—on television, right after he took office," I said. "He seemed like an empty-headed twit, so I switched to another program."

"Zoran's an easy target for Baikov and his clones to lead around by the nose. Or the balls," Opal huffed.

"Until he didn't want to die at the hands of the insurgents he invited into his country," Ilya said, taking the seat next to Opal. "Cabbage, come sit with me," he patted the seat next to his.

I'd been restless and uneasy ever since I'd handed out a death sentence to nearly four hundred insurgents. Ilya was asking me to sit.

"All right." I walked around the island to sit beside him.

"Stop fretting," he said, dropping an arm around my shoulders and pulling me close for a tight hug. "Things will go as they will."

"How soon?" I turned to Opal when Ilya let me go. "How soon will that meeting with President Zoran happen?"

"Don't know, yet. The President has to get the other countries on board without them calling for Russian blood—whether they believe him or not, the Russians are ultimately responsible for the downing of those planes."

"That means the Secretary of State has a tough job to do," I said.

"True. But look at it this way—they may want that meeting soon, so the fires of their grievances will still be hot."

"But getting all of them to agree," Ilya pointed out. "That may not be so easy."

"Also true. We may be here for a while. I have the feeling that Madam President will want us there in one capacity or another."

"Great. I love politics," I said, recalling the meetings I'd gone to when I'd been to Camp David before. "I'll be interested to see whether a Baikov and Mary clone are included in Zoran's entourage."

"We should get a list of attendees before they arrive," Opal observed. "Matt will insist on it."

"Any word on Iraq?" Ilya asked, pulling me into a hug again.

"Matt said Iraqi physicians are still attempting to determine how those men died," Opal said. "It looks to them as if their hearts just stopped, with no discernable reason for it."

"They don't know who to blame for that, whereas they know—or think they know—who to blame for faulty rockets," Ilya offered.

"Do you think the Russian version of the Program will go underground until this mess blows over?" Nick asked after walking into the kitchen and setting a cup beneath the brewer to make coffee.

"If that's the plan, it'll just give them time to create larger problems for us," Ilya said. "I would prefer to eliminate it completely. That will not happen until we find their cache of the drug and destroy it, then destroy all their drug survivors and clones."

"What about our cache?" I asked. "Shouldn't it be destroyed, too?"

"Now we're treading unsteady ground," Nick said, taking a seat on the opposite side of the island. "We can say we want to keep some, just in case, but then what happens when somebody comes along and wants to live longer, or make clones of us?"

"Holy shit," I almost dropped off my barstool, I moved so quickly.

"What?" Ilya was off his seat, too, steadying me before I fell.

"We have to find Merle Askins," I snapped. "Now."

~

Notes—Colonel Hunter

By the time Matt's agents tracked Askins' personal cell phone, Askins was nowhere to be found and his assistant held up the former CIA Director's phone when he raised both hands in surrender.

He was brought back to Matt's office, where Matt and I were waiting—with Rafe and Corinne. Warren Brownlee, the assistant who was sent packing the same day Askins resigned, swallowed uncomfortably when he caught sight of Corinne.

He'd seen her before—when she'd gone to see Askins and offered a cure for his cancer. Askins was likely on his way to getting the drug, if it hadn't happened already. He'd left his cell phone with Warren, to keep up appearances.

"How long has he been gone?" Matt demanded.

"Th-three days," Warren mumbled. Corinne nodded her agreement —he was telling the truth.

~

Corinne

Warren Brownlee, Askins' assistant, was about to wet himself, he was so terrified. He also had no idea where Askins was; he only knew when the phone had been handed to him, with an excuse that Askins just *needed privacy*.

Askins had disappeared off my radar, too—leading me to believe he was with the enemy. That spelled the drug to me—Askins was either going to die or survive—as something other than what he was. It was an easy way to beat the cancer and any charges leveled by the Justice Department.

While he knew Askins had connections, he wasn't aware of who they really were—he only knew code names.

"Who did you think this *Spinner* person was?" Matt demanded after Warren revealed Askins' contact.

"Somebody highly placed who had a reason to hide his identity," Warren shrugged. "I thought we were uncovering vice and illegal activity."

"Let me guess—Matt and I were involved in all that?" Auggie snapped.

"He said as much—Director Askins did. He told me you were involved in very suspicious endeavors."

"What do you know about the Program?" Matt barked.

"He says it was one of your illegal operations," Warren blustered.

"You didn't think to ask about that?"

"Director Askins said it was better if I didn't know—then I couldn't be held accountable."

"Because he was in it up to his neck," Matt said. "I assume you understand that he was in charge of the creature experiments?"

"I came to that conclusion recently, yes," Warren dropped his eyes and stared at the floor.

"Do you know what those creatures used to be?" I asked, causing Auggie to turn a frown in my direction.

"Animals of some kind?" Warren turned to me, then.

"Those were the survivors of the attacks on Montana and Georgia. They used to be people, Mr. Brownlee. Your boss saw to it that they were used to blackmail and then to pose a threat when he thought to send them to the insurgency in Iraq. They're all dead, now, thanks to Mr. Askins."

"But—how?"

"It's complicated," Matt snorted. "Do you understand what you had your hands in, now? I sure as hell hope so. I have a cell with your name on it, and maybe in thirty years, if you're good, you'll get out of it. You can thank Director Askins for that, too."

"You knew you were wandering into illegal waters, didn't you?" I said.

"After a while," he nodded. "But I was loyal to my boss."

"Right. Stand up and put your hands behind your back," Matt said, producing handcuffs. "Bail will be refused—I'll see to that myself."

"If we're lucky, he'll die," Nick snarled.

"Askins always has been a lucky bastard," Opal pointed out. "I don't want to place any bets on this outcome."

"The odds are certainly against him," Richard said. He and Maye sat together on a media-room sofa at our ugly building.

"I hope we don't see him again," Ilya said. "I've had enough of that asshole. Corinne, perhaps you should have killed him when you had the chance."

"He had a choice. He chose to stay with the devil he knew," I sighed. "Rather than choosing what he understood to be right."

"You mean he does know right from wrong?" Maye huffed. "I'd never have guessed that."

"He went so far down the wrong path, he decided not to go back, I guess. I do have a question, though, for Auggie and Matt." I looked at Auggie—he and Matt were sipping Scotch and listening to the rest of us talk after sending Warren Brownlee to jail.

"What's that?" Auggie asked, rattling the ice cubes in his glass.

"Do former President Phillips and Askins have the same blood type?"

"Holy Christ," Ilya muttered.

"No," Matt said after consulting his phone for a few moments. "Not even close."

"Thank goodness," I breathed.

"That's a scary thought," Auggie said. "Stop scaring me, Cori."

"Okay. Want more Scotch?"

"Yeah."

"I'll get it," Nick offered and rose from his chair to wander into the kitchen.

⁓

Video—Drug Subject: Merle Askins

"There are no guarantees," the man holding the syringe said, his accent evident. "The final choice is yours."

"Guarantees?" Merle snorted a laugh. "The guarantee I have is that I'll be charged with treason and face a trial while lung cancer kills me. That's the guarantee I have. Give me the goddam drug. Do it now."

"Suit yourself." Askins watched as the needle was plunged into the IV line attached to his hand. He only had a moment to reflect before everything went dark.

⁓

Corinne

"Three weeks." Auggie set a tablet beside me while I ate a bowl of oatmeal for breakfast. "Three weeks, and they want the meeting at the White House."

I looked at the tablet—it showed his personal schedule. I'd never seen his personal schedule before. "How's Laci?" I asked while reading the list of attendees at the meeting between Madam President and President Zoran. I understood as I read that Auggie intended to bring three guests, as did Matt. Without asking, I knew Ilya, Nick and I would be going with Auggie. Maye, Opal and Richard would go with Matt.

"I'm leaving James out of it," Auggie said. "Besides, he's enjoying his new relationship. I don't want to ruin that."

I understood what he was saying—if the shit hit, he didn't want

James anywhere near it. James was human, after all. At least six guests at that meeting wouldn't be.

I still wanted to see the list that Zoran would bring, but that might not come until the last minute.

"Unless things go wrong before then, I'd like for you and Rafe to have a honeymoon," he added. "We've done nothing to celebrate your wedding, and that's not right."

"We're married under assumed names, Auggie," I stated flatly.

"I'll see to it that it's changed," he said. "I think Matt and I can arrange that, at least."

"What will it say—the amended marriage license?"

"It will say that Rafe Black married Corinne Watson, on the eighteenth of August," he said. "I wish I could put your real names there, but those people are dead, now. I hope you understand."

"I do. Thanks, Auggie. That's a nice wedding present."

"The underground facility near Chernobyl was shut down by the Ukraine government earlier," Auggie said. "They'll be at this meeting, too."

"I saw that," I nodded. So far, everybody of any importance would be there. They all wanted answers. France, Germany, the UK, several South American countries, Italy, Spain, Ukraine, Ireland, Japan, China, Canada, South Africa, Australia and at least a half dozen others would be there.

"I wouldn't want to be Zoran at this meeting," Auggie sighed. "I imagine France and Britain will demand their stolen crown jewels returned."

"He'll lay the blame on those imaginary criminals; you know he will," I huffed. "Besides, those crowns are in somebody else's vault right now—and the proceeds used to fund the insurgency in Iraq."

"Matt and I have shared that information with those attendees in the G20," he said. "They already know that getting their belongings back may be a lost cause."

"Any hint that Phillips may be involved?"

"None. I'm hoping Zoran will be backed into a corner and confess that much."

"I'll know if he's lying," I said.

"And that's why I want you there, giving me advice," he tapped his temple. "Madam President expects the same."

"I want pictures of everybody Zoran is bringing with him, including his."

"I'll arrange it."

"Thanks, Auggie."

"Is everything all right?" Ilya sat next to me on our bed. I'd settled there, just to stare into space.

"Everything just feels wrong, somehow," I said. "I know all those countries want to take their shots at Zoran and what he allowed Baikov and the others to do, likely with his knowledge, but I just don't like it."

"It's done, cabbage. This is what they want—Opal says that most of them can't wait to fling their accusations at Zoran."

"You probably wouldn't mind taking a swing at him," I said.

"I wouldn't swing. I'd crush," Ilya muttered. "His minions killed my son."

"Phillips' minions killed mine," I said.

"Why did Phillips give you the drug?" Ilya asked. "I fail to understand that."

I wanted to laugh at Ilya's question. I didn't.

"Because he was a fan of Harriett Majors," I grated. "He had no idea that I'd live, and likely, when he thought I wasn't a danger to him, he continued to let me live. He knows differently, now."

"You knew of this, although you disliked him as a politician?"

"Yes. I even sent signed books to the White House, per his secretary's request. That was before my trip to France, you understand? Darin decided to stay and visit the Louvre that day, instead of traveling to Wales, like we should have. We had reservations and everything. All that went right out the window."

"No punishment is harsh enough for that bastard," Ilya hissed.

"We have to catch him, first."

"After this meeting, we will hunt him down."

"Sounds good to me. All you have to do is convince Auggie. Where are we going for our honeymoon?" I asked.

"What?"

"Oh, Auggie said that we could have a honeymoon before the meeting."

"There are so many places I'd like to take you," Ilya's arms encircled me and squeezed.

"Too bad your friend who taught you how to make spaghetti sauce is dead. I wouldn't mind meeting him."

"His son is alive and still cooking for his restaurant," Ilya grinned mischievously.

"Want to?"

"Of course I do. There is a nice hotel not far away."

"Let me tell Auggie."

"Please do."

CHAPTER 17

*C**orinne*

We didn't stay at a hotel. We rented a small villa for two weeks. Just seeing Ilya walking through the house naked was worth every penny. He did put on pajama bottoms to cook breakfast, however.

"We will buy something like this when this ordeal is over," he promised, kissing me between bites of fruit and pancakes.

"I like having you all to myself, without somebody walking into the kitchen looking hungry," I said.

"Or sending us somewhere to do something," he grinned. "Promise me that we won't talk business while we're here," he added. "It was something I used to do when I took time away. I learned to cook Italian that way. I never discussed my work with anyone, and it was nice to walk away from it at times."

"I didn't discuss my work with anybody either," I straddled his lap. "Because that would have released spoilers."

"I remember." His hands went to my face and held it gently while he kissed me. "I recall wanting to meet you once, because I liked your books."

"That's nice, honey," I said between kisses. "Is it okay to say I want to fuck you now?" My fingers feathered through his dark hair while I watched a smile curl his mouth.

"All day, cabbage. All day," he replied.

Notes—Colonel Hunter

"This is the most recent photograph we could get of President Zoran," James handed a tablet to me.

"I hate to send this to Corinne," I sighed. "It can wait." I set the tablet aside. "She'll be back a week before the meeting anyway."

"We don't have a list of people Zoran is bringing with him," James said.

"That's what I'm most interested in," I said, tapping my finger on the tablet, which brought Zoran's features into a larger view. "If we see a Baikov clone," I shook my head.

"I say bring him on," James growled. "Rafe won't mind killing another one, I don't think."

"What's the report on Iraq?" I asked.

"Quiet. That worries me," James said. "You can bet they're plotting something, but I don't know what that could be."

My cell phone rang then—Matt Michaels was calling. "I'll guard the door," James said and left the office.

"I have intel from Russia," Matt said.

"What did you hear?"

"That three insurgent leaders were locked up after the attack on the Kremlin, while two others left the country aboard a Russian military plane."

"What the hell is that supposed to mean?" I asked. "I can't believe they don't have all five chained to a wall somewhere."

"It surprises me, too. None of mine know what to make of it, either."

"Any information on where the plane was headed?"

"Not at the moment, although I have people watching satellite feeds."

"Will you keep me informed on this?"

"I intend to. No word has come to the White House on the capture of those responsible for the bombing, so they're keeping everybody out of the loop."

"In case insurgents disappear without a trace?" I asked.

"Probably. I still can't figure out why they sent two out of there, though."

"You think they still have a hand in all that?"

"That would be frightening."

"Sure as hell would."

"Look, we'll talk later. I have a meeting with the President this afternoon."

"Sure thing."

We did talk later—when Matt informed me that we'd lost contact with the Russian military plane an hour earlier.

"There are reports of an explosion," Matt said over our secure cell phones. "No confirmation, yet, but that's the word on the ground."

"Where?"

"Somewhere over Iraq. It makes no sense, really, unless it's an accident of some sort. No word on debris or anything else."

"Survivors?" I asked.

"Not from the information I've gotten so far."

"This just gets stranger as time goes on," I said.

"That's for damn sure."

Corinne

The restaurant was small, with a dark-green awning over the front door next to a brick-lined street. *Trattoria Carano* was spelled out in green neon in the plate glass window. If Ilya hadn't made reservations, we wouldn't have gotten in.

I'd never seen Ilya so happy as when he sat across from me and ordered a bottle of wine in flawless Italian.

"Honey, they have cheese ravioli in a mushroom sauce," I whispered, tapping a finger on the menu.

"Have the spaghetti, too—you'll love it," he smiled. It didn't matter that nearly every woman in the place glanced his way from time to time—I was having my moment with my new husband, who was more relaxed now than I'd ever seen him.

Dressed in a black polo and jeans, he was attired appropriately for the restaurant, where everybody appeared casually untroubled. I'd worn a blue dress—at Ilya's urging. He claimed I looked wonderful, I accepted the compliment and we'd taken a cab to the restaurant.

A fruit and cheese plate, lightly drizzled with honey, was served first, with our wine. "European cheeses are always so good," I sighed, biting into a small wedge of Crotonese.

"Try the Pecorini Toscana," Ilya said.

"I won't have room for dinner," I said.

"Just a bite," he coaxed, lifting a thin wedge of the cheese and teasing me with it before feeding it to me.

"Good," I mumbled around the cheese.

The waiter offered half portions of spaghetti and ravioli, so I gratefully ordered that while Ilya ordered half spaghetti and half lasagna. He also asked whether the restaurant owner was there.

"My father knew his father," Ilya lied with a smile. "He taught my father how to make sauce, but my father's was never as good."

"He's here—I'll ask," the waiter said. The conversation took place in Italian—I was grateful to understand it.

Before long, Giovanni Carano arrived at our table with a huge smile. "Your father knew mine?" he beamed.

"He did. He said Gino taught him everything he knew about making sauce and meatballs."

"Tall?" Giovanni asked. "Blond hair? Russian, maybe?"

"Yes to all those things," Ilya laughed. "My father emigrated. I live in the U.S. This is my wife Cori; we're here on our honeymoon."

"Then the food and wine are my treat," Giovanni said. "Because I remember your father. He brought toys to me from many places."

"I think he was more than grateful for your father's friendship—and for his willingness to share cooking secrets."

"Hah," Giovanni laughed. "I still make salmon pie from a recipe given to my father."

"I'm glad to hear it—I use the same recipe," Ilya chuckled.

Dinner was extraordinary; Giovanni sat at our table to share a glass of wine after we finished eating. We learned his wife was babysitting his second grandchild at home, when she usually worked beside him at the restaurant.

Ilya still attempted to pay for our meal, but his offer was waved away. We were asked to come back, too, before we left Italy.

"That was nice—I felt normal for the first time in a long time," I said as we waited for our cab to arrive.

"Normal is in short supply, cabbage," he said. The cab pulled up, we climbed in and rode back to the villa, Ilya's arm around my shoulders while I leaned contentedly against him.

Notes—Colonel Hunter

"We have this." Matt set his cell phone in front of me—the one Corinne had provided.

"What is it?" I asked, tapping the image to make it larger.

"Just before the plane exploded, that dropped out of the cargo hold." Matt jerked his head toward the image on the phone.

"This looks like those aid packages they drop for needy areas," I said, watching the grainy satellite image of a rather large object falling slowly after a parachute opened above it.

"I might think that, too, if it hadn't dropped out of a Russian cargo plane two minutes before it blew up."

"So this was done deliberately. Any evidence of a distress call?"

"None that I know of."

"What do you think is in that package?"

"It's too big to hold only the bodies of two insurgent leaders. It's also too well packed and secured inside that rope mesh. If they wanted to dispose of bodies, they'd just toss 'em."

"Yeah. I get that. Looks like crates beneath those tarps," I said.

"That's my opinion, too. Here's the big question—what's in those crates?"

"Do you have someone working on approximate sizes and weights?"

"I do, and the numbers worry me. What would it take, do you suppose, to mollify the insurgents, after they found out the whole shipment of miniature rockets was useless? Remember, they wanted to bomb the hell out of something or somebody."

"Or several somethings and somebodies."

"Exactly. How many nuclear warheads might those crates contain?" Matt lifted an eyebrow.

Dropping my eyes back to the images, I blinked. "Six, maybe?" I lifted my eyes to Matt's again, begging him to say I was wrong.

He didn't. "Six to eight is what my experts say. Remember, they saw floppy disks in that underground section where the small rockets were manufactured. We know they've cleared out of there—Ukraine said all the equipment was gone when they went to look."

"So that could be in those crates too—the weapons and the system to launch."

"Possibly."

"You're saying the Russians gave them nuclear weapons to make up for the rocket fiasco? Holy fucking hell."

"My thoughts exactly."

"Colonel Hunter?" Maye stepped into my office, flanked by Nick and Opal.

"I need a message sent to Rafe and Corinne," I sighed.

"I'll do my best," she said.

"Have a seat," I gestured toward the chairs in front of my desk. "I have to explain things to you, first."

~

Corinne

Ilya and I were a tangle of nudity beneath a sheet that only half-covered us. Both of us were asleep when Maye's message came. Without explaining everything, the urgency in her sending forced both of us up in bed, while Ilya's arms wrapped around me in alarm.

Something was terribly wrong and Auggie was calling us back to D.C.

~

"Cori, can you tell me anything about this?" I had to squint in the sudden, bright light of Auggie's office as a tablet was shoved in my face.

My brain froze for several seconds as I stared at the video images. Yes, I knew something about that, and it terrified me. The insurgents now had warheads—plural—and the archaic computer system to launch those weapons. I almost couldn't get intelligible words out to say those things to Auggie.

"Matt says it may take a few weeks for them to build the launch site to send those things very far, and that we may or may not be able to destroy any of them in flight. All it will take is one getting through to its target and millions could die. They'll target us, but what if they target someone closer to home, too?" Auggie asked. I'd just confirmed his worst fears by telling him what I knew.

"Like Israel, perhaps?" Ilya gruffed. He took the tablet away and studied the video, replaying it twice to examine every detail.

"We're concerned about that, yes, but they could also target any number of their neighbors—Saudi Arabia, Jordan, Kuwait—you name it."

"What if they target us and the European Union?" Nick asked. "Won't there be some sort of fallout, even if we shoot those fuckers down?"

"Auggie, has anybody had eyes on these things when they landed?" I asked.

"Matt and I are meeting in half an hour to discuss that," he said, his dark gaze filled with worry. "The President wants to be informed of possible countermeasures soon, and we have to take a viable plan to her."

"Are we included in the meeting with Director Michaels?" Ilya asked.

"Yes."

"Good."

"Cori, we're hoping you can do something about this," Auggie pleaded.

"Auggie, I can't detect those things with my radar. To me, that says the enemy had something to do with that."

"It's almost like he can be in several places at once," Nick growled.

"Nick, that's the scariest thing I've heard today, and that includes nuclear war with the insurgents," I said.

"What about photographs? We have some of Zoran and his aides," Auggie suggested. "Think you can tell anything from those?"

"I sure as hell hope so," I said. "If not, we're working at this problem blindfolded."

Matt was there when the photographs were handed to me. I stared at President Zoran for a long time.

"Cori, you'd better tell me something soon," Auggie begged.

"Auggie—this is fucked up—just like he's fucked up," I handed the photograph back to him, as if he could see what I did in Zoran's eyes. "There's a cloud on his brain, like some of the others I've seen, but there's also some confusion in him, too, that I've never detected in any others. He knows he should be more powerful and in better control, but it's as if something stronger came along and is preventing that, somehow."

"You're right—that's fucked up," Matt agreed. "I don't suppose you can see who the stronger one is?"

"Nope—that's part of the fog on his brain," I confirmed. "Like what he truly is has been completely blocked by that fog. I can't see through it."

"Does he have knowledge of the warheads?" Matt asked.

"If he does, it's hiding behind the fog, too. I get the idea he didn't issue those orders; somebody else did."

"Baikov, or his clone," Auggie sat back in his chair with a shake of his head.

"More than possible," I said. "But it could also be our enemy making his presence known."

"How the hell is he going to take a country back, if important parts of said country have been blown to bits by nuclear warheads?" Auggie's voice was a near-shout.

"A play for time, perhaps?" Ilya suggested. "To mollify the insurgents after the failure of the rockets? After all, those warheads are useless without the proper launch codes."

"True," Matt nodded thoughtfully. "Still, they must want something from the insurgents, other than to keep them from bombing the Kremlin whenever they get their undies in a twist."

"It's a cinch the insurgents didn't pay for those rockets, so it can't be because they paid good money for nothing," Opal said. "We've determined that the mastermind behind all this is funding their operation, anyway."

"With stolen crowns, et cetera and so forth," Nick agreed.

"From the *sale* of stolen crowns, et cetera," I clarified. Sadly, an Asian dictator to be named later was in possession of most of it.

"True," Nick acknowledged my clarification. "Do you think it's all a ploy to discredit Madam President?" He directed the question to Auggie.

"Possibly," Auggie replied. "We've thought that all along, though."

"Six warheads," Opal mused. "Who would be the biggest targets, if they wanted to piss everybody off?" She tapped her chin with a finger as she turned her gaze on Matt.

"I thought they already pissed everybody off with the plane bombings," Nick offered.

"But that's been tied to Russia," Maye began. "Oh. You think?"

"They'll point fingers at the insurgents, and my money's on the fact that they'll make that theory stick, somehow," Matt rose from his chair in a rush. "After all, we never saw the ones on the mountain in Colombia, firing those rockets. The one in Argentina was a known enemy of the Russian government, who could have sided with the insurgents. We only know the Russians were supplying the rockets. Don't we?"

"Coupled with the fact that they're setting their planes down in South America and Cuba—and flying on the edge of U.S. airspace," Ilya added.

"It'll only take a photograph or two—conveniently provided by them or a South American government—to point a finger at the insurgents, who'd just love to put those notches on their belts anyway, regardless of whether they were responsible or not," Auggie nodded.

"This is more than confusing," Richard said.

"Twisted mind, twisted plot," Matt said.

"I'm beginning to agree with that assessment," I said. Ilya's arms draped around me as he pulled me back against his chest. He understood, just as I did, that somewhere, somehow, a madman was in charge and killing as many as possible to further his sick agenda.

"I'm sorry about your honeymoon," Auggie took a seat at the kitchen island, looking droopier than a bloodhound.

"There's no way I could stay on a honeymoon when this sort of crap is happening," I said.

"Corinne, what will you do if those missiles are fired?"

"You know what I'd do," I said, turning away and opening our makeshift liquor cabinet. Ice cubes clinked into a glass as Ilya dropped them in; I poured Scotch for Auggie. Ilya set the glass in front of him, before pouring a glass for himself.

"What if that's what they want—to feel you out?" Auggie asked.

"Auggie, they've seen and heard enough already, I think," I said. "Why would they keep doing dumb stuff after all that?"

"To see if you have a weak spot," Ilya poured Scotch for me and pointed to a barstool.

"So they steal crowns, jewels and artwork, to sell to fund an insurgency," I said. "Then, they attempt to destroy our Program, because they learn we might be able to stop them," I began to tick items off on my fingers.

"When their first several attempts failed, they set the creatures free, assuming we'd be sent to look for them. After we solve that riddle and get rid of all that, they send somebody with a clouded mind against me, because they know I can see through most people. Still, we manage to survive what should have blown us to bits in Alaska. After that, they think they've killed us off and start bombing planes from different countries, possibly intending to point a finger at the insurgents, who'd love to start World War III anyway. When the shipment of rockets they send to the insurgents is rendered harmless by us, they hand over bigger bombs that need floppy drives to work. Is any of this making any sense to anybody?" I asked.

"Is that meeting going to have sufficient security?" Ilya asked.

"The best we can provide."

"They've managed to keep us busy, haven't they?" Richard said. He and Maye walked in and took seats at the island. Ilya held up the bottle of Scotch. Richard nodded and rose to collect two more glasses.

"Fuckers," Auggie huffed, emptying his glass in one swallow and holding it out for a refill.

"We still have to consider where Merle Askins fits into this," Maye said.

"I have an idea he's either dead or a drug survivor," I said. "I can't get a line on him, either way."

"I hope he's dead," Ilya hissed.

"The media says he's in another country with no extradition treaty," Richard said.

"While that could be a probability, we can't say that for certain,"

Auggie supplied. "We have no evidence as to where he is—last we heard, it looked as if his vehicle was headed north."

"Toward Canada, maybe, where Hal Prentice is holed up?"

"Maybe." Auggie's one-word answer was accompanied by a shrug.

"So we wait until they start lobbing missiles, which Corinne will have to deal with?" Opal and Matt joined us at the island.

"Looks that way," Auggie agreed. "I hate this," he added.

~

Video—Drug Subject: Merle Askins

"Too bad about your blood type—we could have created something better if you'd had one of the blood types we've already used," the doctor nodded as Merle Askins held the hand mirror up to examine his face.

"This is beyond fucked up," Merle threw the mirror at the wall with a snarl. It shattered with a crash—its glass and plastic shards spattering across the sterile tile of his hospital room.

"You're stronger, now—much stronger," the doctor pointed out. "Perhaps that will compensate for the scales. Prove yourself to us and we'll enroll you in the replication program."

~

Ilya

"My darling, you must stop worrying." I found Corinne sitting up in bed in the middle of the night, arms wrapped around knees, her head lowered. My hand automatically went to the tender skin at the back of her neck; I massaged those muscles gently, as they were knotted with tension.

"I can't turn it off, honey," she murmured. "I can't shut it out like I did in Alaska. My son died because of that."

This was a conversation we hadn't had, and that worried me. "Cabbage, all of us face terrible things. No matter how good we are, we cannot prevent all of them from happening." The sheets rustled as

I shoved them back and worked myself into a sitting position beside her.

"Will you answer a question for me, then?" she sighed.

"Always."

"What if," she began and then stopped.

"What if what?" I said when she failed to continue.

"Ilya, I love you more than anything," she said.

"And I you."

"But what if—what if I'm faced with a choice—of saving you from something awful, or letting the enemy get away?"

"Cabbage, listen to me," I said, pulling her face around so our eyes met. "Get that piece of excrement. No matter what. I have been taking care of myself for a very long time. Let me worry about me in that situation. Take the bastard down."

"Then you do the same, Ilya," she said before kissing me fiercely and drawing away to speak again. "No matter what my situation is, kill him if you can."

"I have never had a love such as this," I said. "We understand one another."

"I've waited for you my whole life," she said and kissed me again.

"Colonel Hunter, I have questions," I said the following morning. I'd left Corinne asleep in bed—she'd finally succumbed after I loved her into exhaustion.

"About?"

"Harriett Majors. What was her relationship with her husband like? Do you know?"

"I-uh, well, see James. He was curious, you understand."

"Of course. Thank you, Colonel Hunter."

"Rafe," Colonel Hunter's tone stopped me from leaving the kitchen.

"What is it?" I turned to ask.

"Matt and I—want to have a discussion with you. Do you think Corinne will sleep another hour or so?"

"I hope so; she was awake much of the night."

"Good. This is important, and we wouldn't approach you like this if we weren't concerned."

"I understand," I said, although I waited for an explanation. Director Michaels arrived in twenty minutes; we spent the following hour discussing many things before I went looking for James. I still wanted to satisfy my curiosity about Harriett Majors' husband.

"Word has it he was a cold fish—perfect for a trial attorney, not so perfect as a husband or father," James said, copying a file onto a flash drive and handing it to me. "He thought Cori's—well, Harriett's writing was just a quaint little hobby—his words, not mine—until she started making more money than he did. Some of their neighbors were interviewed after the deaths were reported. Even before Darin Sr. was diagnosed with pancreatic cancer, they slept in separate bedrooms."

"Why not get a divorce?" I asked.

"He was Catholic—she wasn't. I don't know that she ever asked for a divorce, but he'd have refused it. She brought him clients, too, once people knew who he was married to."

"So he starved her for attention and love, perhaps?"

"It's possible. Dr. Shaw thinks that's exactly how it was—he did this research and gave it to me because it's all public record anyway. Once Darin Sr. got sick and his time was limited, she bent over backward to see he got everything he wanted, including a visit to the Louvre instead of going to Wales that day."

"And she was still determined to avenge his death, because it was so violent and undeserved," I said.

"She could have killed the original Baikov without thinking too hard about it," James pointed out. "She let you have that honor."

"Yes, she did."

"Because she knew how important that was to you."

"I know this."

"Commander Black," Nathan Cross walked into James' office with an armload of files.

"Commander?"

"You've been given titles—all of you," Nathan smiled. "Madam President has to introduce you formally at the meeting, so you have to have a title."

"Interesting," I responded. "What is Corinne's title?"

"Special Attaché to the Department of Defense."

"Classic," James laughed.

Corinne

"Special Attaché?" I'd wandered into the kitchen to find Auggie, James, Nathan and Ilya there, having coffee. James was grinning as I made coffee for myself. He announced that I had a new title while my coffee dribbled into a waiting cup.

"We can't offer a military title—you could be questioned about your service, of which there is none," Auggie pointed out judiciously. "Rafe probably has all that squirreled away in his head anyway, so it was a cinch for him."

"I am a Lieutenant Colonel, as is Maye," Nick beamed as he walked into the kitchen and headed for the coffee maker.

"Everybody outranks me?" I huffed.

"Christ," Auggie covered his face with a hand.

"Corinne, these titles mean nothing," Leo said as he walked in with Maye and Richard.

"Hey, now," Nick protested.

"Christ," Auggie repeated.

"I don't believe it was meant as a slight, cabbage," Ilya said.

"No? You're a Commander. I'm a glorified secretary or something."

"I'll get it changed," Auggie sighed.

"No, the damage is done." Lifting my coffee cup, I stalked out of the kitchen before transporting myself to Tybee Island.

CHAPTER 18

*I*lya

"She'll come back," Richard attempted to calm everyone. "She always does."

"Why did this upset her so much?" Nathan asked.

"You'd have to know more of Corinne's history to start guessing at that, and most of us are still in the dark about it," Maye responded.

"I think it's when we question her talent or ability that she gets upset," James said. "Remember the Ukraine-Crimea-Baikov thing? Rafe thought she was delusional when she said she'd take care of the bunker and boom—off she went."

"At least she dropped you off in Matt's office first," Opal said. She'd come late to our difficulty, but she'd been updated quickly.

"Exactly. Corinne won't leave us hanging out to dry," Richard said, pointing a finger in Opal's direction.

Cabbage? I sent mindspeech to her.

Go away, she replied. *I'm having a snit.*

My love, the last thing anyone here would do is upset you. It wasn't meant that way.

How was it meant, then?

I have no idea who arranged these titles. You understand that your title will ensure that you stay close to Colonel Hunter? Of all of us, he may be the most vulnerable. He is not a drug survivor, my darling.

What about the President?

Maye and Nick will be with her. You are to be with Colonel Hunter, who will watch a live feed of the meeting from a room close by.

I'm being excluded from the meeting? I could tell she was even more upset by that.

My love, do not look at it that way. There is a reason, I assure you. I will be positioned near President Zoran at the table while the meeting takes place. These are precautionary measures, you understand.

Do you have orders, Ilya? Concerning President Zoran?

In a way. Come home and we will discuss it in private.

Then meet me in our bedroom. I don't want to see the others right now. I fail to understand what keeping me from the meeting will accomplish, other than placing people in danger.

I understand. I'll be in the bedroom soon.

Corinne

"What did they tell you, Ilya?" I demanded the moment he arrived in our bedroom and shut the door. Auggie and Matt had planned this somehow, only I failed to see the reason behind it.

"I am to deliver justice if Zoran makes any attempts or orders his aides to harm anyone," Ilya shrugged.

"Auggie told you to?" With arms crossed tightly over my chest, I refused to move any closer—we had a standoff going while on opposite sides of the bed.

"Colonel Hunter and Director Michaels, yes," he admitted.

"Do you understand how things could go very wrong in all this?" I asked. "What if somebody is waiting to fire warheads if anyone touches a hair on Zoran's head?"

"That has been discussed," he nodded, his eyes half-closed. I fought the urge to drop my shield and read everything in him that I could.

"Who else was in on this discussion? Want to tell me that?"

"Corinne, I think you should allow that to remain secret," he argued. "I'm going against orders to tell you what I have."

"Right. I'm just the secretary. I remember that, now." I turned away, considering where I should go—how far I should transport myself away. After all, it didn't sound as if they wanted me anywhere near the meeting.

"Corinne, they worry about many things. One of those things is you. Surely you understand that."

"Right." He knew I wasn't buying it.

"They're concerned about what might happen if you're injured or killed."

"Because then their asses would be in a sling, is that right?"

"I see I'm only upsetting you further. That is not my intention. I love you. You know this."

"I have a bad feeling about this," I snapped. "Being left out of it makes it worse."

"What's going on in there?" Auggie's voice arrived, followed by pounding on the bedroom door.

"You'd be sorry if we were having sex," I shouted while opening the door with power. It swung open with a screech and hit the doorstop so hard it nearly bounced back in Auggie's face.

"We are merely having a disagreement," Ilya said calmly. I knew he was anything but calm, but then he was a former spy, more than capable of hiding his true feelings.

Colonel August Hunter stood at the threshold of our bedroom, wearing a huge frown. James stood right behind him, and after that came Matt, Opal, Nick, Maye, Richard and Nathan.

"Those people I left alive at the Pilchuck facility?" I said as I shouldered my way past Auggie and the others. "They're dead. They holed up in that train caboose outside Granite Falls and the enemy found them. They were shot to death. There's blood everywhere," I announced as I made my way toward the kitchen.

"Were they questioned? Did they know anything?" Auggie demanded as he followed me.

"They didn't know a damn thing," I yelled. "That's why I left them alive in the first place. They had nothing to give their former boss—except their lives."

"Did you know when it was happening?" Matt asked quietly as I slammed a coffee cup beneath the brewer. Everybody had followed me to the kitchen by that time.

"Director Michaels," I began. "I knew when it was happening. If the enemy is not directly involved with an event like that, I know exactly what is happening. I knew when every one of those planes went down, along with a ton of other things before that. I was overwhelmed for a while in Alaska, so I shut it off for a few hours. My son died during that blackout period. Do you understand how hard it is not to interfere with any of that?"

"Why didn't you interfere?" Auggie was now furious, his voice an angry hiss.

"There are problems with that," I said, "if I'm not directly involved or in physical danger because of it. Destroying those creatures, killing insurgents and disarming those rockets was a stretch at times, but those points can be argued in my favor. Outright interfering can cause ripples in the timeline otherwise and I assure you, that could be a very bad thing. I have to use only the abilities I had last time—I just wasn't aware at the time what all those abilities were. There's a reason—you have to believe me. Going behind my back with Ilya only makes things worse."

"What were you last time?" Richard kept his voice even as he asked.

"You won't recognize it if I told you," I shrugged.

"Tell me anyway. To satisfy my curiosity."

"I was a Karathian Witch last time," I huffed. "A powerful one."

"You can do so much more, this time," Richard pointed out.

"Look—Karathian Witches and Warlocks have to have their power awakened when they're young, or they are limited in what they can do. I was limited last time, because the awakening wasn't performed. I bypassed that little requirement, this time."

"Because?" Leo had arrived and joined the conversation.

"I can't—and won't—tell you that. It's important that I don't."

"What does Karathian even mean? I've never heard that word, before," Nick said.

"Karathia is so far from here you can't even see a glimmer of its sun's light," I said. "Stop asking questions. I'm still pissed."

"We need to deescalate," Matt said. "We're on the same side here, remember?"

Stop acting like you don't know anything, you pretentious schmuck. I slammed those words into his head and stalked out of the kitchen, keeping my coffee cup from spilling by employing power.

Opal

"It can't be," Matt paced inside an empty suite at what Corinne had dubbed the ugly building in Arlington.

"What if it is?" I asked.

"You know there's only supposed to be one."

"Yet we're looking at fallout from the drug," I argued. "After all, her talents in the first incarnation," I didn't get to finish, Matt held up a hand.

"Yeah. You're right," he eventually nodded his agreement. "But you think she can see right through?"

"I think that one hundred percent," I said.

"I don't want to send a message to you know who without being absolutely sure," he pointed out.

"You can say her name, nobody's listening," I said.

"I just don't want to call her attention to this—she asked us to take care of as much of the crap that comes along as we possibly can without interrupting her."

"I think it's time somebody knew that the drug landed here," I released a sigh. "Somebody besides us, that is."

"Fine. You tell 'em," Matt threw his hands up. "Tell them we haven't done one damn thing about sorting this out—that we're blind to the enemy's location and are relying on somebody else to take care of it."

"So far, she's building a case to keep her life," I snapped. "That stuff is illegal everywhere else for a reason. You know how others look at drug recipients—no matter what form they're in."

"It's a death sentence in most places," Matt frowned. "Even the race who created it millennia ago will now destroy what they find and kill the recipients, whether those recipients had anything to do with getting the drug or not. We have volunteers here, who really didn't know what they were signing up for. And then there's Corinne, who never agreed to take it, either time."

"And she's the most talented of all of them," I said. "If anybody gets us out of this mountain of shit, it'll be her."

"You know why I told Hunter it wasn't a good idea to have her at the meeting."

"I do, but you see what kind of problem that created, don't you?"

"We don't need a repeat of what happened the last time someone like her died."

"I hear that, all right."

~

Ilya

A day and a half passed before Corinne came home after disappearing a second time. From an unemotional standpoint, I understood. I couldn't remain unemotional, however, whenever Corinne was involved.

A part of me wanted to continue the argument. Another part wanted only to hold her close. I chose to remain silent as she walked into the kitchen during dinner, which Nathan and I prepared for the others. I'd learned that Nathan liked to cook and was quite good at it.

Corinne went straight for a protein drink inside the refrigerator, uncapped the bottle, drank some of it and turned to walk out of the kitchen again.

"Wait," Colonel Hunter held up a hand.

"You're about to tell me you can't handle any more of my disappearing trick," she waved a hand. "Got it. I'm going to the media room. Carry on."

We watched as she walked out the door and made a turn for the media room, just as she said. "Fuck," I muttered.

"Finish your meal," Dr. Shaw suggested. "Leave her alone for now. She'd have stayed in the kitchen if she wanted company."

"Screw that," James said and rose from his place at the island. I didn't intend for him to get to Corinne before me, so I beat him to the door.

~

Corinne

No matter how much I tried to squash them, panic attacks had threatened to overwhelm me the past two days. Something was wrong, I could feel it, but whatever it was stayed frustratingly outside my search field.

Less than five minutes passed before Ilya and James arrived in the media room, at a near-run. "Cori, please don't leave like that again; I nearly had a heart attack," James rasped.

Ilya, in better shape and breathing more evenly, wore a slight frown as he took a seat beside me on the sofa. I'd settled there, my knees drawn to my chest, while I sipped the protein drink I'd filched from the kitchen.

"Will you talk to me?" Ilya breathed. He hesitated to touch me— worried, no doubt, that I'd disappear again.

"Depends on what you want to talk about," I said, refusing to look at him.

"I know we haven't been completely open with you," he sighed and leaned back on the sofa.

"When were you going to tell me that Auggie will be at the meeting and I'll be the only one watching a live feed from somewhere else?"

"We were working up to that," he admitted.

"I'll uh, just go," James mumbled and walked out of the room, his footsteps muffled by carpet that hadn't been changed in decades.

"I hate the carpet in the hallway," I said.

"We can worry about the carpet later," Ilya said. "You'll be watching a live feed, Corinne. You can rush in if you're needed—you know you can—at the first sign that something is wrong."

"Sure—just magically appear in front of some of the most powerful world leaders? You may as well hang out a neon sign telling all of them that aliens are on the loose."

"Cori, I think you may be fretting over nothing. Maye, Rafe, Opal and I will be there, in case things get out of hand," Nick said as he strode into the room and settled on a nearby chair.

"I disagree." My forehead now bumped against the tops of my knees and I refused to look at him. "Conspiracy theories are everywhere, still, even after all the creatures died. People on those websites and some in the mainstream media still believe they're in danger. They're not wrong, either, they just don't know what they should really be afraid of. If I were still human, I'd be terrified, too."

"I know you worry." Ilya braved my anger and reached out to massage the back of my neck.

"I'm concerned that insurgents will fire nuclear weapons at specific countries while their leaders are tied up in a meeting," Auggie said, taking the chair next to Nick's. "That's why we need you outside the meeting and able to do what you do without anyone noticing."

"Nice try, Auggie," I lifted my head to blink at him. "Now, I'm only going to ask this question once—are you absolutely sure you don't want me in that meeting?"

"Corinne, I am absolutely sure," he said.

"Fine. You live with the consequences, then," I said. Dropping my feet to the floor, I stood and walked away. The ugly carpet changed to wood flooring beneath my feet as I left Ilya, Nick and Auggie behind.

Ilya

Corinne refused to discuss the matter further. It acted as a barrier between us, too, whenever I convinced her to make love. A sadness had come over her, too—one I couldn't banish, no matter how hard I tried.

Every day, Colonel Hunter and Director Michaels had a meeting. I was invited often, to discuss seating at the large table, and how difficult it might be to get to President Zoran from three seats away.

Too, Zoran wanted two guards with him; they'd stand against the wall behind him during the meeting. Nick would be placed five seats to my right, on Madam President's left side, while Maye would sit to her right. Colonel Hunter and Director Michaels would sit on the opposite side of the table, with Opal placed between them.

Colonel Hunter did make a concession, though—he asked Richard Farrell to stay with Corinne inside a smaller room nearby, where the live feed could be seen on several monitors. Hidden cameras would be placed strategically inside the meeting room, so that every attendee would have their image relayed to at least one of the monitors.

I understood why Colonel Hunter wanted Richard with Corinne—he wanted to know if nuclear warheads were launched and Corinne disappeared as a result. Richard was tasked with sending a text if that happened.

I didn't fail to notice that Corinne became quieter after every meeting I attended with Colonel Hunter and Director Michaels. Often, Nick, Maye and Opal were there, too, as they'd be directly involved if pandemonium occurred during the meeting.

Colonel Hunter held off telling Corinne to stand back and let us take care of things unless they went too far—that would come the day of the meeting, which was now two days away.

No additional word had come on the location of the warheads, and the insurgents had settled for beheading two hapless relief workers they'd kidnapped from a small border town; they'd gone to help treat an infection that had run rampant.

Corinne, to distract herself, I'm sure, set about transforming the ugly building. Yes, it still looked the same on the outside. On the inside, it was anyone's dream, from an atrium filled with plants and a fountain to luxurious suites decorated with comfortable furniture and the latest entertainment technology.

Nick attempted to hug her when he found the latest gaming

system and a horrendously large television screen installed in his suite.

She'd brushed him off, choosing to walk away, instead.

Our suite was an area of tranquility. The kitchen was something I'd dreamed of in the past and fully intended to get for myself someday.

Corinne had given it to me now.

She listened while I talked about anything except what was important while we cooked. The others showed up for meals and often attempted to engage her in conversation. They barely received replies to direct questions.

Corinne was cutting herself off from all of us.

Notes—Colonel Hunter

"I've gotten the silent treatment from Laci in the past," I said. "This is worse."

"Yeah." Matt didn't meet my eyes. He felt just as guilty as I did, but wasn't about to back down. For whatever reason, he'd insisted that Corinne be kept from the meeting and the President agreed with him.

Opal, at times, looked as if she'd lost her best friend when Corinne failed to respond or volunteer anything. As badly as Opal was taking this, Rafe was worse. The moment Corinne was out of sight, deadly silence would descend and he'd only respond if spoken to directly.

Even worse, Corinne appeared fragile. Leo Shaw was concerned, but couldn't get her to agree to a session. Unless things changed, I wasn't sure it would do any good anyway.

At least Laci was keeping her appointments with Shaw—she was looking forward to this being over, hoping, I'm sure, that everything would return to normal once the meeting took place.

I wished I could say the same thing. Corinne was upset about it, and if I'd learned anything in the nearly seven years I'd known her, it was to be concerned right along with her.

Rafe refused to discuss any difficulties between him and Cori, which was admirable and frustrating at the same time. Shaw had invited him for a session after Corinne's refusal—Rafe refused as well.

~

Corinne

"Isn't this premature? You've only known one another for a few weeks," Maye said as she, Richard and James walked into the kitchen the morning of the meeting.

Ilya worked nearby, covering a breakfast casserole with shredded cheese and olives before placing it in the oven. Automatically, I began brewing coffee. I understood, too, without asking, that James and Nathan wanted to be married.

"We don't live in the dark ages, anymore," James pointed out.

"That's not what I'm saying," Maye said. "I'm just saying to get engaged and set a date, instead of rushing into it."

"If you set a date, Corinne and I will stand with you," Ilya said after shutting the oven door and turning toward James.

"Cori, will you be there for us?" James implored.

"If you get married, I'll be there," I said. "Even if I have to move Heaven and Earth to do it."

"That's two whole sentences," Richard smiled. "More than anyone's gotten from her in days."

"Hmmph," I muttered and went back to making coffee.

"What's cooking?" Auggie arrived with Leo and sat down at the island.

"Breakfast enchilada casserole," Ilya said.

"I love that," Leo beamed. "Thank you."

Cori, Opal sent while dipping casserole onto her plate twenty minutes later.

Opal? I returned.

Always remember I'm on your side, she said. *Always.*

I appreciate the thought, but I'm not sure how that might help me in the future, I replied.

You never know, she gave a slight shrug. "Aren't you hungry?" she said aloud.

"Not really." I made more coffee. The others were eating, drinking and talking as if the weight of the world hadn't settled like a heavy blanket over the lot of us.

∽

"He's holed up at the Russian Embassy and has refused to see anyone other than his aides and the new Ambassador since his arrival yesterday," Madam President said after we were ushered into the Oval Office and the door was shut behind us.

Repairs to the office had been made in record time, although a few things still remained to be done. Those things were cosmetic only, as Madam President needed the space to work.

She was referring to Russian President Zoran, although she hadn't mentioned names. "The German Chancellor is offended that he refused to talk over dinner last night at his embassy, the French President is angry on many levels and wants a personal apology, of course, along with finding the culprits inside Zoran's government responsible for handing dangerous weapons to terrorists. He wants to put them on trial—in France," Madam President continued. "The UK is understandably upset, and that doesn't include the fact that the same people are likely behind the theft of their crown jewels."

She then went on at length about all the other world leaders— Ukraine and Australia included—who'd been wronged and whose citizens had died on Zoran's watch.

The Secretary of State had been busy, attempting to calm everyone while delivering messages from Zoran—that rogues in his government had somehow been involved in selling secret technology to the insurgents. He'd even gone so far as to offer proof, but that didn't fly with any of us.

It didn't surprise me in the least that Zoran wouldn't take responsibility—somebody had likely told him to do just that. It made me wonder what else they'd told him to do. None of the photographs

I'd been shown even hinted at what that might be, but then the photographs I had weren't recent, either.

I wanted to set my eyes on Zoran the moment the live feed was up and running. Worry still gnawed at me while panic threatened—Leo Shaw had been included on the live feed roster at the last minute, because I'd been shaky after breakfast.

That's when Auggie leveled the last bit of frustration to the heap I'd already dealt with. "I don't want you to come in that room unless there's no other option," he said while Madam President nodded her approval. "Let us handle any problems that arise."

"Is that your final word, Colonel Hunter?" I asked, my voice as cold and emotionless as I could make it.

"By my orders," the President said.

"Fine," I said. I didn't say another thing as we filed out of the Oval Office, Richard, Leo and I going toward a small room equipped with several screens; the rest toward the much larger meeting room.

Notes—Colonel Hunter

Words are things that can never be taken back, no matter how often you might wish it otherwise. Matt exchanged several glances with Opal as we walked down the hall toward the Cabinet Room; Corinne was herded toward the Press Secretary's office farther down the hall, where the live feed would be shown on several screens.

She'd called me Colonel Hunter, in a voice I'd never heard before. Something was broken between us, and I worried that it couldn't be fixed.

Foreign leaders were already arriving; I watched the French President and the German Chancellor arrive, one after the other. They were ushered into the Cabinet Room by White House employees.

Corinne disappeared into the Press Secretary's office. I almost called out to her. I didn't.

≈

Corinne

"Have a seat in here," the Press Secretary smiled as he indicated a small cubicle inside his office. It was lined with six monitors, each designated for a different camera hidden in the Cabinet Room.

They weren't on, yet. I fidgeted. I must have made some sort of frustrated noise, too—Richard held out a hand to touch my shoulder.

"Corinne, they'll be turned on soon," Leo said softly.

Snow appeared on each screen first before images appeared. In fact, I believe I heard the screams and shouts first, before the images appeared on six screens. Richard, poor man, watched as Maye, standing in front of the President to protect her, was nearly cut in half by exploding bullets a half-dozen lizard-like troops fired after appearing from nowhere.

CHAPTER 19

otes—Colonel Hunter

At the time, I had no idea who'd attacked us. Maye was dead, Nick wounded, from their attempts to protect the President. At least four world leaders were already dead, their blood spattered over everything as armored, lizard-like creatures fired among us, the shots silent—the damage their bullets caused anything but.

Opal, still between Matt and me, had pulled a weapon from beneath her jacket and fired back at the creatures. While I might have believed these creatures were part of a force sent by the enemy, I was wrong.

I didn't learn that until later, however.

Zoran stood behind his two guards, who were shooting at the armored intruders, just as Rafe was shooting.

The French President died before my eyes while Opal took aim, her bullets ricocheting off the shield surrounding the creature who'd done the killing.

Rafe, though, his shield up and strong, downed the creature with a shot from the unusual weapon he carried before taking aim at another and killing him, too.

Only one or two of the attendees had managed to get through the door; one of the assassins went after them, shouting in a language I'd never heard. A huge chunk of the doorway was blasted to dust with a terrible noise as Rafe fired at him and missed.

Three were still up and firing as Nick, bleeding from at least two wounds, pulled Madam President to the floor and shoved her beneath the sturdy, wooden table. He was shot in the back for his efforts. He died as Corinne walked through the door.

If I hadn't seen it myself, I'd never have believed it.

She was herself when she walked in; she transformed before my eyes.

Eight feet tall or taller. Blue skin. Pale, blonde hair. Fury in bright blue eyes. All three lizard-like invaders took aim at her. I opened my mouth to shout. Nothing came out. Instead, I watched, filled with terror and wonder as she lifted her hands, weapons firing all around her, each assailant doing his best to take her down.

I'll remember the wash of that power as long as I live.

Each lizard-man disappeared in a storm of glowing sparks, as if he'd been reduced to atoms before winking out of existence.

Dropping to my knees, I fought for breath—discovering that I'd been holding it for what felt like an eternity.

~

Ilya

Zoran's gaze leveled on Corinne—at least she'd been Corinne when she'd walked into the Cabinet Room. What she'd become after that I didn't recognize. Yes, I was motionless in shock when Zoran spoke.

"You," he snapped, drawing my attention away from Corinne. Jerking my head around, I stared into his eyes.

That, as it turned out, was the worst mistake I'd ever made. "You will not harm me," he said. I felt the command grip my mind. It had an ugly, sickening feel to it—I understood, then, what Corinne had meant when she'd described the fog on other's minds. The gun shook in my hand—I wanted to shoot Zoran and found I couldn't. A slow smile formed on Zoran's lips before he turned toward Corinne.

∽

Notes—Colonel Hunter

"Very nicely done," Zoran spoke to Corinne in the sudden silence. "I see now how effective you can be at killing." One of his guards was dead, the other wounded in the shoulder. He was unscathed.

"Hello, President Phillips," Corinne said. She kept the shape she'd transformed into, crossing her arms over her chest as she stared at the one we'd believed to be Zoran.

"Well, I can't let you live after that little announcement," Zoran bared his teeth in a caricature of a smile. With bodies piled around us and blood from the dead and wounded soaking into the rug beneath the table, Zoran wanted to bandy words with Corinne. "Kill yourself," Zoran commanded.

"That means nothing to me," Corinne snapped. Zoran took a step back, a fleeting expression of surprise crossing his features.

Rafe, stunned by what he was seeing, stared at the tall, blue creature before him, speaking with Corinne's voice. I understood, then, why Cori had never revealed her true self to us. Rafe had no idea what to do, now.

"You had the same blood type as Zoran, didn't you?" Corinne asked.

"Yes—right again. That's another nail in your coffin." Zoran took another step backward, placing his one remaining guard between himself and Corinne.

"He was born to a drug survivor, wasn't he?" Corinne hammered at Zoran/Phillips, while Rafe and I blinked stupidly at both of them.

"Colonel Hunter," Opal pulled at my sleeve and spoke softly, attempting to move me toward the door.

"Get Hunter and Madam President out of here," Matt hissed on my other side.

Aside from us, only Madam President and the Ukrainian President had survived the first attack by the lizard-men. The Ukrainian President was already limping toward the door—at least he had the sense to do that.

"You need to come, too," I hissed back at Matt.

"I have a problem with any of you leaving," Zoran/Phillips turned toward us.

"I have a problem with your problem," Corinne announced.

"You are such a fool," Zoran/Phillips laughed humorlessly. "You," he turned toward Rafe. "Kill her."

My heart stopped when Rafe turned his weapon toward Corinne. I think I began to realize at that moment where all the brain fog Corinne spoke about originated.

Phillips, who'd shared a blood type with the Russian President, turned out to be stronger, smarter and ultimately more evil than Zoran could ever be.

Too, he'd asked for this meeting, probably to place a fog on every world leader in the room. If he could command Rafe to kill Corinne, whom he loved, then he could command almost anyone to do anything. He hadn't wanted only the White House, this time. He'd planned to take the planet. Corinne was the only one to defy him.

Get out, Auggie, Corinne sent.

"No," I said. "Rafe, put your weapon down."

"He has my obsession, now," Zoran/Phillips laughed, confirming my fears. "He won't rest until she's dead. What shall I tell you to do, Colonel Hunter?"

Corinne didn't wait to tell me again—she used power to send me, Madam President and the Ukrainian President to the Oval Office, leaving Matt and Opal in the Cabinet room while I shouted at her to stop.

Corinne

"Remove the obsession," I demanded, "and I'll let you live," I snapped at Phillips. Just because he'd taken the drug and now looked like President Zoran meant nothing to me. He was an evil, evil bastard.

"No," Phillips laughed. I watched in horror as Ilya's hand shook—he was ready to fire the weapon I'd given him.

"They're coming," I said, turning Ilya's weapon to sparks that died quickly, leaving him empty-handed and blinking at his fingers in shock.

"They already got here, or did you miss something?" Phillips snapped. "Kill her with your bare hands, you stupid Cossack," he shouted at Ilya.

I was forced to place a heavy shield around Ilya—he'd leapt toward me with murder in his eyes. "Take off the obsession," I demanded as Ilya punched futilely at the invisible wall around him.

"Let me walk out of here and I'll consider it," Phillips examined his fingernails. "Better yet, agree to serve me and I'll see you get him and anyone else you want."

I turned toward Matt Michaels, who stood immobile on the other side of the conference table, as if he couldn't decide what to do. Opal appeared to be having a mental argument with him. I turned back to Phillips.

"Take off the obsession—this is the last time I'll ask. They're coming," I said.

"Who were those who already came?" his wounded guard asked.

"The descendants of the ones who created the drug," I said. "They've outlawed it and are on a quest to destroy any of it that's left," I shrugged. "Last chance," I said to Phillips. "They're coming."

"I refuse," he said.

His particles separated as he grinned.

I'd made a promise to Ilya.

I kept it.

Auggie skidded to a stop in the hallway outside the door as they landed all around me. Blinking tears away, I saw that Ilya had beaten his hands bloody, attempting to punch his way through my shield.

～

Notes—Colonel Hunter

Six tall, blue men surrounded Corinne, all of them with close-cropped blond hair, except the tallest. His hair was deep red and hung in waves to his shoulders.

I still don't understand how I could decipher their language, but for a moment, that's what happened.

"You will come with us, and if you wish to live, you will not resist," the red-haired alien spoke to Corinne.

"I understand," Corinne replied, hanging her head. I watched as a crystalline tear fell to the floor, followed by another. Corinne wept.

"Who?" I said, struggling to keep my voice steady while stepping into the bloody, bullet-riddled room.

"We are Larentii," one of the others said. "It is what this one has become, after the drug was administered. We have never seen such and must decide whether she will live or be subjected to particle separation."

"Auggie, don't argue. There's nothing you can do, now," Corinne quavered. "Good-bye, Ilya." Those words were accompanied by a sob.

The Larentii disappeared with Corinne. The shield around Rafe dropped at the same time. I will never forget his scream of rage and loss as he dropped to his knees on the blood-soaked floor.

Ilya

I can't even think her name without going into a terrible rage. Doctor Shaw showed me her photograph once.

I destroyed his office as a result.

The truth that I see—in his eyes and others around me—is that they fear she is dead anyway.

Nevertheless, the obsession stands. If I were to see her again, I'd attempt to kill her.

Madam President survived the attack, as did the Ukrainian President. All the others died—if not during the initial attack, then later, at a hospital.

The lizard-like attackers also had other targets—six locations in Russia and one in Canada were destroyed. In all, more than four hundred bodies were discovered—both drug survivors and civilians—including Hal Prentice, whom everyone believed to be former President Phillips. The alien attackers in Russia and Canada managed to escape—at least that's what appears to have happened. She and I—we'd killed those who'd appeared at the White House.

At a terrible, terrible cost.

Nick and Maye—both dead.

President Zoran—the real one—was found dead at a facility in Russia hit by the attackers. That information wasn't released to the public. Instead, the public believes the man in the meeting room was the one responsible for all the deaths. Either way, both died. There was little sorrow expressed at their passing.

Sorrow was saved for world leaders who'd died at the White House meeting. State funerals were held, one after another. Madam President attended several of those. Director Michaels was forced to find additional guards for her.

I know the President discussed *her* death with Colonel Hunter.

I was left out of that conversation—for obvious reasons.

Six months have passed since she was taken away. Colonel Hunter turns pale every time anyone speaks of her. Maye and Nick received highest honors and a burial in Arlington for saving Madam President's life.

Richard Farrell is little more than a ghost. He and I—we are the only known survivors of the U.S. Program. Both of us are empty shells, our love torn away from us. We have no idea if any of the Russian drug recipients survive, although Colonel Hunter and Matt Michaels are watching constantly for any sign. As for the drug—every grain of dust is missing and presumably destroyed. Perhaps it is just as well.

After all, we have no idea whether there are more Zoran clones out there. If there are and they have the same talent as Phillips, we could all be in very deep trouble.

In my dreams, however, I see her.

Love her.

Touch her.

When I wake, I find my suite destroyed.

There is no escaping this affliction—it consumes me in my waking hours and in my sleep. I have to destroy what I love; that is the nature of Zoran's curse.

I weep.

Not for myself, but for her.

Notes—Colonel Hunter

I told Laci I had to go to Seattle to shut down the Pilchuck facility once and for all.

It was an excuse.

I'd taken a rental car as far as I could drive before leaving it in a clearing and climbing up the rest of the way. When I arrived at a peak near the summit, I stopped to catch my breath and look about me.

The night was clear, with a sliver of moon shining low over Puget Sound in the west. Stars so close they appeared to be woven together, wheeled overhead. I drew a ragged breath and breathed it out again.

"Cori," I said. "I'm so sorry. I hope I can see the stars of your world from here. I wish—I pray—that you're alive, and that the Larentii welcomed you home."

The End